FUTILITY FORETOLD

A VOICE FROM THE PAST RETURNS

CHRISTO A. CHANEY

First eBook Impression: March 2026

First Paperback Impression: March 2026

First Hardback Impression: June 2026

979-8-9934574-0-6 (ebook)

979-8-9934574-1-3 (hardback)

979-8-9934574-2-0 (paperback)

979-8-9934574-3-7 (audio-forthcoming)

Library of Congress Control Number: 2025927937

Disclaimer: This is a work of historical fiction. While it draws upon real events, people, and publications of the time—including the sinking of the RMS *Titanic* and Morgan Robertson's novella *Futility*—the main character, his journal entries, and interpretations herein are fictionalized. Any resemblance to actual persons, living or deceased, is purely coincidental. The author has taken creative liberties to explore the philosophical, emotional, and speculative dimensions of the available historical record.

The views expressed by characters regarding faith, prophecy, or spiritual belief do not represent any particular historical figure, religious doctrine, or institution.

Formatted with Vellum

IN MEMORIAM

Morgan Robertson wrote 'Futility' in May 1898. Fourteen years later, the Titanic sank under circumstances eerily matching his fictional Titan. Without him, this book couldn't be possible.
The steamship Titan was fiction.
The Royal Mail Steamer Titanic was not.
Fiction, sooner or later, becomes fact. Sometimes too late.
May he be remembered only for good.

September 30, 1861 ~ March 24, 1915

In life it's imperative to get accurate information right from the old horse's mouth, and don't ever listen to the lies coming from some jackass!

— SAMMY RAY CHANEY (MY DAD)

Sometimes all you need is some proverbial wisdom and just a little bit of common sense!

— CHRISTO ALLEN CHANEY

With gratitude to all my helpful test readers:

My mother, Linda W. Dickenson
Shoshanah Bina
Simone Gordon
Marc I. Esper
Joshua Salmans
Michael Atkins
David Pillath

Thank you, Rabbi Stuart Federow, who insisted I write a book and publish it. Yes, I know this wasn't the one you had in mind!

Professional Editing by Stuart Budgen

"It has been instilled within us that when we die, we take nothing with us. It's what we leave behind that counts: a good name, doing kind deeds, and all the love we give to others."
~Dr. Leon Cohen

ONE BOOK SAW THE FUTURE

History didn't repeat—it was published first.

A book from 1898.
A ship from 1912.
A collision foreseen.

The *steamship Titan* was fiction.
But the *Royal Mail Steamer Titanic* was fact.

Fiction sooner or later becomes fact…sometimes too late.

With thanks and
acknowledgments
I am
Sincerely yours
Morgan Robertson

IT'S JUST A NOVEL...ISN'T IT?

Hidden within the silent archives of long-forgotten libraries, some crumbling with age, others merely overlooked, secrets remain. The air smells faintly of dust and fading ink; the light, if any, is thin and golden, filtering through cracked shutters. Some shelves sag beneath the weight of forgotten truths, while others stand almost pristine, not left untouched by time, but by indifference. In these quiet corners, stories await. Not to entertain, but to awaken. They whisper of destinies that defy time, of stories not merely read but lived, and sometimes, just barely, survived.

This is one of those stories.

Some stories warn. Others experience. This one does both.

In May 1898, an American writer named Morgan Robertson produced one such tale—a work now classified as a novella—that would eerily foreshadow one of history's greatest maritime disasters. It was as if a voice from the past had returned to warn us.

At just 20,614 words, this slim volume told the story of a massive ocean liner, far larger than any ship then afloat. In an age when most vessels were proud to cross the Atlantic in slightly over a week, the imagined speed and scale were absurd. The public was still marveling over ships like Cunard's *Lucania* and *Campania*. Both were grand in their own right, but barely half the size of Robertson's vision. The ship was filled with the world's wealthiest passengers. On a cold April night, it struck an iceberg in the North Atlantic shipping lane, and its sinking led to terrible loss of life.

That story, meant to illustrate the futility of human ambition, bore a fitting title: *Futility*. It was first published that same year by the firm, *M. F Mansfield & Co.*

Long overlooked, *Futility* now lingers in the public domain, free to read or sold cheaply on many eBook platforms.

Its initial reception was modest. The reading public, if they noticed the book at all, treated it as a curiosity: a maritime melodrama with a hint of moralism. Very few, if any, reviewers commented on the technological foresight of its author. Most simply shrugged it off. After all, who could believe that a ship so vast could also be so vulnerable?

No one could have guessed that real events would soon echo fiction. Not just in outline, but in stunning, ship-for-ship detail.

Over ten years later, a British company called the White Star Line launched a new Atlantic liner that bore an uncanny resemblance to Morgan's fictional vessel, not just in its immense size but in its specific dimensions and capabilities. It was the second of three ships in what would be called the Olympic class. According to some, it was intended as the company's flagship. Although all three ships were more alike than different, this ship would become the most well-known. Even today, everyone knows her name.

Their new vessel, at over 46,000 tons, was nearly the twin of Robertson's imagined ship at 45,000 tons, though that number was increased in later printings. The real ship measured 882.5 feet long; Morgan's was slightly shorter at 800 feet. The parallels were chilling: triple-screw propulsion, a speed of 24–25 knots, and a capacity for roughly 3,000 souls.

Both ships met the maritime standards of their time. Yet neither carried lifeboats sufficient for all aboard. This was considered a seemingly minor concern at the time, as both were widely believed to be "practically unsinkable." A detail some would later deem prophetic, while others saw it as unforgivable.

Just after noon on Wednesday, April 10, 1912, this real ship set sail from Southampton, England, bound for Cherbourg, France. After a final stop in Queenstown, Ireland (known today as Cobh since 1920), she continued on her maiden voyage to New York. But she would never arrive.

Like her fictional counterpart, she also struck an iceberg at her starboard side on a frigid April night, and sank with tremendous loss of human life. Morgan Robertson had named his doomed vessel the S.S. *Titan.* White Star's would be known as the R.M.S. *Titanic.*[*]

Understandably, the world was stunned. Newspapers scrambled for headlines. Survivors arrived ashore in donated clothing, their faces hollow with disbelief. Among the mourners, theorists, mechanical engineers, and poets, a few curious minds turned back to the shelves.

Morgan Robertson was a former sailor who claimed no prophetic gift. Only a desire to warn against unchecked ambition. Few remembered the book. Fewer still reached into the dust of obscurity to retrieve it. Those stiff pages were now carrying the weight of a terrible echo, as if warning and tragedy were already intertwined. And it

---

* Historical note: S.S. denotes steam-powered propulsion. R.M.S. identifies a vessel contracted to carry mail for the British Royal Crown—a mark long associated with prestige and dependable service.

prompted the question that still haunts some even today: **How did he know?** In this book, I'll attempt to answer it.

While *Futility*, later republished as *The Wreck of the Titan* with some minor edits in May 1912, was a haunting work of fiction, this book is somewhat different. It is a story of hindsight, of echoes across time, and of a young man who narrowly lived through what Robertson could have only imagined.

This novel builds on *Futility: The Wreck of the Titan* and the real events that echoed it. What follows is a work of historical fiction, the journey of Robert A. Morganson, a second-class passenger sailing aboard the *Titanic*. From among the many who sailed, his voice finally emerged. Not in official reports, not in testimony to a court, but in a journal meant for no one's eyes but his own. Robert was not a man of great renown. He carried no titles or wealth. Only a satchel, a journal, and a mind attuned to patterns others ignored.

With a first-edition unedited copy of *Futility* and a new journal in hand, he encounters real historical figures. As Robert records his observations, he begins to perceive chilling parallels between his lived experience and a long-forgotten, eerily prophetic book.

But he is not a clairvoyant. Nor is he a prophet. At first, he is merely a man reading a book. Yet something stirs within him. It's a nagging thread of recognition he cannot quite name. When he opens the cover of *Futility*, he begins to see a pattern forming in the fog. As the voyage progresses, Robert begins to suspect that this work of fiction may be only the first draft of his own reality.

Author's Note: Though my book is also a work of fiction, it is deeply rooted in historical maritime events. I have drawn extensively from eyewitness testimonies, including survivor accounts published shortly after the disaster. My research included examination of available blueprints of the three sister ships built by Harland and Wolff in Belfast, Ireland, for the White Star Line: the *Olympic*, *Titanic*, and *Britannic*. As of this publication, Harland and Wolf remain in the shipbuilding business.

My goal is to offer as historically accurate a portrayal as possible of the real ship, the only voyage, the people, the disaster, and its aftermath as it was experienced by those who survived it.

For clarity, whenever *Futility* is quoted in this novel, those excerpts are drawn directly from the May 1912 edition, jointly published by *McClure's and Metropolitan Magazine*. Released just weeks after the sinking, that edition, a republication of Robertson's original 1898 text with some slight revisions, was revived by public interest.

When possible, I also consulted the few fragile remains of the original 1898 printings before any revisions were made. As of this publication, the 1912 facsimile edition remains in print today. It's available in softcover, hardcover, and ebook through SeaWolf Press. Historical information about that publication is provided in the appendix.

This edition is almost the exact same as the one that Robert Morganson might have carried in his satchel and read aboard the *Titanic*. I have carefully retained its original phrasing, layout, and spelling variants as faithfully as possible. Certain words and expressions will feel very antique to our modern ears. Please let them.

These words, like the rusted remains of the great ship, must be preserved for as long as possible. Their resonance lies not in polish, but in the lessons they still carry.

Perhaps the true message lies not just in written words, but in the echoes they create. Look closely at what stands apart from the rest, and you just might find it. Not written between the lines exactly, but hinted at from the very beginning, scattered like stray letters or dissonant notes across the chapters, waiting for someone to listen closely enough to piece it together. You may not see it at first. But if you look closely, it will begin to reveal itself. Your first hint is in this very prologue.

Perhaps you've already brushed past it without noticing. Go on. See if you can find it before someone else does. As you read this story, you will discover a shocking twist no one ever saw coming. Because when these events were unfolding, something else was already taking shape.

AFTER ALL, *Futility* was just a novel… Or was it?

1

THE NEW TITAN

Wednesday, April 10th, 1912—5:30 PM
Cherbourg, France—English Channel

Mist clung to the harbor like a whispered secret, softening the outline of the vessel ahead. One of the White Star Line's new tenders, the *S.S. Nomadic*, cut through the sparkling waters, ferrying two groups of passengers, First Class and Second Class, to their awaiting ship. Robert A. Morganson sat at a table against the wall, his journal in hand, as the small craft sailed gracefully over the evening swell. Its lone funnel released a steady stream of black smoke that matched the rhythm of the twin propellers.

Ahead, the massive silhouette of the new Olympic-class liner loomed offshore, anchored in waters deep enough to accommodate her tremendous size. Nearby, Robert spotted the identical twin tender, the *S.S. Traffic*, carrying mail and third-class passengers. Through another window, he saw rare Atlantic puffins soaring over the waves, several diving and resurfacing with fish in their beaks.

Now settled on a cushioned bench near the upper-deck stairs, Robert dipped his pen into an inkwell set carefully on the armrest. He closed the top before writing with a satisfied smirk:

'And so, for this reason we travel, not to escape life, but for life not to escape us. Give me a satchel of well-thumbed journals and a

passport smudged with signatures of foreign ink over a house cluttered with baubles and bric-a-brac.'

He let the ink dry for a moment, his fingers drumming lightly on the worn leather of his satchel. Somewhere behind him, the lone engine hummed softly. Travel and writing had always been his twin passions, and this journey, though unexpected, offered a welcome return to both.

On his first Atlantic crossing, Robert had booked passage on Cunard's now nearly five-year-old *R.M.S. Mauretania.* But for the return voyage, he'd been reassigned to White Star's newest and most ambitious liner at no additional cost. The news had come as a surprise, a last-minute shuffle amidst a strike-induced chaos. He'd imagined a more predictable return on a well-experienced liner, but the sheer coincidence of finding passage, let alone on this ship, had quickly overshadowed any issues. He wasn't complaining. If he had to spend a whole week alone at sea, he might as well enjoy it. Besides, it wasn't every day someone got to experience a maiden voyage.

On the table lay a newspaper detailing the recent worker strike due to a coal shortage that had disrupted crossings, forcing passengers onto whatever ships still had space and enough fuel to sail. On the same page, another article mentioned rumors that Ireland could soon gain its independence from England due to a new movement they called Home Rule.

A loud voice interrupted his thoughts. It was boastful and brimming with pride. "There she is, men! The pride of the White Star Line! She is the sister ship to the *Olympic*. Behold, the largest moving object ever built! Now, let's see how those fools back at Cunard respond to this mighty vessel!" The man's loud words reverberated through the paneled walls of the first-class accommodations and into the second-class area.

Robert glanced up from his journal, shocked and offended by not only the shouting but also the sheer arrogance. His feelings were conflicted between irritation at the man's boorishness, and a genuine sense of sadness, not for himself, but for someone so seemingly lost in his own inflated ego.

Some years prior, a new friend, a man whose quiet strength had once pulled Robert from the cold streets, brought him into his home, and helped get him back on his feet, had offered a simple, profound lesson. When Robert had been bullied by someone, his friend, a close associate of Mark Twain during his time working on Mississippi River steamboats, kept a calm gaze that belied his power and had taught Robert: '*It's better to keep your mouth shut and allow everyone to think you're a fool, rather than say something and remove all doubt.*'

He felt the familiar hot surge of indignation, a prickle behind his eyes. It was an old battle, one he'd fought many times in different settings, always against the loud and the entitled. But then, his friend's calm, steady gaze flashed in his mind, a silent, ever-patient reminder. *Control*, the gaze seemed to say. *Control the impulse, and let their own words be their undoing.* Robert took a quiet, steadying breath.

Just past the Bostwick Gate, he saw a tall, impeccably dressed first-class gentleman, his mustache curled to perfection. He held a glass of alcohol in one hand and a cigarette in the other, blowing gray smoke from his nostrils. Robert noticed the wealthy man was not scrawny but slightly thick in a few areas, likely proving that he had never missed a good-sized meal in his life. Something Robert could never claim.

Noticing Robert sitting alone with his journal, the man took a few steps toward Robert and made an overt effort to impress him. "She's a marvel of engineering, indeed. As you can clearly see, I have the pleasure of traveling first class. One might even find oneself dining with Captain Smith, you know." Looking over Robert's more plain clothing, he gave a slight laugh and added with a very condescending tone, "A very different class of travel for you, I perceive."

Robert smirked. Unable to resist, he decided to calmly respond: "You would be correct to think so. I have no doubt you'll make it quite evident to any poor soul obliged to hear it."

The man's jaw visibly clenched, but he forced a chuckle. "Ah yes, the envy of second class, I can see. Clearly one of those on the lower rungs of society. Still, count yourself lucky to have secured passage at all. I daresay many would give a king's ransom for any class of ticket on this maiden voyage."

Robert arched a brow. "Most certainly. I am quite aware. However, you will find no envy from my side, sir. I daresay we all have our own particular reasons for undertaking this voyage. Now, if I may be honest with you, I prefer to listen to what others have to say rather than boast about myself."

The man sniffed with a smile. "Quite. After all, listening is very well and good, young man, but I rather doubt it will take you very far in this life. See where you are at this moment, and notice the position I'm in."

Robert tilted his head. "That's a fair observation. It's rather curious that the two words 'listen' and 'silent' share all the same letters, but in a different order. Something for us both to ponder, wouldn't you think?"

The wealthy man, agitated, took a few more steps toward Robert, clearly bothered. "I say, you're not speaking to me in that fashion, are you? Do you have any notion of the sort of person I am?"

Robert had an idea. "Actually, sir, I believe I have a fair understanding of your sort. As Plato cautioned, 'The emptiest vessel gives off the loudest din, and those of the least wit are often the most inclined to be the loudest babblers.'"

The rich man's face turned a deep pink as someone else in first class let out a low, soft whistle. Another person, a woman possibly, gave a soft laugh of agreement.

"Oh, a philosopher, I gather. Well, allow me to offer a bit of advice. I am a man of science. My understanding of how this world operates likely surpasses anything you could imagine."

Despite the locked gate separating them, Robert knew that he had to be careful with his next response. "I do admire that. Then, as a man of science, you will no doubt be well aware that light travels much faster than sound, which explains why some individuals appear to be rather bright. That is, until they choose to speak."

A steward on Robert's side of the partition failed at covering up his snort-filled laugh as he walked away. Some of the passengers on his side were listening to the exchange, but he didn't notice them; he was never one to seek out an audience.

Several of the wealthy passengers on the other side started to laugh softly, with at least one of them giving a soft, steady applause of approval. The man thought he would put Robert in his place and have the last word.

"You may not appreciate it, but the accommodations in second class are quite modest. Even those poor souls in Steerage will likely find more room than you. Your movements and activities will be considerably restricted. What you see here on this tiny thing will likely be the height of your experiences. I, however, shall be traveling in considerable style, wouldn't you agree?"

Robert calmly placed his pen down next to his journal and turned slightly to face the man for his next response. "I can't prove you wrong in that regard. If everything must always be better, then nothing will ever be good enough. We only have so long to live. My late father used to say, 'We take nothing with us when we die. It's what we leave behind that matters: a good name, the good we've done for the less fortunate, and the love we leave behind.' Sir, I know that I will never have everything I want. But I've always had all I need. And that's far more than what I am owed."

Giving a frustrated glare with a defeated huff, the man took a final, prolonged draw of his cigarette and intentionally blew the thick smoke through the bars of the gate into Robert's breathing space. Then, throwing his cigarette butt into the sea, he walked off to finish his scotch or headed to the bar for another round, apparently already a bit inebriated.

Robert held his breath for a moment, then exhaled slowly, blowing the cloud of stench away from his face. He turned in his seat to focus on the potted plants nearby. "Good heavens, Robert, do conduct yourself better. You've always let your tongue outpace your judgment. One day, it may cost you more than a bruised ego," he said to himself.

"Excuse me, young man," a firm yet kindly voice interrupted.

He turned, startled. The woman walking up to the gate wore a dark traveling coat with embroidered trim and a feathered hat tipped smartly to the side. She had the air of someone accustomed to speaking her mind and having anyone within hearing range listen.

"I hope you weren't telling yourself to behave after that unacceptable display of pomposity."

Robert blinked. "It's quite all right. I had no wish to stir up trouble."

"Well, you didn't. He did. Now, as far as I'm concerned, you carry yourself just fine, Mr....?"

"Morganson, but please call me Robert, ma'am." He stood up and approached the gate.

"Happy to meet you. Margaret Brown. But most folks call me Molly." She smiled warmly and extended a hand through the bars. Robert didn't hesitate to return the respectful greeting. She had a noticeably firm grip. "There's no shame in traveling second or even third class. A person's worth isn't measured by their ticket. There's dignity owed in every class."

"I've no argument with that. Those born to comfort often don't know the meaning of hardship. It wasn't very long ago that I didn't have a bed to sleep in or hardly any food to eat. That is, until someone took me into his home and helped me."

"Oh my gracious. I hope your struggles didn't last too long. But look at you now," she said with a knowing glance. "You've been to France and probably a few more places, judging by your nice American accent. Now about to be on the grandest ship in the world. I wasn't always wealthy myself, you know. My husband, J.J., struck gold recently out west back in the States. Not only that, but we also found a deposit of copper as well. Even though we have separated, we're not getting divorced due to our being Catholic. But I've never met a finer, more worthwhile man than J.J. Now, men like that blowhard who disrespected you don't much care for me either. 'New money,' they call it."

Robert tilted his head slightly. "Then it seems our fortunes have both turned for the better, Miss Molly. I'm pleased to know it. But I do regret that your marriage has had some problems leading to the separation."

Molly's smile brightened. "Thank you. We still get along well and do care for each other very much. Mind this, son, don't let the loud ones shake your confidence. There's room on every ship, and in the world, for more than their sort. Always remember that no matter how difficult times are, they can get better with the help of others. See you on board, then." She looked behind her for a moment, then gave Robert soft, knowing applause. Just a few gentle claps, more encouragement than spectacle.

He lifted his second-class ticket in a small salute. "Yes, ma'am. Thank you kindly for speaking with me this evening."

Molly smiled as she walked up the nearby stairs to tend to her luggage. Robert returned to his journal and leaned over the table to record a quiet thought: '*Life improves only when people are together. Patience, perhaps, is merely what one displays when there are too many witnesses. A silence born not of peace, but of pressure. I wonder how often such restraint is mistaken for virtue?*'

Robert paused for a moment, the exchange lingering in his thoughts like the salt air on his skin. He'd never met Margaret Brown before, but something about her, that confidence, her kindness, her clarity, had settled the rising tension in his chest. Perhaps this voyage would offer more than just ocean views and time to write. Maybe it would hold the kind of encounters that could reshape a man if he allowed them to.

The boastful fellow was correct about one thing. Robert walked to the nearest window and looked out the side. The air, crisp and tasting of the sea, held a tangible chill, yet a thrill ran through him, warmer than any coat.

There, dominating the horizon, was the largest ship he

had ever seen. A behemoth against the evening sky. Even from this distance, it was staggering in scale, less a vessel and more a floating city. Even in the fading light, the great ship's sheer scale defied imagination.

Illuminated portholes and large windows stretched like constellations along her sides. Her hull, a deep, polished jet-black, gleamed almost liquid in the fading light, stretching nearly a sixth of a mile from stem to stern.

A thin gold stripe, barely visible but perfectly straight, traced the length of both sides just beneath the brilliant white of her superstructure, a stark contrast that hinted at the luxury within.

At the front of the ship, Robert could see a short row of only four lifeboats. He also noticed another row of the same number near the stern. But there were none in between. Assuming there would be the same amount on the other side, that would make sixteen. Sixteen. It seemed so few. Like a concession to appearances rather than safety.

But she had passed her sea trials earlier before being allowed to take on passengers. That meant the safety regulations were met. But if they were sufficient, why did Robert feel very unsettled? For a ship that could carry around three thousand people, would that really be enough? Shouldn't there be more? Or were there others secured nearby that Robert couldn't see? Hopefully, there were. Cunard's two largest ships had the same number of lifeboats, but each were much smaller. Almost one hundred feet shorter, actually, and not quite as high up.

Above it all, four enormous funnels, each wide enough to drive a train carriage through, rose like the stately towers of a grand, majestic sanctuary. From the third funnel, a faint plume of smoke curled lazily into the evening air, probably just to keep the electricity on while anchored; a visible breath of the immense power contained beneath her decks.

The sheer audacity of her design, her almost impossible proportions, made his breath catch. He had been very impressed by the *Mauretania*, a swift and proud monarch of the Atlantic, but she seemed a mere toy beside this colossal creation. This wasn't just a ship; it was a defiant statement, a monument to human ambition, built to conquer the very ocean on which it now peacefully rested.

Noticing the top quarter of the funnels was painted black to hide the stains of the black soot, Robert smiled to himself. He imagined the gentlemen in first class tipping their black top hats in approval, as they observed the ship's pristine paintwork and fine wood carvings.

The ship's newly applied red antifouling paint on the bottom could be seen just above the waterline, preventing marine growth from clinging to her steel belly beneath. It was all meticulously crafted. Not only for function but also for grandeur.

This wasn't just a ship. It was a monument to modern ambition. It was gorgeous, bold, and, perhaps, unaware of its own hubris. But grandeur, thought Robert, did not always equate to wisdom. This was a floating palace. And palaces, history had taught him, often forgot or even ignored the people outside their gates. The very ones who made that palace possible.

The *Nomadic* gave a soft lurch as its engine began to slow, its approach to the towering hull of the giant bringing them ever closer.

Robert returned to his seat, leaving his journal open, and looked out through the window. First-class passengers were preparing to board, guided toward their exclusive reception area on D Deck. Once they had boarded, the tender would reposition for second class to embark through their own entrance farther behind.

Robert's gaze drifted to the name displayed proudly on the bow; the letters deeply etched into thick steel and filled with a bright shade of golden-yellow paint. That name was unmistakable: **TITANIC**.

Robert took a deep breath and softly whistled. He had once thought the two Cunard vessels, nicknamed the Greyhounds of the Atlantic, were massive, and indeed they were. But this one? It was on another level entirely. There was no denying her magnificence, yet something simmered in the back of his mind. Even as awe settled over him, a flicker of unease returned just for a moment. He couldn't explain it. He didn't believe in omens, not really. And yet…

He turned from the window and looked at his satchel, unsettled by a thought he couldn't quite name. Not fear, exactly. Not yet. But something about those sixteen lifeboats lingered.

He reached in, fingers brushing against the small, tattered book tucked inside a side pocket. The cover, faded and slightly scuffed, depicted a large, multi-funneled ship sinking beneath the waves, an iceberg towering ominously behind it. The author's name was strikingly similar to his own: Morgan Robertson. The title, printed in bold red letters, read simply: **FUTILITY**.

The short novel had intrigued him ever since he'd stumbled across it abandoned on a shelf in the *Mauretania's* second-class lounge. He'd been told it was unpopular, and since it had been consigned to the trash bin, it was his to keep at no cost. It felt less like he had found the book and more like the book had been patiently waiting for him. The similarities between the fictional vessel and the real ship he was about to board couldn't be dismissed so easily.

He flipped through the early pages until he found the

passage that had unsettled him most: '*From the bridge, engine room, and a dozen places on her deck, the ninety-two doors of nineteen watertight compartments could be closed in half a minute by turning a lever. These doors would also close automatically in the presence of water. With nine compartments flooded, the ship would still float, and as no known accident of the sea could possibly fill this many, the steamship* "Titan" *was considered practically unsinkable.*'

The automatically closing doors were not what worried him, as many ships had the new safety features. Robert trembled, the words "*steamship*" and "*Titan*" echoing in his mind. He pulled out a folded advertisement from the White Star Line. '*Royal Mail Steamship*' or, for short, '*R.M.S. Titanic.*'

True, most passenger ships were powered by steam. But even the names of these two vessels bore a chilling resemblance. He checked the copyright page. No month or day. Just the publisher, '*M. F. Mansfield & Co.*' and the year: '*1898.*' About fourteen years ago. It was very intriguing.

And yet something else tightened in the center of his chest. Something unbidden. Unlike the *Titanic*, which was contracted to carry both cargo and mail, *Futility* described the *Titan* as a ship built solely for passenger service. Still, the likeness was uncanny.

Robert scanned through the chapter. The words in certain paragraphs were slightly unsettling: '*Unsinkable—indestructible, she carried as few boats as would satisfy the laws… that in case of an end-on collision with an iceberg—the only thing afloat that she could not conquer… She had beaten all records… had not lowered the time between Sandy Hook and Daunt's Rock to the five-day limit; and it was unofficially rumored among the two thousand passengers who had embarked… that an effort would now be made to do so.*'

Next to one mention of '*Titan*,' he underlined the

name and scribbled two small letters next to it in the margin: '*-ic.*'

With a faint hiss of steam, a blast of the whistle, and the low rumble of ropes being released, the small tender eased back from the *Titanic's* hull and made its way in reverse toward the second-class entrance.

Once secured, a gangway was extended, and crewmen moved into position to assist passengers with boarding. Robert waited his turn, watching as stewards took coats and luggage and offered assistance up the swaying steps.

Then, snapping the book shut, he jotted a brief note in his journal. With care, he added a final thought beneath his earlier quote: *'We pursue wonder not for where it leads, but for the stillness it grants amidst the noise within. I do not claim to believe in fate—but this curious volume raises questions I cannot easily set aside. And as for this ship? She is, for certain, a new* Titan, *in every sense of her great name.'*

Then, securing his inkwell and pen, he slipped the journal and the novel back into his satchel and stood.

He approached the threshold of the *Nomadic*, taking another look up at the towering hull before stepping closer. With each step toward the gangway, the deck beneath his feet seemed to hum. An anticipation, a breath held between history and the unknown. He was going aboard the grandest ship in the world.

How small a person feels when standing in the shadow of giants. First *Olympic* and now *Titanic*. Their names alone carried immense weight, spoken with a mixture of admiration and awe at the sheer size. To behold these two ships was to stand before the might of an empire forged in steel. Robert craned his neck, examining the towering side that stretched into the distance. Nearly 100 feet longer than Cunard's twin ships, she was so long that he couldn't see either end. Robert adjusted his coat. Whatever lay ahead, it was bound to be a journey worth writing about.

Even among the other great liners, this ship stood apart, a marvel beyond anything he'd ever seen. Everywhere within this ship, from prow to stern, she was a triumph of both Irish craftsmanship and British engineering. A floating city on her maiden voyage. Somewhere behind those thick steel walls lay his temporary home for the next week.

Far beneath her steel bones, time itself held its breath. Because somewhere between fiction and fact, a long-forgotten story was soon preparing to repeat itself. Robert unknowingly had stepped aboard history, entering the very pages he had just begun to read.

Holding his breath without meaning to, Robert gripped his passport and his boarding ticket, feeling his journal and the novel in his satchel tucked under his arm. The irony of that book's title, not to mention its very existence, also being in his possession wasn't lost on him. He had brought it along as light reading. A curiosity more than anything. But now, as he stood before the *Titanic*, its title carried an eerie weight. He had heard of the sister ship, *Olympic*.

Robert recalled the stories from the Greek classics about the ancient Titans who challenged their rivals, the Olympians. Losing the war, the Titans were cast down into the eternal darkness. This ship, cleverly named, seemed to embody the same hubris as the mythical deities, despite being a running mate to the *Olympic*. Not only that, but the third ship to complete the trio was already under construction.

The Second-Class Gangway bustled with activity as passengers checked in. It was no mere ladder but a solid ramp leading into a brightly lit entryway. The air within the giant was markedly different from the breezy open deck of the tender. It was warmer, hushed, and filled with the faint, comforting scent of polished wood and fresh paint. Robert could sense the distant, rhythmic thrum of machinery deep below, a vibration that spoke of immense power barely contained.

His footsteps felt strangely light as he approached the threshold, the feeling of what felt like solid ground beneath his feet now replaced by the subtle, almost imperceptible sway of the massive liner. He was no longer looking at the marvel; he was inside it.

"Good evening, sir. Second-class, are we?" A uniformed steward approached, eyeing Robert's papers with a polite nod.

"Yes, sir." Robert handed them over, watching as the young man compared the information to the passenger manifest.

The customs officer glanced down at Robert's paperwork, then up again. He began making some small notations on a few documents. Robert began feeling nervous. *Remember, assume nothing, Robert*, he silently told himself, trying to mask his anxiety.

"Very interesting. Not many Americans are aboard this voyage, certainly not in second class. Returning home, are you? Business trip, sir?"

Robert hesitated only slightly, offering a small nod. "In part, yes. But mostly for a personal course of study."

"Understood, sir. Very good then. All appears to be in order. Welcome aboard, Mr. Morganson."

Robert took a deep, calming breath and adjusted the strap of his satchel, feeling the familiar weight of the journal inside. A course of study, he'd said, which was true enough. Not all lessons came from a classroom. He had long decided not to disclose too much of his real reason for traveling. He was better now. That was what mattered.

The steward returned the documents and handed him a folded map. "We are presently on E Deck. Your cabin is situated above us on D Deck just down the corridor from the Second-Class Dining Saloon. I've marked it here for you. If you would be so kind as to use this staircase directly behind me, you'll find your way with ease. Should you be seeking a quiet spot for reading and writing, there's a rather agreeable small library just above the saloon, on C Deck, also known as the Shelter Deck. And if you partake in a pipe or cigar, the Second-Class Smoke Room is located further up, on B Deck."

A library? That was a welcome surprise. "Thank you, young man. I'll be sure to visit the library more than once and browse the fine books," Robert said with a smile, tucking the map into his coat before offering a handshake. "But please, call me Robert."

The ship was a genuine titan indeed. Made real in millions of iron rivets and thick steel plates. The moment he crossed the threshold; a wave of warmth enveloped him. Solid. Unshakable. A marvel of modern construction. He'd spent many nights in anonymous hotels or cramped ship cabins during his travels. One night, he'd even slept under a bridge in the rain. But this felt deliberately personal. As if someone had cared enough to craft not just a ship, but a memory.

A quiet tremor vibrated through the enormous frame, a living pulse beneath his worn leather shoes. It was the collective heartbeat of thousands of souls, a testament to human ingenuity, to mankind's enduring belief in its own mastery over nature. He felt a part of something monumental, unaware that this very monument was all too soon destined to become a legend of a very different kind.

Robert had stepped aboard a ship. But perhaps, without knowing it, he had also stepped into a story already written. And the world, though no one knew it yet, was about to change.

2

GREETING THE NEW OLYMPIAN

He took a few steps inside and paused just past the entrance, momentarily overcome by the sheer elegance surrounding him: polished wood paneling, brass fixtures gleaming under electric lights, and decorative floor tiles underfoot. Almost identical to those on the *Nomadic*, the pattern featured a barbed cross design within nine-inch square borders, alternating cream tiles with red backgrounds, and matching cream crosses. Each one a negative image of its surrounding neighbors.

His shoes echoed softly against the tile and wood with each careful step. The scent of fresh paint still lingered. It was a quiet reminder of how new everything was. Spotless. Untouched by time or wear. It felt as though he were stepping into a dream someone had dared to make real.

This was no ordinary steamship; it was a legend in the making. And to think there was already another one just like it, and a third in the process of rising into scaffolding from the blueprints. No doubt, the next member of the Olympic class would be even grander.

Robert took in the gleaming furnishings and the hum of excitement in the air as passengers admired the grandeur of the world's largest ship. The polished brass fittings and towering funnels spoke of progress, of man's triumph over nature.

Passengers filtered past, some admiring the fine aesthetics of the environment, others eager to settle into their cabins.

As Robert stepped further inside, voices from a nearby

corridor caught his sharp ear. Two slightly older gentlemen in first-class attire stood just beyond a decorative glass partition, deep in conversation over a crumpled newspaper. Though he couldn't enter their section, the low barrier and well-lit room beyond made it easy to overhear. Curiosity drew Robert closer.

"Take a look at this," one said, tapping a photograph showing *Olympic*'s hull, badly scarred from her collision with *HMS Hawke*. "She stayed afloat, thanks to those watertight compartments. She even returned to port under her own steam."

"A testament to the shipbuilders over at Harland and Wolff, I'd say," the other replied. "This one's even more advanced, mind you. If *Olympic* could withstand that, these ships must be nigh unsinkable!"

Robert paused to allow his eyes to take in the details: the jagged triangle-shaped hole in *Olympic's* right side was a stark contrast against her thick hull. He could see parts of the frame exposed. On the same page, a worker in the shipyard posed next to the damaged area on the side of *Titanic's* sister. It was recent. One of the men mentioned the date was September of last year. For a moment, Robert didn't feel perfectly safe. An uneasy thought settled within his mind. If *Olympic*, mighty as she was, could be torn open like that… what did that say of *Titanic's* promise?

But then again, this was a newer ship. Stronger, better, surely. He forced a mental shrug, pushing the disquiet aside. Superstition belonged to a bygone era, not to the age of steel and logic. Yet, the image of the gash in *Olympic's* side persisted, a dark stain on the gleaming promise of this new vessel. He brushed it aside. This was *Titanic*, the pinnacle of modern engineering. An improvement over her older sibling.

The photograph showed that *Olympic's* damage was in

two large compartments in the stern, directly forward of the engines. How did that ship still manage to make it back for repairs without assistance? "*Futility* indeed," he thought. Robert clutched the small novel through the satchel as if to reassure himself those words would stay trapped in the book. Even as he tried to dismiss the image of the ruptured hull, a strange unease crept in. The kind a novel shouldn't be able to evoke.

As he continued toward his cabin, the image of the wounded sister ship faded though not entirely from his thoughts. The deeper Robert moved into the *Titanic*, the more he marveled at the attention to detail. Taking the second-class staircase to the next deck, he noticed the same barbed cross tile pattern recurring in various areas. On the steps, however, the border design was absent, replaced with simpler tiling more suited to foot traffic and smaller spacing.

Outside the Second-Class Dining Saloon, the flooring shifted noticeably. The tiles were of a different design. Slightly more understated, with an alternating pattern of browns and grays. A more modest aesthetic, but still deliberate in its refinement.

The corridor leading to his cabin was lined with neatly carved wood paneling, far more elegant than he had anticipated. He reached out and ran his hand along the wall. The surface was perfectly smooth. Polished, yet not overly lacquered. He could still catch the natural scent of the wood beneath a light trace of oil or wax. For a moment, Robert wondered if he'd wandered into the first-class section by mistake.

It was clear the designers of this ship had taken great care to make even the second-class accommodations feel thoughtful and welcoming, almost proud of what they offered.

He soon reached his cabin which was a modest yet comfortable room. Not the most spacious, but far from cramped. His berth was neatly made: a wood-framed bed with the company logo embroidered on the neatly folded blanket. A bed no one had ever slept in, a couch opposite it for sitting, a small writing desk tucked under a porthole, and a polished washbasin gleaming in the corner. It was comfortable; a private haven after the bustling journey.

As he set his satchel down, the copy of *Futility* already seemed to draw his eye from where it rested on top. The book's presence on the *Mauretania* had felt like a coincidence; its presence here, on *this* ship, felt like something more.

A single porthole let in the daylight, with drapes pinned neatly to the sides. The ceramic washbasin, simple yet cleverly made, folded up to drain the water and funnel it out the side of the ship. A mechanism that was both practical and refined.

Since he was traveling alone, he had booked a smaller cabin at a lower price. Not that it mattered. There was too much to see aboard this great ship. He didn't plan to spend much time in his cabin when the world outside was so full of wonder.

Setting his bag onto the couch, he unfolded the map once more. The Second-Class Dining Saloon was within eyesight of his door, which meant he wouldn't have to go far for meals. Above that, the library called to him, promising pleasant times of quiet reading and writing as the ship steamed through the open waters. The Smoking Room didn't interest him much, as he was not a fan of such habits. If it were not very crowded, he might sit in for a bit.

After a few minutes of settling in, he stepped back into the corridor. The ship's complex layout intrigued him, and he wanted to explore for a while. His curiosity sometimes got the better of him. Robert made sure he had the map in his pocket, as he knew he was likely to get lost on a ship this massive.

After glancing around his cabin once more, he felt an unexpected tug of obligation. He had promised to send word. And keeping his promise mattered more now than ever.

Robert approached the Second-Class Purser's Office and lightly knocked on the wooden frame of the window. A clerk looked up from his ledger as Robert offered a polite nod.

"Pardon me. I should like to send a wireless, if I may."

The man smiled. "Certainly, sir. If you'll write it out. Recipient's name and address at the top, please. I'll see that it reaches the Marconi Room."

Robert pulled a folded slip from his pocket, filled in the information, and passed it across. The words had been carefully chosen beforehand.

To: Prof. S. Freud

Berggasse 19, Vienna

'Safe on board the Titanic. *En route to New York. The journal is a nice gift! Writing in it daily. Thank you for meeting with me.' ~ R.M.*

He considered signing with his full name but thought better of it. Freud would recognize the initials.

The purser glanced over the message, then dipped his pen. "I'll add the charges to your account. It shall be sent at the earliest opportunity."

"Actually, I'd prefer to pay now, if I may."

"As you wish, sir."

"Thank you kindly," Robert said, then hesitated. "Please see that it reaches my friend without delay. It's important."

The purser gave a knowing nod and tucked the message away. A few hours later, it would be translated into dots and dashes, making its silent way across the relay stations.

Freud hadn't offered answers so much as a mirror, but sometimes, that was all Robert had needed. Just knowing someone had listened and cared.

He hadn't told Freud everything. Not even close. But even the little he had shared had stirred up more than he'd expected. Old guilt, restless thoughts, and questions he still wasn't sure how to ask.

Sending the message made it feel real. Anchored. A man thinking clearly, making rational choices. Not some fractured soul trying to outrun shadows Freud barely understood. The memories, sharp and unbidden, still pricked at the edges of his calm. He'd come to Europe to find a path forward, to silence the echoes of a past he couldn't change but that still haunted his present.

He still heard the words, "*You couldn't have known.*" But even Freud hadn't said them with certainty. Only as a suggestion. As if Robert might never truly be free of it. What else had Freud said? "*The past is never past. It only hides in the present.*" Robert wasn't sure he believed that. But part of him was afraid it might be true.

Robert glanced at a Special Notice written opposite from the first page of the passenger manifest for a moment.

'The attention of the Managers has been called to the fact that certain persons, believed to be Professional Gamblers, are in the habit of traveling to and fro in Atlantic Steamships.

In bringing this to the knowledge of Travelers, the Managers, while not wishing in the slightest degree to interfere with the freedom of action of Patrons of the White Star Line, desire to invite their assistance in discouraging Games of Chance, as being likely to afford these individuals special opportunities for taking unfair advantage of others.'

The man noticed Robert was reading the memo. "Understood. Would you like to check any valuables into the safe? I can secure your funds in there."

Robert nervously drummed his fingers next to the ledger. "Not yet. I shall give it some thought. Thank you for offering."

That wasn't entirely true. He already knew he wouldn't; the thought of handing over all his funds made him uneasy. And he hated lying. But Robert had already lost so much in the past.

But he was honestly trying to prove, even if only to himself, that he was thinking clearly. That he remained rational.

Remember what Dr. Freud taught you, he told himself silently.

Finishing up and moving toward the stern, Robert came across a staircase leading further down and also up to the Aft Well Deck. Behind that was where third-class passengers had their promenade space. He ascended the stairs of his section one level and walked outside to get a view of the back. The two massive electric cranes had their arms raised into position and locked in place.

Unlike the grand promenades reserved for first-class travelers, the open area for third class was tucked at the very back of the ship, just above the propellers. Families, young men, and lone travelers were already gathered there, some staring in awe at the ship towering high above the water.

Robert leaned against the railing, gazing at the skyline of Cherbourg, now slightly faded in the distance.

Nearby, on the Aft Well Deck, a third-class boy

clutched his mother's hand, his wide eyes filled with wonder as he stared up at *Titanic's* towering structure.

The mother noticed Robert watching, and he gave a polite wave. She returned the gesture with a warm smile before speaking to her son in a language Robert didn't recognize. He heard the woman say, "*Yallah, yallah.*" Apparently, that meant "hurry up." The language sounded Middle Eastern. Maybe from Northern Africa. They'd likely come from far away, chasing some glimmer of hope across the Atlantic. He wondered what they'd find in New York. Wondered if, like him, they'd find something altogether different.

Seeing this, made Robert think of an experience he had shortly after arriving in Europe. Pulling out his journal, he balanced it on the rail to steady his writing: '*I have often wondered if a language exists that does not depend upon the ear. One that requires no vibration of the air, no voice raised to be heard. Watching the passengers converse in so many tongues reminded me of a little girl I once saw in a London park, conversing with her parents using signs. I could not understand their words, but the gestures were graceful, like birds in flight. Spoken languages travel at the speed of sound, but not this one. No, the signs travel faster still. Faster than the Atlantic Greyhounds. It moves at the speed of light.*

Perhaps this is the answer. A language that requires no sound, only light and motion, and meaning made visible. Maybe that is the only language quick enough to outrun sorrow. For though the deaf may not hear, even they may listen.'

He sighed, a little heavier than normal, and put his journal away. Robert understood that third-class passengers were kept completely separate from others due to immigration laws. Single men were accommodated in the bow and women and families in the stern.

Glancing at the map again, he saw that Scotland Road,

a long corridor on E Deck, ran nearly the entire length of the ship. Robert traced the route with his finger, realizing it allowed third-class passengers and crew to move unseen past the lavish areas of first class. Since it had few turns, he wondered how often second-class passengers like himself used it, or if they even realized it was there. Noticing he could access Scotland Road via the second-class stairs, he made a mental note. Convenient. The nickname made him think of detective stories by Arthur Conan Doyle. "They might almost have called it Scotland Yard, like that major street back in Liverpool," he murmured with a faint smile.

He took the short stairs down to the Aft Well Deck and looked around, spotting the Number 5 and 6 cargo hatches. On the opposite side, a pair of stairs led up to the Third-Class Open Promenade. Robert felt his adrenaline rise. He knew he wasn't supposed to be there, but so long as he had his passport and ticket, would it really cause any trouble?

Crossing the well deck toward the stairs, he finally began to feel the deep vibrations of the engines beneath him. He looked at the signs over the doors behind the stairs. To his left, the Third-Class General Room; to his right, the Third-Class Smoke Room.

He ascended to the Stern Deck, where one of the electric cranes stood directly before the stairway, their twin arms raised as if in silent salute. The entire deck, covered in medium brown pitch pine, was spacious, with several benches near the center. Toward the back stood an elevated platform housing navigation equipment.

That's when he saw him. A young man stood with squared shoulders, gazing toward the open sea, holding a small brown book and standing beside a Trot-man anchor laid on its side. His lips moved silently and rhythmically, and his frame swayed gently with an unseen cadence. It wasn't a language Robert understood, but it didn't matter. The ritual spoke through posture alone, without words, as if the ship itself were being praised or warned.

Drawn by something he couldn't name, Robert inched closer. The man was praying. Beginning to feel guilty, Robert turned to head back toward Second Class when a crewman descended the stairs from the elevated platform of the Aft Docking Bridge.

"What's all this?" the crewman asked.

Robert turned, half-startled. The man made his way up to Robert, wiping his hands with a cloth.

"Apologies," Robert said, lifting a hand. "Just taking a look. Curious sort of fellow, I suppose."

"Aren't we all on this ship?" the young man replied. "She's a floating wonder. Certainly draws the mind outward, through steel and smoke."

His expression was neither angry nor confrontational. Just somewhat weary, with a hint of wry amusement.

"You're not the first. This ship draws the eye in all directions." He looked past Robert. "Third-Class Promenade is not strictly off-limits for second-class passengers. But it raises eyebrows. You do hold a second-class ticket, correct?"

Robert quickly pulled out his ticket and unfolded it. The crewman nodded.

"Not likely I'll be seeing much of First Class, if any," Robert said, gesturing toward the upper decks ahead. "Unless someone decides to extend an invitation."

The man laughed, shaking his head. "Wouldn't recommend trying. You shan't get half so far up there as you have here. First-Class doesn't often send envoys. But you've already seen more than most would dare."

Robert began to breathe a bit heavier. "Would that be a warning, sir?"

"Let's call it friendly advice. Ship this size, there's always someone watching and not all of them smile."

They both nodded and grinned.

"My name is Robert Morganson."

"Pleased to meet you, sir. I'm Sidney Daniels. Steward for Third Class. Previously worked on the *Olympic*. Just started here six days ago."

The young man with the book standing at the ensign staff, with the British national banner fluttering softly in the breeze, had noticed the exchange but didn't let on that he'd heard them.

After a pause, Sidney gestured casually toward the lower deck.

"But if it's the rest of the ship you're curious about…" he said, giving a slight nod toward the companionway, "Third class is a sight in itself. Might not be chandeliers and string quartets, but it's got a lively kind of spirit you won't find up there."

Robert raised an eyebrow. "Are you offering me a guided tour?"

Sidney glanced around as he smirked. "Let's say I'm steering your curiosity somewhere a little more welcome. I'm headed that way. Might as well show you a bit before anyone else comes around. Come along then, but mind your manners and your footing."

As they moved toward the stairs, the praying man turned briefly to watch them leave. *Curious… very curious*, he thought. Then, shrugging, he returned to his prayers.

Before entering through the Third-Class General Room, Robert noticed that the last passengers had boarded. Now those who were getting off were preparing to step onto the *Nomadic*.

Robert and Sidney descended a few levels, passing simple white-painted corridors, exposed pipes, and electric lights that flickered slightly. Along the way, Sidney gave short explanations. They were nothing dramatic, but just enough, tinged with subtle warning. Robert loved hearing the various languages being spoken by the Steerage passengers.

"Third-class isn't quite the hardship some might expect, Mr. Morganson. For the next week, families live down here. Workers. Many of them are dreamers. Not so different, really. Just a different kind of ticket."

They passed a simple dining room, glanced into an open dormitory-style berth, where the wool blankets had a very large knitted design of the company logo, and even saw the men's communal lavatory.

"It's not as bleak as I expected. It's actually quite nice here," Robert said.

"Yes. We've made improvements over the years. You should've seen Steerage ten years ago. Even second-class on other ships not much older are not as good."

A quiet moment passed. Robert looked into a brightly lit common area where many were socializing. Some were playing music on instruments they owned.

"Do you think they know? I mean… about how little space they have on deck?"

Sidney paused and thought for a moment. "Some know. Others don't. Many won't care. The accommodations here are far better than they've ever experienced in their entire lives. They've got hope. And they've got each other. For these people, that's all that really matters."

At the end of the walk, he led Robert up a narrow stairwell and back to the edge of Second Class. Robert offered his thanks.

"My pleasure. But best not to make a habit of wandering. Curiosity's fine, so long as you don't forget which side of the gate you belong to."

"I understand, sir. Thank you again."

The man gave a small, cryptic smile. "This ship is full of stories, sir. You look like the sort who'll write one of them down."

"I'm actually keeping a journal during my travels. I suppose you've seen the ship from top to bottom."

"More or less." He nodded. "But even I don't see everything. There are quite a few places I'm not allowed to see either. There's something strange about this ship. Not bad, of course. It's just... well, it's hard to put into words."

Robert smiled. "Still wandering about like a certain second-class passenger who got caught today?"

Sidney couldn't hide his grin. "Exactly." He tipped his cap. "But mind you, if any of the others catch you, you'll have more explaining to do than I will."

After shaking the man's hand, Robert made his way back up the stairs to Second Class. Noticing out of the corner of his eye that Sidney kept watching closely, Robert continued up to the top of the stairway, where the Promenade Deck offered its own vantage point. It encircled the fourth funnel, catching the wind like a crown upon the ship's great spine.

Unlike First Class, which had an uninterrupted ocean view, the Second-Class Promenade was largely blocked on both sides by eight of the ship's sixteen lifeboats. The view aft remained open, but otherwise the towering wooden hulls crowded the railing, a silent reminder of the limits even in second-class luxury.

Robert stepped closer to one of them, eyeing the thick ropes that held it in place and the heavy canvas stretched taut across its frame. Each boat rested in a cradle-like stand on the deck, surrounded by a short removable railing. Curiously, they weren't suspended from the davits at all. Just secured alongside them.

He recognized the davits as the new Welin double-acting quadrant type were recently introduced on some of the larger liners. They could swing into the boat deck as well as out. Unlike older models, these were designed to hold more boats than were actually mounted, up to four per set. It was a modest improvement over what he'd seen on Cunard liners.

He leaned in, studying the metal arms and pulleys. The davits didn't just pivot out. They seemed built to swing inward as well. Could it be…? An inner row of lifeboats might be stored on deck beside the first, then lifted into place and swung outward for launch. Ingenious, in theory. But only if more boats were actually provided.

Robert took some time to examine the map carefully. Attached to the fourth funnel in the center, he saw the pipes leading from the First-Class Lounge, which had the only functional fireplace. There were other pipes connecting to the funnel from the galleys where food was prepared.

The engineers had their own small promenade, a narrow walkway that served as a buffer between the wealthy and the working class. Forward of that was the First-Class Open-Air Promenade Deck, which was the largest and grandest of them all, stretching from just behind the third funnel all the way past the first.

Titanic was deemed an indestructible marvel, built with the latest safety measures. A ship destined for the history books. It was a masterfully designed ship, even if some passengers grumbled about the arrangement.

As Robert returned to the entrance of the Second-

Class Stairs, he slipped his hand into his satchel, and his fingers instinctively traced the book's worn cover.

Pulling the novel out, he found the page he'd discreetly marked earlier: *'The same professional standard applied to the personnel of the engine room, and the steward's department was equal to that of a first-class hotel… In short, she was a floating city—containing within her steel walls all that tends to minimize the dangers and discomforts of the Atlantic voyage—all that makes life enjoyable. Unsinkable—indestructible, she carried as few boats as would satisfy the laws.'*

Well, that was very unsettling.

Glancing back at the lifeboats again, the words felt extremely familiar. But *Olympic* didn't sink due to the watertight compartments sealing automatically. *Titanic* had the same capabilities. Only better. With improvements that *Olympic* did not have.

Robert shook his head, fighting the stirrings of superstition that threatened to take root. He was never a superstitious person. But he looked again at the row of only four lifeboats in front of him. Eight here in the stern with the other half in the bow. Just sixteen. For a ship that could carry almost 3,000 people.

Robert did some rough math in his head. "If each lifeboat holds between 60 and 70 souls, that would make… what? Roughly a thousand?" he mused. "Were these new leviathans becoming too large for their own good?"

Almost dropping the novel from his shaking hands, he stole one more glance at the towering stern. Somewhere beneath the surface, three great propellers lay still. Soon to begin turning for the journey. The *Titanic* hadn't even begun her voyage, and yet, a strange weight settled in Robert's chest. He shook it off. The future was for another day.

A voice, lightly touched with an Irish lilt, broke through his thoughts.

"Young man, is that book worth the reading?"

Robert turned and saw a man, seemingly his own age, leaning casually against the rail. One hand was tucked into his overcoat; the other cradled a curved pipe, its silver ring near the bowl shined in the orange light despite a small amount of tarnish, still trailing a faint curl of blue smoke. He gestured toward *Futility*, still resting in Robert's hand.

Robert hesitated, then gave a modest smile. "I believe so. It's… quite interesting, actually."

The man stepped forward and gave a low chuckle.

"Ah, yes *Futility*. I believe I've heard of it. An American fellow penned it, didn't he? Intelligent chap, I've no doubt. Bit of a shame, that one. Couldn't hardly give the blasted thing away last I heard. That's the tale about a ship that founders at sea, isn't it?"

"It does?" Robert blinked, surprised. "I've not read far yet. Only came across it recently. Someone meant to throw it out." He turned the book over in his hands. "It's remarkable, truly. How authors can summon such visions from imagination alone."

The man nodded thoughtfully, inhaling from his pipe and exhaling to the side to keep the smoke out of Robert's face before replying.

"Fiction's a curious business, wouldn't you say? Seems some books know more than the men who write them. It's uncanny sometimes how close it runs to life. And every so often, mark my words, fiction sooner or later, becomes fact."

He inclined his head and pointed to the book with his pipe. "What's the name of that ship again?"

Robert opened the book and read aloud, "The *Titan*."

The man stepped a bit closer, peering at the page. Was

Robert losing his hearing? He had expected to hear the man's footsteps. But he didn't.

"Well now… that *is* something. Considering that we now find ourselves aboard a ship called *Titanic*…"

His voice drifted off, as though carried on the salt wind.

Robert's eyes caught another line on the page. *Built of steel throughout and for passenger traffic only… She was eight hundred feet long, forty-five thousand tons' displacement…*

Titanic was just over 882 feet. The advertisements noted the displacement of exceeding 46 thousand tons.

Robert said nothing, turning toward the horizon. The sun had dipped low, streaking the sky with deep orange, and a few deck lights flickered to life. He tried to think of any rational explanation. But nothing came.

For a fleeting moment, a ripple of panic stirred in his chest. He glanced toward the dock. What if he got off now after he grabbed his things and left? Did he have time?

But the small *Nomadic* had already cast off. It was on its way to the shore. Too late. The decision had already been made for him.

One of the *Titanic's* whistles bellowed through the air. A deep, resonant, commanding voice that trembled through the soles of his feet. It was preparing to depart. Robert exhaled and watched the swirling churn of the water below. Though he couldn't see it, he knew the bow anchor had already been raised.

Taking a breath, he caught the smell of the man's pipe and turned to ask him a question.

But he was gone. No footsteps, no echo of retreat. Just silence. That, and faint, unnatural stillness, as if the ship itself had briefly held its breath. Only the soft scent of pipe smoke lingered, curling gently away into the open air.

Robert looked down the deck. Nothing. He stepped around the corner, but again, no trace. Had he imagined the whole thing? A cold prickle ran down his spine, despite the relative warmth of the evening. His gaze darted left, then right, scanning the empty deck, searching for any sign, any distant figure. The faint scent of pipe smoke, now a ghostly reminder, was the only evidence of the encounter.

"Oh no. Not again," he murmured. "Please… not again."

Even on the largest ship in the world, there were only so many places someone could vanish. Had the man slipped inside? No footsteps. No creaking stairs. He hadn't heard the lift. It had felt like a chance encounter, but now it felt like something else.

Had he imagined it? Freud would call it projection, the mind inventing what it feared to see. But Robert could still smell the smoke. Why?

You're going home, he reminded himself. *Steady yourself.*

Indestructible. Unsinkable. That's what people were saying.

He tucked the book back into his satchel and stepped inside, trying to shake off the unease that clung to him like mist. "It's best not to dwell on phantoms," he told himself. He had a long journey ahead, and hunger was a far more immediate and tangible concern.

Descending the stairs, Robert took deep, calming breaths, letting his fingers brush against the smooth wood paneling. Using one of the calming methods that Dr. Freud had taught him. He knew the *Titanic* was already underway, but it felt as if the ship were perfectly still.

On the *Mauretania*, the obvious vibrations of the powerful turbines through the flooring were always a subtle reminder of the speed beneath his feet. But now, nothing. It seemed like the engines were not even running. After descending the steps another few decks, he could hear the engines and feel the slight movement under his feet.

Robert's fears finally faded as he stepped into the Second-Class Dining Saloon. The scent of freshly cooked food. He noticed a hint of fish and some kind of meat he couldn't place. The scents were mixed with the rhythmic sound of someone cutting produce and the aroma of warm bread. The dining saloon felt alive, mingling with the quiet hum of conversations.

After days of travel, it was a welcome moment of warmth. He had never been so far from home before. Certainly not for this long. Traveling alone had its advantages, but at times, it was very isolating. Tonight, though, as he found a place to sit near the wall and breathed an audible sigh of relief, the passage of time finally slowed to a calm. The world outside of *Titanic* faded, if only for a little while. The projected phantom might haunt the deck above, but here, among inviting fragrances and murmured conversation, life was ordinary again. Finally.

Around him, the low murmur of conversations filled the air, a blend of English accents, scattered German, and what sounded like Scandinavian. Families settled at tables, children excitedly pointing at the silverware, while a few lone gentlemen, like himself, found quiet corners, already deep in thought or lost in their own worlds. It was a comforting experience, a slice of life transported across the sea.

After a few moments, Robert heard the voice of a woman. "Honestly, Benjamin, I shan't sleep a wink this entire voyage. That anyone could build such a vessel and call her unsinkable. It flies in the face of God. Especially after what happened leaving Southampton."

Piqued by this, Robert stood to introduce himself as the couple walked by with their young daughter.

"Benjamin Hart. This is my wife, Esther, and our daughter, Eva. She's seven."

Robert smiled warmly as he greeted their child with a wave. "As I'm traveling alone this voyage, might you join me for dinner if you've no objection?"

Esther thanked him but still looked unsettled. "It was the incident this morning that left me uneasy."

"Is that so?" Robert asked. "What occurred, exactly?"

Benjamin explained, "A smaller liner called the *New York* was moored nearby. When *Titanic*'s engines engaged, the suction drew her toward us. The mooring lines snapped like string, and the stern swung perilously close. It looked to be within feet of the hull."

Robert raised his brows. "And how was a collision avoided?"

"I'm not sure. A crewman explained that one of the tugs responded quickly, which managed to catch a line to the *New York* and pulled her back. The captain ordered the port propeller reversed as well, if I'm not mistaken. Created a wash that helped push her away."

"But neither ship was damaged?"

"Thankfully, no," Esther said. "But I cannot shake the feeling that something dreadful lies ahead. That this ship will not reach New York… the city, I mean… not the vessel we nearly struck."

Suddenly, Robert's concern returned. A near disaster with a ship called the *New York*? Their destination was New York City. Robert had not read much of the novel in his satchel, but for some unknown man to tell him that the ship sank and it was named the *Titan*. He wasn't sure how it sank in the book. The image on the cover hinted at how, but he wasn't sure he wanted to know just yet.

He was trying not to think of the photo of the *Olympic*'s damage. Accidents happen. *Olympic* didn't sink, and *Titanic* averted a collision. Surely people were learning from past mistakes?

Before long, the stewards provided menus. Robert scanned the options, expecting something simple. Perhaps roast beef, a soup, or a cold meat salad. What caught his eye instead made him pause.

Among the offerings was a dish styled after a traditional American Thanksgiving meal. It wasn't elaborate. Just roast turkey with a light dressing, cranberry relish, and mashed potatoes. But the familiarity caught him off guard. He pointed it out with a soft chuckle, explaining to the Harts that Thanksgiving had always been the most important holiday in his family growing up.

They listened with interest. Eva, curious, asked what it was like. Her mother commented that the dish was likely a novelty abroad meant to amuse or accommodate Americans en route back home.

"We've heard of Thanksgiving," she said, "but it's never quite made its way across the Atlantic, being an American celebration of its founding."

Robert nodded. The presentation was simpler than what he remembered from home, but something about it still reassured him. In the midst of the unfamiliar of the ship, the journey, and the ache of everything left behind, it was a small reminder of who he was and where he came from.

And that, despite everything, he still had much to be grateful for. Every day. Not just the fourth Thursday in November.

After dinner, Robert noticed that Esther wasn't returning to her cabin. Curious, he watched as she ascended the stairs and quietly followed at a distance to see where she was going. She walked outside to the Boat Deck and eventually sat on one of the benches near the lifeboats.

Keeping back, Robert watched her from the shadows. His heart raced and he found it hard to control his breathing. He felt terrible for spying on her this way.

She looked worried. She was trying not to cry. Robert was concerned as to why she was so upset.

Then, standing up and bowing her head in prayer, Esther walked over and placed her hands gently on the side of the nearest lifeboat, perhaps anchoring her fears to something solid or seeking comfort and expressing gratitude for the presence of some safety measures. Several minutes passed, and then softly, she began to sing.

The tune was familiar, though Robert couldn't quite place its name or origin. One line echoed in his memory as she sang it gently into the night: "For those in peril on the sea…"

At this point, her prayer was very quiet, and though he was unable to hear what she was saying, Robert felt it was not appropriate to eavesdrop on her.

He quietly turned away, giving her the dignity of that moment. Yet something about it lingered. A kind of solemnity that echoed faintly in his own unsettled thoughts. She had reached for the lifeboat like it was a tether, and although he hid in the shadows of the night, he realized he too was searching for something to hold onto.

But it had to be something he could see and touch. Faith alone would not be enough for his rational mind. He was not opposed to religions so long as they made people kinder. Belief was only as acceptable as the good it inspired, he often thought. He cared more about what people did in response to their beliefs.

Maybe it was the book still in his satchel or the feeling that this voyage had already begun to ask questions he wasn't ready to answer. As he descended the stairs back to his cabin, the image of her framed by the lifeboat and starlight stayed with him as a soft, steady, and strangely haunting feeling.

He could understand her concerns. *Perhaps she knows something we don't*, Robert thought to himself. If he were being honest with himself, he would admit he was still a bit on edge, too. He was very scared on his first transatlantic crossing. Knowing he would be away from his relatives for so long and heavily dependent on the kindness of others made him feel like he would never be an adult.

But now something else bothered him. The novel in his satchel weighed heavily on his mind. Its very existence puzzled him. Fourteen years ago, there had been no ship near the size of the *Titanic*. He tried to remember if he had ever heard of a real ship named *Titan*. Nothing came to mind.

Cunard and White Star had listings of their various ships in active service. Robert had noticed that as a naming convention, Cunard vessels ended in "*ia*," and White Star's ended in "*ic*." German liners were named with the prefix *Kaiser*, German for Emperor, then the name of the national leader.

The vessel may be designated as a Royal Mail Steamship, but underneath, it was just really "*steamship Titanic*." Even the plaques on the lifeboats said so. *S.S. Titanic*.

Then there was the name of the author. So similar to his own. Could it be a pen name?

And that cover image. It unsettled him. A towering iceberg loomed in the background as a multi-funneled liner slipped beneath the waves.

Should he ask her about the novel? Had she ever heard of it? Would it put her fears at ease? Or cause distress? Perhaps it's best not to tell her about it. Better not to burden her with tales of doom from a book that might be just that. A book.

With all these thoughts in mind, Robert found his cabin door. He wanted to write a little before going to sleep. Checking the time, he made a note of it and the date before writing.

'A welcome surprise on the dinner menu this evening: roast turkey with cranberry sauce, accompanied by mashed potatoes and green beans. No doubt a nod to American travelers. For a moment, it didn't feel as though I were thousands of miles from home. Strange to think that, in less than a week, I will be back in America.

The principal topic was the near-collision with a smaller ship earlier today, shortly after we left Southampton. It reminded several of the incident between Olympic *and* Hawke *last year. I was told it was no cause for alarm. Simply the natural effects of water displacement by so large a vessel. Later, I overheard passengers on the First-Class Promenade recounting the same, with varying degrees of concern and amusement. A close call, to be sure, even before reaching open water. Surely not an ill omen. Though some have already begun to mutter of bad luck.*

These two sister ships, both hailed as invincible, each beginning their service with misfortune? It seems unlikely. And yet… I do wonder. How close did each truly come to calamity? There was laughter among some. But I would be dishonest if I claimed the matter did not weigh on me. It does. Still, I cannot disembark. So I shall leave superstitions to sailors and poets.

A new acquaintance I met refuses to sleep in her cabin. Her husband is insistent that she rest. But she refuses. Said she will sleep during the day. Right now she stays at the lifeboats. She sang to the sea tonight. Not with hope, but with warning. Her voice, soft as prayer, carved into the calm quiet of the night. I watched from the shadows and felt the shape of my own doubts take form.

If faith is a tether, I still reach for what is visible. But what if visibility deceives? I do not fear drowning. I fear misunderstanding the depths.

After closing his journal and putting it away, Robert hesitated for a moment before he pulled out *Futility* to read a few more pages. He was still only on the first chapter. The words didn't concern him much that night. But they would later.

'...*that in case of an end-on collision with an iceberg—the only thing afloat that she could not conquer—her bow would be crushed in but a few feet further at full than at half speed, and at the most three compartments would be flooded, which would not matter with six more to spare...*'

A cold shiver pricked Robert's skin despite the warmth of the cabin. An iceberg. The very thought felt ludicrous. A ship of the *Titanic*'s strength striking something so inert and raw? He tried to dismiss it, to remind himself of the multiple layers of steel, the reinforced bow, and the very physics of such a collision rendering it survivable, as the book claimed. These ocean liners were built to withstand the worst the Atlantic could throw at them. To be profitable for their companies, they had to be able to sail year-round on strict schedules, no matter the weather or the season.

Three compartments at most. Six more to spare. The words were meant to be reassuring, a testament to the *Titan's* (and, by extension, the *Titanic*'s) resilience. But the image of that vast, white mountain of ice, portrayed almost as if it were a monster, still lingered at the edge of his vision.

Robert kept reading into the next chapter. The *Titan* was departing New York, bound for England. The opposite direction of his own voyage. The author introduced a few key characters and detailed the ship's impressive capabilities with renewed precision. Strangely, Robert began to feel a little more at ease. The thought of the *Titan* departing New York, bound for England, was a comforting disconnect for him.

Robert imagined the two ships passing each other like dignified gentlemen of the sea in the vast Atlantic, perhaps tipping their massive hats in silent acknowledgment or exchanging greetings with a dignified blast of their steam whistles. It was a pleasant image, a far cry from the unsettling premonitions that had plagued him earlier.

The descriptions of the fictional ship, as he read on, seemed to diverge subtly from the reality of the *Titanic*'s own formidable structure, making the whole prophetic angle feel a little less potent; a little more like... well, like fiction. In fact, as the descriptions unfolded, he found himself thinking less of the ship he was on and more of his previous time aboard the familiar, if less grand, *Mauretania*.

Feeling sleep beginning to claim him, he pushed on to the end of the paragraph: '*...the passengers dispersed themselves as suited their several tastes. Some were seated in steamer chairs, well wrapped—for, though it was April, the salt air was chilly—some paced the deck, acquiring their sea legs; others listened to the orchestra in the music-room, or read or wrote in the library, and a few took to their berths...*'

Ah, yes. The library. He was looking forward to visiting it tomorrow. The ship still felt perfectly still, though he could faintly hear the low rhythm of the engines from his vantage point. Not loud, but unmistakably present.

Robert set the book aside on the small writing desk, the faint scent of its aged paper mingling with the newness of the cabin. He stretched his legs and arms out with a yawn as he reached out to extinguish the lamp, plunging the small room into a soft, comforting darkness.

As he leaned back against the headboard, the hum of the engines, a low, steady heartbeat of the behemoth, became more noticeable in the quiet. He closed his eyes, letting sleep quietly overtake him, allowing himself a small, private smile.

Perhaps the old professor was right after all. Maybe a change of scenery was precisely what he needed. The grand ship, a testament to human will, he was confident, would carry him home. And for tonight, that was enough. He closed his eyes, the image of the vast, open ocean just beyond his porthole a promise of safe passage.

Outside, the countless stars blinked silently above the vast Atlantic, watching the *Titanic* slip farther into the dark, silent night, carrying its unwitting passengers deeper into the unknown.

3

HAPPY MEDIUM—SECOND CLASS

Thursday, April 11th—Breakfast—Celtic Sea

Stars from the night before had long since faded by the time the morning light entered Robert's cabin. The low pulse of the engines was still there, unchanged, as yellow morning rays streamed through the thick glass of the porthole, gently waking him from his rest. Surprised by the cabin's stillness, Robert stretched, then got out of bed and walked over to look outside. The ship was still moving. How could it be so stable in the water?

He had slept surprisingly well. Much better than he had on the *Mauretania*. On the *Mauretania*, he had only sponge-bathed, unwilling to risk vulnerability, and even that had felt unsafe. Here, aboard the *Titanic*, he had dared something more, even if it may be just the once: to use the showers.

The warmth of the water had surprised him, almost as if it were a balm. The simple act of at least rinsing was very soothing. But the moment he'd heard footsteps echoing nearby, the old dread returned, sharp and sudden. He'd chosen to remain in stillness, but the echoes continued.

The low hum of the ship, a passing footstep, the sound of water flowing through the pipes, the clang of metal nearby—any one sound could tighten his chest. He had whispered to himself the same words that had often carried him through the worst: "You're safe now, Robert. You know you're safe."

Looking out past the curtain, he only saw a crewman restocking supplies before turning to leave. The silence had answered back. But even silence, at times, can feel like a physical presence. Robert hurried to finish so he could get dressed.

Taking some time to reassure himself, he brought his journal, wanting to capture everything while it was still fresh in his mind. The Second-Class Dining Saloon had surprised him yesterday. It was larger than he expected, stretching the full width of the ship. Wooden doors framed like those of a fine country club welcomed passengers inside. Four long rows of tables sat under a finely detailed ceiling, while large portholes set into recesses let in plenty of daylight. The mahogany chairs with crimson upholstery were bolted to the floor and swiveled easily, which was a luxury unheard of on many ships.

White Star couldn't compete with Cunard's speed, so they'd invested in comfort. Unlike the two speedy Greyhounds of the Atlantic, the company prided itself on luxury. Since passengers were limited to the confines of a ship until they reached their destination, they might as well enjoy the journey.

Similar to the night before, tables were draped in white linens, with polished silverware and bowls of fresh fruit. Dining at sea was a social affair. Passengers exchanged stories, discussed business, and played games. Among the passengers Robert met, one in particular stood out: a rather intelligent science teacher and journalist. Well-educated yet unpretentious, carrying himself with humility.

Lawrence Beesley brought up the incident in Southampton upon learning that Robert boarded at Cherbourg the prior evening.

"Well, I've just spoken with the Hart family, and from

what their daughter told me, you missed quite the excitement back in Southampton. But boarding at Cherbourg gave you the unique chance to experience the *Nomadic*. You seem a touch preoccupied. Is something troubling you?"

Robert hesitated. He was honest, though he withheld certain details. He chose not to mention the novel or his recent consultations with Dr. Freud.

"I had heard about the *Olympic's* accident last year when I first boarded. Then Benjamin and Esther told me about the near miss yesterday in Southampton. It gave me pause. Ships have never been built on this scale before. And I've read that even larger ones are now being planned.

But I wouldn't call myself superstitious. I strive to remain rational. I suppose what I'm struggling with most at present is the distance. I've never been this far from home, and I'm traveling alone. There's a certain loneliness to it.

My father died just recently while I've been overseas. He was, well, to be polite about it, very difficult. I could never seem to meet his expectations. We had not been on speaking terms when I left. He and my mother divorced when I was quite young, and she later remarried. She and my stepfather both live nearby still and are retired. But I've recently learned he's having back problems. I have a younger brother and sister, but neither lives close. We don't correspond much.

I beg your pardon. I've never been especially skilled at social conversation. I often find myself thinking or behaving very differently from what others expect, and I don't always understand why."

Lawrence nodded thoughtfully. "I've seen you writing in a book a few times. A journal, I take it?"

"Yes, sir. A new one. Writing has always come more easily to me than conversation. It comes more naturally to me. I've always been something of a solitary soul, I suppose."

"Young man," Lawrence said, leaning forward and resting his hands on the table, "there's nothing wrong with needing solitude. Some require more of it than others. But from what I gather, you observe the world with unusual care. That is not a flaw. When one notices what others do not, it simply means one is more attuned to what matters. There is, after all, a difference between hearing and truly listening."

Robert couldn't help smiling. His shoulders relaxed as he let out a quiet breath. "Thank you. That brings me some comfort. I had begun to wonder whether I was being unreasonable. I've been known to leap to conclusions without fully weighing the consequences."

Lawrence offered a kindly expression. "We've all done as much. But I can tell you think in your own way and the world needs that. I take it, from your accent, that you're American? Then this must be your return crossing?"

"Correct. I live in New Mexico, now a state, as of this past January. We were a territory for many years. I confess, it still feels odd calling it a state. Especially since I left for Europe some time before the change was made official.

It's been a long-held dream of mine to travel so I could see distant places and visit the lands my ancestors once called home before they made their way to America more than a century ago."

"And what have you thought of your travels thus far?" Lawrence asked, clearly pleased.

Robert smiled. "I mean to travel again at the first opportunity. And much farther next time."

Robert took an immediate liking to Lawrence. They both loved books and writing, and in their easy conversation, Robert felt something rare: a quiet sense of belonging. For the first time in a long while, he didn't feel so odd, so adrift in a world that often seemed to move without him.

When their talk faded into a companionable silence, Robert leaned back in his chair and glanced toward the windows. The *Titanic* was already well underway, yet the dining saloon felt still, almost suspended between the sky and sea. It was a strange and comforting illusion. That something so massive could glide so quietly through the ocean.

Whenever the weather allowed, he spent time outside, drawn again and again to the endless blue horizon. On his first crossing, he couldn't get enough of the ocean view. It amazed him how sailors could navigate such vast spaces with little more than a compass and the stars. Fragile tools against an ocean where landmarks and leaving breadcrumbs would never be possible. Yet somehow, people found their way.

Later that same morning, after another stretch of quiet reflection on deck, Robert wandered into the Second-Class Library. He intended to browse the shelves but paused when he spotted a chess set arranged neatly on one of the tables, waiting.

A familiar voice echoed from long ago. His father's steady tone: *"Remember, assume nothing, question everything."*

Robert grinned, a small, unguarded smile. He missed the good times he had shared with his father, few though they were; moments like learning chess, where patience and foresight mattered more than speed or strength.

Similar concepts were imparted to him when his father took him fishing on the Elephant Butte Lake, formed by the recent dam construction that began in 1906. Although it was the last time he and his father ever spoke, they were lessons that still, somehow, continued to endure.

Turning to the bookshelves, his gaze wandered the inventory, until a slender spine caught his eye. Edward Fitzgerald's English translation of *The Rubáiyát of Omar Khayyám*. Published in 1859, it was a very thin book and organized into quatrains, which were sections of four lines each. Suddenly, Robert recalled reading in the local papers that a priceless jeweled copy of this book was won at a recent auction at Sotheby's in London. Now, it was in one of the cargo holds being delivered to New York.

Robert thought of a saying his uncle had taught him when he and his cousin were children. "*Never judge a book by its cover until you've read the pages found within it.*"

Pulling the book off the shelf and opening it, the rhythmic verses of the *Rubáiyát* drew him in:

'Irám indeed is gone with all its Rose,
And Jamshýd's Sev'n-ring'd Cup, where no one knows;
But still the Vine her ancient Ruby yields,
And still a Garden by the Water blows.'

By the twenty-sixth quatrain, his interest began to fade, until he paused at the last few lines:

'Oh, come with old Khayyám, and leave the Wise
To talk; one thing is certain, that Life flies;
One thing is certain, and the Rest is Lies;
The Flower that once has blown for ever dies.'

Robert wondered what, if anything, anyone could ever be certain about. Apparently, there were a few other translations of the text included to thicken the volume somewhat. Closing the book and placing it back, Robert was surprised to find a parallel Greek-English edition of the *Apocrypha*.

He remembered using a similar copy years ago to practice his Greek while reading classics by Plato and Homer in the attic. Out of habit, he checked the copyright. Published by S. Bagster in London, 1871. Same edition he learned Greek from. But not feeling drawn to anything religious at the moment, he continued browsing.

Next, he found a volume of poems by George Gordon Byron titled *Childe Harold's Pilgrimage*. Robert was surprised at the book's age. Clearly a much later reprint, as the book was in such good condition. The years of publication were listed between 1812 and 1818. Sitting at a table near the bookshelf, Robert quickly lost himself in the words until his worries came flooding back at a particularly brief poem:

'Roll on, thou deep and dark blue Ocean—roll!
Ten thousand fleets sweep over thee in vain.
Man marks the earth with ruin.
His control stops at the shore.'

A cold knot tightened in his stomach. He tried to tell himself it was just poetry, a dramatic flourish of language and interpretation. But the words echoed with a chilling resonance, striking too close to the unspoken fears already simmering beneath his calm façade. He read it twice. Then a third time. The words stirred something nameless inside him. A shiver, perhaps. But only a passing one.

The sea beyond the windows was calm, endless, and unknowable. This ship felt like she could conquer it all. The floor under his feet felt as still as solid earth. He forced his eyes to scan other lines, but the rhythm of the ocean's relentless power, and Byron's grim assertion of man's limited control clung to his thoughts. Robert closed the book and returned it to the shelf.

Then his eyes fell on *Hesiod's Theogony*, one of the best-known Greek classics. He flipped through it, reading of the ten-year war between the elder gods—the Titans—and their younger challengers, the Olympians. A footnote at the bottom of the page gave it a name: the *Titanomachy*. Greek for *War of Titans*.

A shiver traced his spine. ***Titanomachy:*** *defiance punished by the gods.*

He slammed the book shut louder than he intended and tried to breathe. *It was just mythology… just coincidence. Right?*

Robert recalled passing mentions of the Titans in *The Iliad* and *The Odyssey*, but this was something else. More vivid, more *personally impacting*, perhaps even *ominous*.

The Titans fell for their arrogance. And what of those who built this modern one?

The Titans lost the war, he thought, and Zeus imprisoned them in the dark depths of the earth never to rise, never to see daylight again.

Just like the R.M.S. Titanic … *no* … *the* S.S. Titan*!*

The thought gnawed at him. The names kept blurring in his mind. Fable and fact, memory and myth.

He rubbed his temples. Dr. Freud, during one of their sessions in Vienna, had once warned him about symbols that return uninvited. "*Repetitive compulsion*," he called it. The mind's way of forcing a confrontation with something buried deep.

He tried to recall how "*Titan*" and "*Titanic*" might have been rendered in ancient Greek. His memory of the language was faint, but he opened his journal and scribbled them down as best he could. '*A war between gods—an arrogance punished. How fitting that the name* Τιτᾶν "Titan" *keeps following me…*'

Another word came to mind. Something from the same root, he thought. It had meant straining, overreaching. He considered writing it too. But the ink hadn't dried before he muttered, "Snap out of it, Robert. You're going to drive yourself mad… again."

Robert retreated back to his journal: '*I find it is a curious thing, the pride some seem to take, simply in standing aboard this ship.*

A somewhat older man on the deck above me earlier. British, judging by the accent. He remarked, "No one's ever built anything this big before. It's a floating city." He also mentioned that he looked forward to dining with Captain Smith himself. I believe it was the same fellow who tried to impress me aboard the Nomadic yesterday. I suppose I ought to feel the same sense of awe. The Titan *is… why did I do that again!? I mean, the* Titanic *is impressive, certainly. Yet something in all this grandeur unsettles me. There is a kind of overconfidence in the air. Passengers boasting of the ship's size, its strength, and even its supposed unsinkability.'*

Robert hovered his pen over the written error "*The Titan,*" meaning to cross it out. But he hesitated. What was holding him back? He resumed writing.

'It puts me in mind of something Dr. Freud once said. At least, something I recall from one of our conversations in Vienna: "When a man must speak constantly of his power, it is not power that truly concerns him." He said it with a faint smile, but I knew he meant it. I am not one to boast. My life has never been shaped by achievements so grand they required public praise. Perhaps that is why I feel more the observer here than a true participant. Let others marvel at the chandeliers and endless corridors. I find myself more interested in what lies beneath me. The heartbeat of the ship and the many souls few ever speak of. The ones who keep this vessel alive. Without them, she would not stir.

Perhaps I shall yet find something more to admire before the week is through. But today, I find myself wondering whether this ship is too proud for its own good. I keep thinking of the man I saw last night. Or thought I saw. Would that I could be sure. A figure who seemed to know things that unsettled me. I try to reason it away with my fatigue, shadows, the imagination stirred by this novel still tucked in my satchel. But the encounter clings to my thoughts like fog upon the sea.'

He tried to reconstruct the encounter, searching for a flaw in his memory, a logical explanation for the man's abrupt disappearance. Yet each time, the same chilling impossibility remained, leaving him with the creeping sensation of being watched or, more disturbingly, of teetering on the edge of something far stranger than he cared to admit.

'It called to mind something else Dr. Freud once said during my brief time under his care in Vienna: "You can unlock any door if only you have the right key." At the time, I believed he spoke of dreams, traumas, and fears. But what if he meant more? What if the door is not merely of the mind, but of time itself? Memory, intuition, warning… what if they are all bound together?

I boarded this ship in search of distance from the past and to return home with some measure of peace. But now I wonder: did the past follow me? Or worse, has the future begun to speak?

Perhaps I am simply tired. Perhaps I imagine it all. And yet… perhaps a door is indeed beginning to open. While I strive in vain to keep it shut.'

Robert closed his journal and sat still for a long moment, listening to the quiet shuffle of pages and footsteps in the library. The ship hummed beneath him, steady and sure, but something in him felt unmoored. He glanced once more at the shelf where the books remained on display, then turned away. There were doors he wasn't ready to open. Not yet. Outside, the Atlantic waited. Vast, indifferent, and ancient. And somewhere within its silence, Robert felt the faintest pull, as if something had begun to stir.

Later that afternoon—1:30 PM—Queenstown, Ireland

Needing time to decompress from all the intellectual correspondence, Robert enjoyed sitting on the B-Deck Promenade, which offered a generous view of the ship's stern, or higher up on the Second-Class section of the Boat

Deck. It gave him time to process what he had seen and heard from his fellow passengers.

While near one of the covered lifeboats, he noticed the fourth funnel barely emitted any smoke, unlike the other three. A bit of white mist mixed with a faint trace of black. Could it really serve a purpose beyond simply aesthetics? He had seen engineering diagrams of the Olympic Class. It was evident that these ships only required three funnels. Upon closer examination, he had seen brief mentions of a fireplace in the First-Class Men's Smoking Room and nearby kitchens. Apparently having a spare just for some added ventilation gave a visual impression of tremendous size and more power. Yet with only three of them needed, the ships were apparently much more fuel efficient.

He recalled while on the *Mauritania* that all four funnels were heavy with black smoke once the voyage had begun. While passing near the sister ship, the *Lusitania*, all four of those funnels likewise emitted a lot of smoke.

He squinted. For a brief moment, he thought he saw a figure at the top. Was it a crew member? Were there ladders inside? A stairway? It seemed ridiculous, so he decided not to write it down. However, beneath the funnel's crown, he realized that even here, at the edge of wonder, the ship had eyes.

As they cleared the coast, the central propeller was engaged, boosting the speed to a steady 21 knots. The ship remained remarkably stable.

Noticing the slight increase in speed, Robert stood near the railing, gazing at the endless Atlantic. No land in sight. He placed his hands on top of the rail. Unlike on the *Mauritania*, there wasn't even a tremor from the engines deep below.

"Amazing! So much progress in just a few years," he

marveled, taking in the crisp ocean air. The wind felt amazing against his skin. Smiling, his mind returned to the novel in his satchel. He looked again at the lifeboats nearby. "*Unsinkable—indestructible, she carried as few boats as would satisfy the laws.*"

Feeling the panic rising again, Robert carefully leaned over the railing, resting his chest on the top rail, and wrapped his arms around the lower rung on the opposite side. Gazing toward the water, he spotted what he thought was a whale far off, and some type of dolphins leaping over the waves. Trying to give the outward impression that he was only relaxing, he squeezed his hands to keep his balance so he didn't collapse from the sudden panic attack. "It's only a novel… mere fiction. None of it is real," he murmured, attempting to steady his thoughts. "What ever could possibly go wrong?"

Friday, April 12th—Late Afternoon—North Atlantic Ocean

Despite the comforts of Second Class, Robert noticed how its reserved areas, while elegant, felt contained compared to the lavish sprawl of First Class or the vast communal quarters of Steerage. It was the most expansive section, filled with those emigrating to Canada and the United States in search of a better life. Many of them only owned what they could carry in their hands, and most likely never saw friends or relatives again. Immigrants were the main source of financial income for ship companies like White Star and Cunard. As long as immigration was open and viable, company profits would be too. Meanwhile, those who were better off financially would travel overseas mainly for business. Very few could do so for pleasure. Robert certainly couldn't.

From his vantage point, Robert noticed both First-Class Promenades bustling with passengers. The barriers separating Second Class and the Engineer's Promenade kept him from getting any closer. Just beyond the partition, he spotted one of the expansion joints directly behind the third funnel.

For a moment, the joint opened slightly then partially closed. Then it happened again. Robert looked over the side and noticed the large waves. As the ship "entered" a wave, the joint closed as the middle of the ship rose slightly, maintaining its buoyancy, and as it "exited" the wave, it then opened and closed slightly. The same would happen at the bow section just seconds before.

The innovation reduced stress by allowing the ship to flex and bend with the gentle swell of the waves.

Robert thought back on his religious upbringing. Rather than providing the freedom it promised, he felt more constrained by the unwavering dogma. Briefly recalling the Sermon on the Mount in the Gospels, he playfully paraphrased one of the verses: *Blessed are the flexible for they will not get bent out of shape!* he thought, a smile playing on his lips. His parents would have never approved of such sass.

The sign in front of him read, ***NOTICE: Passengers Are Not Allowed on the Engineer's Promenade.*** Seeing a crewman step outside, Robert quickly turned around and faced toward the ocean. He didn't want to give the impression that he was a troublemaker. The upper Second-Class Promenade on the Boat Deck had numerous people enjoying the view and fresh sea air.

Walking around the corner, he looked over the railing to the lower First-Class Promenade and noticed two men and a young boy who was holding something in his hands. One of the men was instructing the boy what to do, while the voice of a noticeably older fellow standing directly below Robert announced something he couldn't quite catch. The child followed the instructions, and a wooden top spun for a long moment on the deck. The older man then began explaining a simplified lesson of physics to the boy.

Smiling, Robert turned back so as not to interrupt the lesson. He then descended the stairs to the lower Second-Class Promenade where it seemed to be quieter.

He found a bench by the railing directly forward of the Aft Well Deck on the port side, which was accessible from below by third-class passengers at the very back. He was about to step down to the Aft Well Deck when he noticed another sign posted near the gate: ***NOTICE: 2nd Class Passengers Are Not Allowed Forward of This***. He saw yet another on the opposite side of the stairs, facing away from him. Robert turned his back to the railing and leaned against it, resting his elbows behind him, which gave him a wide view of the area. Waiting until no one was looking, he discreetly opened the gate and stepped on top of the stairway to read what it said. ***NOTICE: 3rd Class Passengers Are Not Allowed on This Deck.***

Suddenly, Robert heard someone approaching and quickly returned to his area and closed the gate, making sure it was latched. He found a bench on his side of the railing with a decent view of the Aft Well Deck and the Third-Class Promenade at the very back of the ship. Apparently, even the people in Steerage had a lot of open space to congregate outside. He got comfortable on the bench and took a bite of a fresh pear, its sweetness a small comfort against the lingering unease.

He opened up *Futility* to read; the story was somewhat interesting about a disgraced sailor who had a run-in with a prior love interest. At one point, the crew attempted to cover up a major accident when the *Titan* sliced through a smaller vessel in a fog bank at high speed. No attempt was made to help the victims. The evidence was covered up so that the passengers could not learn what had happened. The details seemed outlandish, truly absurd.

Robert looked around from his vantage point. The day was clear, and the horizon could easily be seen in the bright sunlight. Maybe it was just a coincidence. "Maybe fiction only echoes truth when we look too intensely for patterns. It's just a novel, after all. Just fiction. Nothing more. Isn't it?" he said softly to himself, but skimming ahead, a line caught his eye, standing out from the page: '*A few hours of bright sunshine had brought the passengers on deck like bees from a hive, and the two broad promenades resembled, in color and life, the streets of a city.*'

Robert noted the chapter and page number in his journal and refilled his fountain pen with fresh ink. Around him, the faint hum of the engines vibrated through the ship. He closed his eyes, taking slow, deep breaths, grounding himself in that steady rhythm. Finding reassurance in the fact that, deep within the giant, the engine crew labored, surrounded by the deafening yet stable pulse of the mighty *Titan's*… I mean… *Titanic's* beating heart.

Leaning back and running his fingers through his hair, he felt his slightly long locks, and he recalled seeing a sign for a barbershop near the Second-Class Entrance on E Deck. Realizing his hair was getting a bit long for his liking, he decided to get a cut and a shave. The sun, mild but warming, pressed gently at his back as he rose and closed the book for now. Robert made his way inside. It was time for a trim.

As he descended toward E Deck, the ship's interior grew warmer and more enclosed. The scent of shaving cream, soap, and tobacco drifted faintly from the barbershop, mingling with the hum of conversation and the rhythmic clink of razors being cleaned. Robert paused at the doorway, watching a young steward sweep hair from the floor. It was a simple ritual, but something about it felt important. A kind of shedding, a trimming away of the weight he had carried. He stepped inside, ready to be made new.

Most of the time between him and Herbert Klein passed in silence. There was no expectation for conversation, which suited both men just fine. Robert's mind was too full of worries to entertain small talk. The air in the barbershop was thick with the scent of bay rum, soap, and lather. Robert leaned back, hearing the crisp snip of the shears near his ears and the soft bristle of the brush against his neck, a comforting ritual amidst the vastness of the ship. The low hum of the *Titanic's* engines vibrated gently through the floor, a steady, almost imperceptible rhythm.

Glancing around, Robert noted the various souvenirs available for purchase. He had tucked away the dinner menu from his first night. He decided to keep a copy of the writing stationery from the library that was given out for free. Sometimes the best keepsakes cost nothing.

After a few moments, the shears snipped away the last stray hairs from his neck. Robert gazed into the mirror, appreciating the clean trim and the fresh shave. His skin was soothed by the warm towel. Small touches that made him feel just a bit more polished for the voyage ahead.

"Perfect, Mr. Klein. Thank you," he said, paying the barber and stepping into the lit corridor. He paused briefly to feel his now shortened hair and was pleasantly surprised by the new sensation.

As he strolled toward the staircase leading to the working passage, a faint, melodic voice echoed from just beyond the walls. The words were unfamiliar; sung in a language he couldn't place. German? No, not quite. Though it was somewhat similar. Something vaguely Germanic, though softer and more lyrical. Certainly not Russian. The tone carried a quiet joy, almost wistful, stirring something in him. It came from the direction of Scotland Road.

He paused, listening. The tune was brief, fading as quickly as it had come, but one phrase: *"Tum-ba-la, tum-ba-la, tum-ba-la-laika, shpiel balalaika, tumbalalaika, freylach zol zayn,"* lingered in his mind, its cadence gently haunting. The melody, in its gentle rhythms, refused to leave Robert's thoughts. How many different cultures and languages could be found on this grand ship?

The melody, rich with a quiet joy, felt out of place and yet profoundly resonant amidst the polished wood and distant hum of the engines. It was a fragment of another world, carried across the Atlantic on the breath of someone's song.

Interested, yet unwilling to intrude, he hesitated for a moment, thoughtful, then quietly moved on. As Robert ascended the stairs, the melody lingered in his thoughts like a half-remembered dream. He didn't know the words, but the feeling remained. It was a kind of ache, sweet and sorrowful. It reminded him of something Dr. Freud once said about music: that it bypasses the intellect and speaks directly to the unconscious. Perhaps that was why it unsettled him. Not because he didn't understand it, but because some part of him could.

Later that day, while exploring more of the ship near the Second-Class Stairwell close to Scotland Road, he heard the same voice again. But in a different language. This time it was clearer. The soft cadence of meditation filling the corridor in rhythmic waves. He followed the sound until he spotted a young man in third-class attire standing in a quiet corner, head bowed over a brown book that was small enough to fit into a coat pocket.

Recognition dawned. He was certain it was the same voice he'd heard earlier. Not just from that hallway but from the Aft Well Deck. The man by the smaller stern anchor. Robert had only caught a glimpse of him back then. Their paths had nearly crossed but not quite. And now, here they were.

Respectfully, he waited, enjoying the pleasant musical intonations of the stranger's voice, until the man closed the small brown-covered book before stepping forward.

"Pardon me," Robert said gently. "I couldn't help but overhear your prayers. May I ask what that lovely language is?"

The young man looked up, eyes bright with mild surprise. "Hebrew," he said. "I was *davening Minha;* that means praying the afternoon service."

Robert extended a hand. "I'm Robert Morganson. From New Mexico in the United States."

"Shalom, Robert. I'm Leo Zimmermann, from Austria," the man replied with a warm smile as he accepted the gesture.

"Happy to meet you. I have spent some time in Vienna recently. I hope I haven't intruded."

Leo shook his head. "No apology necessary. I came to this area because the third-class decks are rather crowded just now, and I didn't wish to disturb anyone. You're from Second Class, yes?"

"I suppose the clothes give me away. But I've found the ship's design doesn't always respect the barriers between classes or people. I've been sitting out on C Deck, near the electric cranes," Robert replied. "One of the best views Second Class can claim."

Leo nodded. "Is that why you were exploring the

Steerage section yesterday? It seems that you got a private tour from one of the workers."

Robert began to blush from embarrassment. "Oh my! Yes, that was me yesterday. I know I shouldn't have done that, but I've been very sheltered much of my life and wasn't always given an explanation for *why* when I was a child. Similar to my later years actually."

He shifted a bit, then added, "If I may ask, your prayers sounded quite personal, though I've heard Jewish customs are very ancient and centered around community."

"They are. But my family is part of a newer tradition. I was raised very Orthodox, but now we follow what is called *Reform Judaism*. It seeks to balance our customs with the modern world. Our prayers are now recited in the local language so they may be understood by everyone, especially visitors. It's more important to understand the prayers than simply saying them. We believe in engaging with the broader world while keeping our faith intact."

Robert was intrigued. "I had no idea there were different movements within Judaism. Does that mean you see things differently from those who follow the more traditional ways?"

"In some ways, yes. But in other aspects we don't. You see, Orthodox Jews follow very strict rituals and dietary laws. Their prayers are only in Hebrew, with some in Aramaic. But we Reform Jews focus much more on ethics and actively working to make the world better for others. But all Jews teach that living a righteous life matters more than rigid observance of ancient customs alone."

"That actually makes a great deal of sense. I promise, if I ever hear you nearby again, it won't be a distraction in the least."

"Very well, Robert," Leo said. "I noticed there are

some stairs that connect your area with the Aft Well Deck. If you happen to notice me under the stairs, feel free to listen in. That way you cannot be reprimanded as long as you stay in your area of the ship and I stay in mine."

And there, in the quiet heart of a ship built to divide them, a bridge was quietly built. Stronger than the ship's anchor chains and just as enduring. It was a rare and unexpected comfort. For once, Robert felt accepted, not condemned, and the conversation flowed with an ease he hadn't known was possible with a stranger. "Perhaps," he mused, "some connections were destined to form, even on a ship so vast that anonymity seemed its default state."

Afterwards, while sitting on the Second-Class Promenade near the lifeboats, Robert made a few notes in his journal about Leo. Placing the journal back into his satchel next to *Futility*, he felt a pull to explore farther aft than he knew he should, his curiosity often leading him to the edges of places others avoided.

After a while, he spotted Leo emerging from one of the rooms beneath the Third-Class Promenade, heading toward the stairs to the Second-Class decks. Their planned meeting spot. Robert couldn't resist. He tried to remain discreet as he descended the Second-Class Stairs to the entrance of the library, before hurrying outside into the warm, bright sun.

He'd hoped for a quiet moment to simply observe Leo from a distance, when he spotted the man near the railing, swaying gently with the rhythm of the ship, murmuring softly, but this time in English. Robert recognized the moment as private, even sacred, and thought about turning to leave, but he bumped into one of the deck chairs and knocked it over.

Leo looked up, startled but not angry. Robert hesitated, unsure whether to apologize or simply disappear.

Standing at the top of the stairs for a moment, noticing the signs once again, Robert spoke clearly but respectfully. "I didn't mean to disturb you."

Leo offered a smile. "No harm done. I'm happy to see you again."

Robert shifted awkwardly. "Thank you. The feeling is mutual."

A moment passed between them before Robert stepped closer, lowering his voice. "I don't believe I've ever heard Jewish prayers before. I thought they were only said in synagogues."

Leo's voice contained a touch of warmth. "Many do attend synagogues… or *'shul'* if you prefer the Yiddish term. Judaism says that prayer can and really should happen almost anywhere. The Eternal One is not bound by walls or rituals. We still honor the same ancient traditions, but with a more modern approach."

Robert's curiosity deepened. "So it's not only about rules and rituals, but living an upright life?"

"Exactly," Leo said. "While rituals are important as a guide, we Jews believe that what people do in response to what they believe matters more than outward appearances."

Robert considered this. "I think I understand. There's an obvious respect in that."

Leo smiled. "I find peace in it. Especially on a ship like this."

The hum of the *Titanic's* engines filled the silence between them, the vast Atlantic stretching out before them. Robert sensed that, despite the differences in their backgrounds, they shared something intangible. A search for meaning, for hope, and perhaps for something else.

"Would you mind if I joined you for a little while?" Robert asked.

Leo's smile widened. "Please do. I'd be honored."

As the engines vibrated softly through the steel frame, Robert made his way down the stairs onto the Well Deck directly forward of the Third-Class Promenade and lingered beside Leo, feeling a quiet respect for the young man's devotion.

Suddenly feeling worried, Robert slipped a hand into his coat pocket, fingertips brushing his passport and the second-class ticket tucked there just in case a crewman questioned his presence.

The final prayer Leo recited struck Robert as very odd, as well as needless on a ship like this.

"Your last prayer, asking God to bring you to your destination safely and to keep you from harm. Do you really think it's needed on a ship like the *Titanic*?"

"Honestly, it couldn't hurt. Besides, there's an old Yiddish proverb: 'Man plans, and God laughs.' No ship is too mighty to sink. Not even this one. In the Bible, even the mighty giant Goliath fell to young David's stone."

Robert brushed it off, but a moment later, felt terrible about his attitude. "Leo, I apologize for my behavior. I want to learn more," he said, "but only with your permission."

Leo's eyes softened. "I pray every afternoon and evening. Sometimes later at night also. The morning prayers are the longest, so I normally don't do those in full if I decide to pray at all. Usually here under the stairs on this deck, where it's quieter. If it's too busy with people, the entrance to Scotland Road from the Second-Class Stairs is also an option. There are a few side corners where I am not directly in the hallway. You're welcome to join me or simply observe, if you prefer."

Robert hesitated, thinking about how he had scoffed at

Leo's prayers for safety while traveling. "Would that be disrespectful? Especially after what I just said to you?"

"Not at all," Leo assured him. "In fact, in our tradition, we welcome those who seek understanding. The prayers are ancient, but their meaning is timeless, especially on a journey like this. And if you want, you can add your own words aloud or silently. It's not about being perfect. It's about being aware. Doubt is not an obstacle to faith. It could be the beginning of it. I believe this could be an ideal place to meet. It's one of the few quiet spots where second- and third-class folks can *schmooze*... er, converse."

Robert nodded, surprised by how deeply he wanted to return. Not for the ship's marvels but for this. For something that made sense beyond steel and splendor. Something deeper than the grandeur of the ship or the excitement of the voyage. Saying the word silently in his mind, his eyes sparkled.

"I do like that word. Then *schmooze* we shall! I shall find you here again after dinner is served?" Robert asked.

Leo smiled. "Good. I'll be here."

Robert sat on the bench forward of the Aft Well Deck thinking about his experiences. In some ways, he preferred this over the nicer Second-Class Promenade, as he could have a closer look at the Steerage passengers. His world was rapidly opening to new ideas he never thought of considering before. Things he never imagined possible.

Dr. Freud had explained to him that much of his healing would only be possible by understanding his mind. That recovering from his trauma was possible by simply changing the way he thought. Robert took notes of his more recent observations while watching the passengers in Third Class, who seemed to be the happiest people on the ship despite how little they had in comparison to him.

As usual, his mind began filling with thoughts. Each

time he wrote them down, it felt like his mind was becoming less cluttered. As if the very thoughts themselves could be removed from his head and stored in a book:

'In considering the marvels of this vessel, such as its grand staircases, the Turkish bath, the swimming pool, most of which didn't exist on ships not more than a few years ago, and many other manners of refinement afforded to those above, it occurs to me that our cleverness in forging steel and harnessing power does not seem to have tempered the restlessness within.

The world grows ever more mechanized and magnificent. Just two years ago Casimir Funk discovered something in rice he calls a 'vitamine.' He thinks it is crucial in order for the human body to survive. He says there could be many more of these 'vitamines' that we don't even know of. If that is the case, I'll be requesting rice at the next meal.

Yet I cannot say we are truly any happier for all this progress. The good folk in Steerage carry heavy burdens, those in first class wear their wealth with polish, and we here are somewhere between aspiration and restraint. If our ingenuity alone were the measure of contentment, surely we would be brimming with peace by now. Yet still I hear rumors of impending wars in the coming future. Concerns of a global conflict much larger than history has ever known. It seems, even aboard this floating city, that sorrow has not been cast overboard.

The area was quiet, save for the creak of ropes and the distant hum of engines. Robert leaned against the railing next to the gate, thinking of the two signs on each side notifying second- and third-class passengers not to mix. His eyes focused on the nearest lifeboat above. He had come here for air and for silence, but it rarely lasted.

A voice drifted from the deck above, crisp and disdainful. A woman in her fine dinner clothes was speaking to someone just out of Robert's view.

"I am glad they keep the steerage passengers well

below. The idea of just being near such people, unwashed, uncultured, it's simply revolting."

Robert looked up. She was in a lightly shaded dress with her gloves on, standing at the railing directly above him. Her voice carried the practiced harshness of someone who'd rarely been contradicted.

Robert spoke calmly but firmly up to the woman. "I've known a fine man in Steerage who's shown more kindness toward me in a single day than some first-class passengers manage in a lifetime."

The woman scoffed. "Kindness? From that lot? Romanticizing poverty, are you? America's drowning in foreigners already."

Robert's gaze didn't waver. "With all due respect intended, madam, without Steerage passengers these ships would have no business. It's their immigration that makes this possible. I've met some of these good people. A steward was even kind enough to show me around their areas of the ship."

The woman scoffed. "You've been in Steerage? And they let you back into Second Class? Oh my, what a terrible shame. One never knows who might end up beside you these days such as miners, immigrants; even Jews."

Robert was stung. His pride pricked. He clenched his jaw, attempting to hold back his anger.

"You don't like Jews?"

"Not in the slightest. If you knew any of them, you would understand. There are few worse than Jews."

"I've not known many Jews in my life that I'm aware of, but I do assure you that every interaction I've had with one has been very pleasant. I've even had a pleasant conversation with one of your fellow passengers in First Class. Mrs. Brown, to be precise. At least she lives by the proper example people should notice."

"That horrid Brown woman? She made her money in mining. Her jokes are highly inappropriate. How vulgar. She doesn't even live with her husband any longer. Quite the scandal if you ask me. Oh, and the Strausses, well, you know what *they* are. I don't care if they do own Macy's Department Store. I do know they and Margaret will not be sitting at our table. Best to reflect proper standards. And as for any Jews, apparently you don't know enough of them then. Just ask my husband here."

The man near her turned and looked over the railing, stepping forward into the light. Robert's breath caught, not from surprise, but recognition.

The curled mustache. The smug tilt of the chin. The voice that once boomed through paneled walls.

It was the same man he had verbally sparred with. With a sneer and a dismissive wave, the man said, "Still slumming it with the unwashed, Morganson? I'd have thought a man of your... *aspirations*... would be climbing higher on the social ladder by now."

"You are mistaken once again, sir. I'm remembering dignity. It's not confined to any deck. If not for them, these ships would never sail."

"Well, then. The lowly philosopher speaks again. Still defending the lower ranks, I see."

Robert didn't flinch. He stepped closer to their railing, glancing up toward them.

"Still looking down, I see."

The man's smile widened, his wife nodding in approval.

Robert continued, voice low but clear. "I find the sea quite fair to everyone. It doesn't ask for nor accept any pedigree." He looked at the lifeboat hanging nearby. "Interesting thing about lifeboats also. They don't ask what class you're in. They just float, or we hope they do at least."

A silence settled over them, thick as fog. The woman looked between the two men, confused, sensing something she couldn't name.

Robert turned slightly, addressing her now.

"I do hope not, but if you ever find yourself in need of them, ma'am, I hope someone from Steerage is nearby. You might be surprised who reaches out first."

The woman laughed. "If those lifeboats were to ever be needed, which is highly unlikely on this unsinkable ship, then I would make certain the officers would seat them according to class."

Robert looked toward the deck above them and had an idea. He nodded once, then he gathered his things and walked away, leaving the man staring after him. No longer above, no longer certain.

"That's right, go back indoors where you belong. Hidden is fine by me." The man chuckled.

We'll see who stays hidden, Robert thought silently to himself.

Driven by a mixture of piqued curiosity and a desire to assert himself, Robert decided to ascend. Though technically still second-class territory, it offered a commanding view. One that now served a different kind of reckoning. He didn't go into First Class, but instead, he took the Second Class Stairs up to the Boat Deck Aft Promenade, which was still his part of the ship. He knew how to choose a spot that was physically above where he saw them.

As he stepped out onto this upper promenade, hurrying to the railing, he looked down. He scanned the faces below for the man and his wife, a sense of petty triumph forming. Then, he saw them, standing where he left them, and the irony suddenly hit him. He was *literally* looking down on them from a higher vantage point within Second Class, but the man's earlier jab implied that Robert was somehow "lower."

"You know, you're absolutely right, sir. The view is much better up here. But I must say, the company is not quite as endearing," he called out. Then, he walked away before the couple could think of something else to say. He felt the wind shift, cool against his face. Triumph flickered, then faded. Pride, also, was a kind of disguise. This forced Robert to confront his own lingering arrogance. He'd just been not only offended but angered by being looked down upon.

But now he'd done the same, even if subtly, by seeking a higher position. It provided a rich moment for his internal reflection on class, humility, and the true meaning of status. But Robert meant what he said. Much of the company in First Class was not as endearing as his conversations with Leo. He made an exception for Molly Brown, though.

Sitting on one of the benches near the fourth funnel, Robert escaped to his journal for a sense of calm.

'I heard two people speak today, not of ideas, but of bloodlines. As if decency were inherited and dignity reserved for the few who decide for all others. One of them whispered 'Jew' like it was a stain or a foul word, not a heritage. Yet, it is a kind Jew down in Steerage who has treated me better than most Christians ever did. Never look down on others unless you're reaching your hand out to help them get up.'

The wind had settled by the time Robert found himself calmly strolling back and forth directly in front of the Aft Well Deck later that day. It was quieter here, tucked behind the Second-Class Smoke Room and far enough from the brass and chatter of the First-Class Promenades.

The only sound was the rhythmic push of the ocean far below.

He paused, hearing a faint melody that was gentle, almost joyful. Following it, he spotted a familiar figure sitting alone near the rail, coat buttoned, collar up, hands resting in his lap holding a small brown-covered book. Leo.

"They who go down to the sea in ships,
who do work upon the mighty waters:
They have seen the works of the Lord, and His wonders on the deep.
For He spoke, and He raised the stormy wind,
which lifteth up its waves… they would go down to the depths,
their soul was melted because of their danger.
They would reel to and fro, and stagger… and all their skill was gone.
Then they cried unto the Lord in their distress…
He calmed the storm into a whisper,
and stilled were the waves of the sea.
They rejoiced when all was calm:
and then He guided them unto their desired haven.
Let them acknowledge unto the Lord His kindness,
and His wonders to the children of men!
The waters saw Thee, O God, the waters saw Thee and trembled:
The clouds poured down torrents; the skies sent forth thunders;
yea… The voice of Thy thunder was in the whirlwind;
lightnings gave light to the world; the earth trembled and quaked.
Through the sea led Thy way,
and Thy path was through mighty waters;
yea, Thy footsteps could not be traced."

Robert hesitated, then stepped closer. "Do you often sing to the sea?"

Leo smiled without looking up, knowing that Robert could understand. "Praised is the Eternal One, our God,

Master of Creation, who has made the great sea. But no. Those selections from the Psalms are for the weekdays. This melody is a traditional way of greeting the Sabbath. Which is about to begin."

"The Sabbath?" Robert walked down the stairs to stand beside him. "Isn't that on Sunday?"

"The Christian Sabbath is Sunday. The Jewish Sabbath begins at sundown on Friday. It ends at nightfall on Saturday. In Genesis, when God creates everything, the Bible says, '... and then there was evening, and then there was morning, day number so-and-so.'"

Leo reached into his coat pocket and withdrew a small cloth bundle. Inside were two small white candles, unlit. "Normally, I'd light these to observe and remember. Some Jews say the glow reminds us that the world is still good even when it does not seem to be."

Robert looked at the candles. "But you won't light them now?"

Leo shook his head. "Against the rules on ships. Fire hazard." He lightly tapped his foot on the brown pitch pine planks of the wooden deck and pointed at the railing, chuckling softly. "Even tradition must bend to others' safety."

"What can you do instead?"

"I always remember." Leo leaned back, gaze fixed on the horizon, now stained amber as the sun lowered. "We sing certain prayers. Like Psalm 92. Or a song called *Lekha Dodi*; it means 'Come, my beloved.' It's like welcoming a guest. The Sabbath is described as a bride in Jewish thought. Beautiful. Gentle. Holy."

Robert's eyes drifted toward the edge of the world where the sky met the sea. "Sounds very peaceful."

"It is. Or at least it's supposed to be." Leo looked down, then offered the cloth to Robert so he could see the candles up close. "Even when the world is so loud, Sabbath is quiet."

Robert held the bundle a moment longer than he expected. "I had not known any religion could ever feel… like this."

Leo turned to him, eyebrows raised. "Like what, Robert?"

"Being invited, rather than demanded."

As the sun slipped fully beneath the horizon, the deck lights flickered on, displaying warm halos in the dark. The stars above began to appear one by one, bold and clear in the cold Atlantic sky.

Robert leaned against the rail beside Leo. "Do you suppose God listens more closely on the Sabbath?"

Leo smiled, his breath misting in the air. "Maybe we just stop long enough to listen better."

"The two words 'listen' and 'silent' are spelled with all the same letters for a good reason," Robert said softly, remembering he made that comment on the *Nomadic*. Leo nodded in agreement, and they stood together in silence for a moment.

"You know," Robert said, after a pause, "I used to think religion, at least the one I was raised in, was about fear. Never being good enough. Or rules. My father left my mother when I was a boy. After that, church didn't help me feel better. Each Sunday, seeing all the other boys with their fathers, a hollow ache would settle in my chest, and I stopped going. I never missed it after that, not truly. What really hurt was no one ever reached out to me, as if they were relieved, glad to be rid of the silent, withdrawn boy who reminded them of something broken. My Bible, untouched for years, is still at home in a closed drawer, gathering dust like the memories."

Leo nodded. "A lot of people feel that way. Many Jews

feel the same about going to *shul.* I certainly did when my family's 150-year-old home completely burned down to the ground. Then five years after that my mother passed away suddenly. My father is now a farmer but is quite destitute. So I'm making my way to Saskatchewan in Canada, where two of my five brothers, Arnold and Edwin, have already settled. I don't know when or if I will ever see my four sisters or three other brothers again."

"My gosh. I had no idea, Leo. It makes all of my own sufferings very minor in comparison. But tonight, out here with candles that can't be lit and songs in a language I don't understand… I don't know. It feels like something's been remembered I didn't know even existed."

Leo said nothing, but the quiet between them felt full, not empty. Eventually, he pulled a small folded page from his coat. "This is part of the *Union Prayer Book for Friday Nights*," he said. "Do you want to hear something from it?"

"Yes, please."

Leo read softly in Hebrew and then repeated it for Robert in English. Leo's voice was a gentle murmur against the vastness of the ocean:

"*Peace be to him who arrives, peace be to him who departs.*

Blessed be they who bring peace, and blessed be they who accept it."

The words settled over Robert like a soft blanket, finally silencing many of the persistent anxieties that usually clamored in his mind. He felt the cold touch of the railing beneath his fingers, anchoring him to the present, while Leo's voice seemed to reach something far deeper than the ocean itself.

When Leo looked up, Robert's eyes were fixed on the page.

"That's from your prayer book?" Robert asked.

Leo nodded.

"You said this was published in the United States. I'd like to read more of it sometime. If you don't mind."

"You'd be welcome to," Leo said, smiling. He showed Robert the inside of the title page. The copyright year and publisher were listed. *'1908, Central Conference of American Rabbis, Cincinnati, Ohio.'*

"Part one? So there is another volume to this wonderful prayer book?"

"Yes, there is. It's for the High Holy Days we Jews observe in the autumn. But I don't have one yet. I'll acquire a copy once I'm settled in Canada, where I have some family waiting for me. Each week, *Shabbes* is for resting the body. But also for remembering who we are when no one's watching. If you want to know more, tomorrow night after dark, I'll tell you about the Sabbath conclusion called *Havdalah.*"

4

A COLD MOONLESS NIGHT

Bundling his coat tight, Robert walked up the stairs to return to his cabin. Turning back for a moment, he watched Leo walk in the opposite direction to use the Third-Class Main Stairs down. That Leo had to take the long, lonely walk through the length of the ship just to reach his cabin, E-58, and that he would have to share it with five other men saddened Robert. But he knew Leo wouldn't be allowed to take a shortcut through Second Class. Nor could he invite Leo over to his cabin to continue their conversation after the quiet symbolism of the unlit candles. Because he knew the rigid rules of the ship would never allow it.

It was a stark reminder of the many invisible walls that crisscrossed this floating city, dividing lives, restricting movement, and enforcing a hierarchy that felt painfully arbitrary, even though the reasons were understandable, especially after such a moment of shared humanity. He thought about writing in his journal outside, but it was getting too cold to stay out long. Instead, he sat in one of the chairs just inside the entrance to his area of the ship, pulling out his journal and a pen.

'Today, I stood beside a man I only recently met, and watched him not light candles he wasn't allowed to use on the ship. Somehow, that meant more than if he had. He read words meant for a people I've rarely heard about and never belonged to. Yet they felt comforting for me. His religion doesn't proselytize like mine does. It was a most welcome reprieve from my unease over reading that strange book. The eerie parallels, the lurking premonition, had gnawed at me constantly.

But tonight, listening to words of ancient peace felt like a powerful counterpoint; a reminder that there is more to existence than just the looming threat of the unknown. I wonder if I rejected the faith of my youth not because I didn't believe in God, but because I only ever saw Him through the lens of judgment. However, tonight Leo showed me something else. Something that listens instead of accuses. Truly, I do not know what I believe, but I know I believe in peace. I'm trying to make that be enough for now.'

He closed the journal and tucked it back into his satchel, the leather warm from his hands. The corridor was quiet now, lit by the soft glow of electric lamps that hummed faintly nearby on the walls. Somewhere below, Leo was likely making his way down the long corridor or already settling into his crowded berth, the hum of the engines beneath him a lullaby of steel and motion. Robert stood, stretched, and made his way toward his cabin. The ship moved forward through the dark, but something in Robert had stilled. Not silenced, but softened. And for tonight, that was finally enough.

Saturday, April 13th—North Atlantic

After the lingering calm of last night's prayers, Robert found a different kind of stillness in a part of the ship he wasn't much a fan of. The air was no longer as thick with the lingering scent of fine tobacco and leather from the day prior, as the calming quiet wrapped around him like a familiar cloak. The deep, cushioned chairs and polished wood paneling exuded an old-world comfort; a gentlemen's retreat where hushed conversations usually remained private.

After lunch, few people would be in the Second-Class Smoke Room on B Deck, so Robert purchased a hot lemonade and began reviewing his previous journal entries. But then, the low murmurs from a nearby table cut through the quiet, pulling him from his thoughts. A pair of hushed voices from a nearby table where two men were playing cards caught his attention. Robert was glad to notice one of the windows was opened slightly, allowing a breeze to blow the smoke from the men's pipes away from his direction.

"It appears she overheard the entire business," one of the men muttered, leaning closer to his companion. "Mrs. Lines is up in First Class, you know. She avows she heard Ismay himself, the company chairman, urging Captain Smith to make better speed, trying to shave a day off the crossing."

His companion responded with, "Some say he's obsessed with the papers and wants to make a grand impression in New York as a show of power. And our captain? What did he say?" The second man's tone was laced with skepticism.

"Declined, of course. Said it wasn't necessary; no good reason to push a new ship." A soft sigh.

"Still, the pressure's there, isn't it? Always pushing, always more; and in our case, always bigger." The second man shook his head as they returned to their cards.

Robert stared down at the blank page before him. '*Wasn't necessary…*' He had been reading *Futility*, and the words of that short novel haunted him. The *Titan*, doomed by people's carelessness and arrogance, pushed recklessly across the Atlantic at full speed, attempting to surpass all prior speed records, causing the numerous needless deaths of those on a smaller ship. Now, here on the *Titanic*, men in positions of authority and some passengers were discussing the very same thing.

The Smoke Room steward, James W. C. Witter, walked by. Robert seized the opportunity. "Sir, excuse me, please," he said. "Is it true that all of the boilers are not yet lit?"

The surprised man hesitated before replying, thinking of how to appropriately respond to the odd question. "Yes, that is correct, sir. It's Captain Smith's orders. We're keeping a few of them banked, four, I'm told, to conserve coal. No need to strain the new engines unduly on this maiden voyage, eh? But I assure you we are making excellent time."

Robert considered that. So the ship wasn't at full speed after all. That should have reassured him, yet an uneasy feeling lingered.

"Thank you. Not that I'm concerned, but may I inquire as to the reason for this?" he asked.

With a noticeably confused look on his face, James glanced around first, being sure no one was listening in, then leaned in slightly and spoke softly. "The word going around is the captain is taking a more southerly route than customary. He's hoping to steer clear of the ice field, which reports from other ships closer to it say is quite extensive."

Robert felt a flicker of relief. A momentary breath of fresh air. Until the man added, "The only difficulty is, other reports we've been receiving today indicate that the ice is drifting further south than is typical for this time of year. Considerably further than any seasoned seaman has ever encountered."

The words landed like a blow. Robert decided not to pry any further. "Thank you, Mr. Witter. I'm grateful for your honesty and discretion."

"Glad to be of service. Will there be anything else?"

Robert shook his head. "Thank you for speaking with me for a moment."

"My pleasure, sir."

As James continued with his assigned tasks, Robert

swallowed hard, his mouth suddenly dry. Taking another sip of his lemonade, he let the liquid remain in his mouth for a moment as his fingers tightened around his pen so fiercely his knuckles went white. He wrote another thought, with his hand trembling; the ink blurring slightly against the page: *'Now I wonder if perhaps* Futility *may have already been foretold?'*

The entire room was nearly empty, so Robert stayed inside. He needed to stop focusing on his journal and the novel for a while. His anxiety was heightened. His breath felt shallow, catching in his throat, and a knot tightened in his stomach. The harder he tried to explain it away, to dismiss the mounting coincidences as mere fancy, the worse he felt. A prickle of cold sweat traced his spine despite the warmth of the room.

Pulling out his folded map, he checked the details of the boat deck. Sure enough, there were sixteen lifeboats. But noticing numbers one and two on opposing sides of the ship's command center, Robert suddenly realized that both were notably smaller. Labeled "Emergency Cutters," they were left uncovered and swung out.

Next to Emergency Cutter 1 was one labeled "*Engelhardt Boat C.*" Checking what was next to Emergency Cutter 2 was the same type labeled D. Where were A and B? Nearby? Readily available? So six of the total available lifeboats were not even full-sized. Robert questioned how that could be acceptable. Unable to keep his journal closed, he recorded his observations with a question: *'Are the maritime safety regulations truly this out of date?'*

This mounting unease defied all his attempts at rationalization. A soft haze lingered in the air. It was remnants of an earlier gathering of men and their cigars. But now, with the room silent and cleared out, only the quiet tick of the clock nearby remained. Robert looked at the time. The days seemed to pass so quickly. *Titanic* may not have been at full speed, but it felt like time itself was.

Robert needed his thoughts to slow for a bit. He needed something he could do alone for a while. He looked around the room for any ideas. He wasn't fond of smoking, not really. But he appreciated the solitude the space offered now, especially at this hour.

One of the tables by a window caught his eye, already set with a deck of cards someone had left behind. He walked over to it and sat down at the empty spot. Robert's hand was trembling slightly as he picked up the deck and began to shuffle. Not with the brisk efficiency of a practiced gambler, but with a method his father had once taught him: "milking" the cards, or pulling one from the top and one from the bottom simultaneously, then placing them together in a new stack. Then repeating until the entire deck was "milked." He repeated the process once more. A kind of slow symmetry.

True, it wasn't the fastest way to shuffle, but Robert never cared for speed. There was something calming in the methodical nature of it, the feel of the cards sliding between his fingers, and the gentle rhythm. The soft, calming sound of cards sliding over each other. Controlled randomness, someone described it as. Order, drawn out of chaos.

There was a strange kind of comfort in that, a momentary reprieve from the swirling anxieties about Ismay's ambitions or the unpredictable ice. Robert had noticed during his travels that people shuffled quickly to mix things up, to invite chance as part of their strategic planning.

Robert did it to make sense of things, to find the underlying structure.

He began to deal them out in the all too familiar

pattern of Klondike. Simple rules. A single player. No noise, no conversation. Just logic, quiet, and patience.

As he moved the cards, his thoughts finally slowed to a calm; each placement a deliberate act of choosing, of seeking an answer. The order and the structure brought a kind of peace. A puzzle with only one solution, if played just right. A sharp contrast to the uncertainty he still felt since coming aboard, a chaos he struggled to avoid. Every card turned over reminded him of how little was truly visible until it was revealed, like the hidden depths beneath the vast surfaces of ocean outside.

Robert thought of each card as a moment in time. The random, slow draw was like life's uncertainties. Robert's slow, deliberate method of shuffling reflected his search for stability in a world that refused to sit still, as well as calming the mental chaos he found himself trapped in. Much like how he was trying to make sense of this novel in his satchel. In a way, milking the cards was like he was drawing meaning from the past of *Futility* and the present as recorded in his own journal.

Solitaire. Solitude. This quiet moment was what Robert needed. It wasn't just about being alone. It was about being aware. He thought about how even shuffled cards follow rules and patterns. Then he wondered if the same could be said for the events happening to him.

He sat cross-legged in the chair with the cards laid out in a quiet pattern before him. It was his private sanctuary of order amid the endless swell of the Atlantic. Few passengers were out at this hour, and the deck lights would soon flicker on. Robert moved the queen of diamonds onto the king of spades, then paused. The rhythm of the cards brought him little peace.

After playing a few rounds, he reached into his satchel and pulled out the worn copy, its spine soft from frequent reading. Something had drawn him back to a particular passage that unsettled him more with each reading. He had dog-eared the page earlier, marking it for future reference.

Opening it again, he read slowly, his eyes scanning the protagonist's tortured reasoning: *"'And they talk," went on Rowland, as the three watched and listened, "of the wonderful love and care of a merciful God, who controls all things—who has given me my defects, and my capacity for loving, and then placed Myra Gaunt in my way. Is there mercy to me in this?… On the supposition that He exists, I deny it! And on the complete lack of evidence that He does exist, I affirm to myself the integrity of cause and effect—which is enough to explain the Universe, and me…'"*

Robert let the book rest in his lap. The words were bitter and furious. But also too familiar for comfort. He had once said something like that himself, years ago.

Unable to keep a job for long, Robert had spent much of his time volunteering. That way, when people asked him what he did for work, he could answer but omit the part that he wasn't paid. At least it gave him something to do most days. Then after a time, even that was no longer possible due to a series of events far out of his control. Everyone in his social circles began to learn more secrets about him than he wanted others to know. The most important people in his life, the ones he connected so well with, no longer trusted him. Those connections he depended on were damaged beyond repair.

Then, after the loss of a friend, the only person he could confide in, the entire world felt cruelly ordered by chance. Losing his father at a young age, his congregation, and then his communities; losing any sense of purpose. Ashamed, he wanted to end his life. Writing turned out to be one of the few methods that kept him from following through with that plan.

'When you add to the truth, you always subtract from it.

Subtracting from the truth also adds to the lie,' he recalled Dr. Freud telling him in one of their sessions.

Robert read on, even as the words felt like tearing open a fresh wound: *"'What ails me?" he gasped; "I feel as though I had swallowed hot coals—and my head—and my eyes. I can't see… What's wrong with the starboard anchor? It's moving. It's changing… and the windlass—and the spare anchors, and the davits—all alive, all moving."'*

Robert exhaled slowly, his spine tingling. The strange vision. The language of madness was fictional, yes, but wasn't there something disturbingly true in it? The anchor, the davits, the machinery coming to life. It felt eerily like a hallucination brought on by too much knowledge and too much knowing. A man cracking under the weight of a truth too vast to bear.

Understanding that anguish all too well, he closed the book and stared at the ceiling. What kind of mind writes something like this and calls it fiction?

He was suddenly chilled despite his coat. The words haunted him, not just because of their intense anger, but because they echoed thoughts he'd had himself, though never spoken aloud.

Was that what this journey was for? To run from the God who had never answered him… or to find that God was listening in the silence?

Somewhere, distantly, the ocean would soon meet the stars again. And the ship pressed onward with relentless certainty. But in Robert's mind, the anchor had begun to move. And the deck beneath him no longer felt steady.

After resuming the game, Robert at last placed the final card in the suit stack. Order was established. He reorganized the suit stacks slightly for a nice appearance. Faces up, it almost felt like an unspoken gift to the next person. Robert imagined it as a silent note for anyone who would come after. An invitation for them to also pause, reflect, and hopefully find calm in something so simple.

On the surface, just a simple game. But for Robert, it was a momentary escape he needed.

Robert stood up slowly, surveying the completed game of solitaire he'd neatly stacked into the four foundation piles. He left the cards in perfect order, as if to say, "Someone else may try next." With a quiet sigh, he began straightening the table by aligning the deck box, brushing a few crumbs to the side, and setting the used cards square against one another.

A steward working nearby paused just briefly, watching with a slight nod.

"Thank you, sir," he said softly. "That makes our job just a bit easier."

Robert glanced up and offered a modest smile. "My pleasure. Happy to return the favor. Please call me Robert."

The steward smiled. "Very good then. John Hardy, I'm the chief steward for second class. I try to keep this place looking respectable."

Robert gave a small nod, surprised by the formality but appreciating the gesture. "A pleasure to know you, Mr. Hardy. It's obvious you're succeeding at that."

John excused himself before stepping away to tend to other tasks, leaving Robert alone again with his thoughts and the distant hum of the ship. Glancing at the clock, Robert was surprised at how much time had passed. Another day aboard the *Titanic* was drawing to a close. The twilight had already deepened into night, and the ship pressed steadily onward beneath a sky littered with stars.

Feeling thoughtful, Robert pulled out his journal. He wrote: *'The truth of a man is found in the quiet, beneath the surface. Some light might reveal only what one wishes the world to see—a practiced part, a polished pretense. That's the part that performs, the carefully constructed façade for the world. But below, in the quiet, unobserved corners of the soul, that's where truth resides, raw and unvarnished. Maybe that's why I'm drawn to the quiet, the solitude, and these late-night musings. It's easier to be honest with myself, to peel back the layers of pretense, when no one's watching, when the only witness is the endless dark sea outside.'*

Feeling calmer now, he couldn't resist the urge to pull out *Futility* and read through an earlier part of the novel a bit more. He found his makeshift bookmark and was surprised to see he'd already reached chapter six.

The book described a strong wind following the *Titan*, creating an unnatural calm on deck despite a thick fog. The sky above was clear and star-filled; the cold, biting. Moonless? The novel didn't say. Robert glanced toward the nearest windows. The night outside was dark. No moon.

He continued reading. In the story, at 9:30 p.m., the main character, John Rowland, was engaged in a quiet conversation with a crewman whose name was not given.

"'Rowland," he said as he drew near, "I hear you've walked the quarter-deck."

"I cannot imagine how you learned it, sir," replied Rowland…

"You told the captain. I suppose the curriculum is as complete at Annapolis as at the Royal Naval College. What do you think of Maury's theories of currents?"

"They seem plausible," said Rowland, "… but I think that in particulars he has been proven wrong."

"I think so myself. Did you ever follow up another idea of his—of locating the position of ice in fog by the rate of decrease in temperature as approached?"

"Not to any definite result. But it seems to be only a matter of calculation, and time to calculate. Cold is negative heat, and can be treated like radiant energy, decreasing as the square of the distance."

The officer stood a moment, humming to himself, then returned to his post."'

Robert blinked. For a moment, it felt more like reading a science manual than a novel. Could it really be possible to detect ice in fog by tracking temperature?

"... *only a matter of calculation*," Robert murmured aloud. He tapped the page softly with his finger, unsettled. "And enough time to calculate it."

Yet no one aboard the *Titanic* seemed terribly worried about ice tonight.

The idea lingered in his mind. Technical, but strangely poetic. And chilling, in more ways than one. He would be seeing Leo again soon. And he knew exactly who to confide in. Not wanting to forget, he pulled out his journal and scribbled a few notes, referencing the chapter and the theory. Then he rose from his seat and hurried for the stairs.

He descended quickly, the cold biting through his coat, but he barely noticed. The theory lingered in his mind like frost on glass. Visible, delicate, and threatening to crack. If ice could be tracked by temperature, then why wasn't anyone doing it? Was it ignorance, arrogance, or simply the illusion of control? He thought again of Rowland's bitterness, of machinery coming alive, of anchors shifting. Fiction, yes. But fiction that felt like memory. Or a warning.

He didn't care how cold it was getting, he needed to speak with someone. The book wasn't finished with him yet and neither, he sensed, was the night.

The faint glow of the *Titanic's* stern lamps cast long shadows across the quiet expanse of the Aft Well Deck, where a night breeze carried a chill off the open sea. The ship moved steadily, her massive form slicing through the dark waters with an elegance only passengers in quiet moments like this could truly appreciate. Most had already gone below, but the night air felt different, like it was charged with something unspoken, wrapped in a strange anticipation.

Robert made his way to the far edge of the lower Second-Class section by the stairs leading down, exactly where he'd agreed to meet Leo. He paused by the railing, a flicker of unease stirring in his chest. The scent of the sea mingled with something old, yet still familiar. A tradition he never expected to find on this modern marvel. He and Leo came from totally different worlds. Not just different localities, but also traditions, languages, faiths, social backgrounds, and likely much more. He had never expected to connect so well with someone so different. He felt conflicted in a way. Part of him wanted to know more, but another part felt like he was intruding into an area he was not permitted to enter.

His eyes caught Leo emerging from the Third-Class General Room beneath the poop deck. The young man crossed to the railing at the edge of the Steerage section, cradling a small silver box. It was very ornate, well-worn, and gleaming faintly in the dim light. It had traveled far, from the Old World toward the New, and now it rested in his hands on this grand ship.

Humming softly, Leo stepped beneath the staircase, not far from where Robert now stood. His voice rose into a quiet prayer, threadbare against the wind. In his other hand, he held a braided, multi-wicked candle. Unlit for now, but ready.

Robert imagined the braided candle flickering in the night breeze, its uncertain flame defying the cold Atlantic air. That small light, unlit though it was, seemed a rebellion against the dark. A quiet resistance made holy by ancient tradition. Its metaphorical light flickering uncertainly against the vastness of the ocean, casting shifting shadows across Leo's face. There was something strangely comforting about the act. About the simple, sacred moment amidst the tumult of time and place.

Raised on sparse sermons and silent doubts, Robert had never felt faith like this woven into life, tangible and shared. The rest of the world, with all its noise and chaos, seemed suspended in that instant.

Leo's voice continued, steady and rhythmic. When he noticed Robert nearby, he waved his friend over and continued praying in English.

Robert's hands, unaccustomed to rituals, nervously hovered in front of the cup of wine in Leo's hand. A sense of unfamiliarity mingled with awe. He had always known that such customs were out of reach for him in his small, distant town in the mountains of the Lincoln Forest in New Mexico. But tonight, something seemed to guide him toward a deeper understanding, something larger than himself.

The moment stretched. Then, as Leo recited the final blessing, he extended the cup to Robert. Without thinking, Robert reached out and took it, his fingers brushing against Leo's. And for a brief instant, he paused and felt a human connection unlike any other he had ever known form between them. He raised the cup, allowing its contents to catch the reflection of the starlit sky above.

"*L'Hayim*, it means 'to life.'" Leo said softly, his eyes meeting Robert's.

"Thank you, Leo. *L… L'Hayim*." Robert repeated the unfamiliar word, tasting the wine, feeling it warm him in more ways than one. The sea around them seemed almost reverential, as if the very ship was aware of the sacredness of the moment. Temporarily putting the concerns out of his mind, in the warmth of wine and imagined candlelight, the cold seemed held at bay. For now.

The air was cool, with the hum of distant engines beneath the Well Deck. Robert leaned up against the wall underneath the stairs, shoulders tucked into his coat. Leo stood near the railing, gazing at the sea, hands in his pockets.

"You've been asking a lot of questions. Which is fine, so don't apologize. I'm glad to answer them. Do you ever think about faith? Not the kind one inherits, but the kind one chooses?"

Robert gave a dry chuckle. "Lately? Yes. More than I used to."

Leo finally turned. "When someone wants to convert, to Judaism, I mean, it's not just about learning the prayers or reading the Torah. It's a whole shift in how you live. Who you live among. There's a lot of study. The soonest it can happen is a little over a year after the learning began. Community is essential. Toward the end of that process comes being immersed a few times in a ritual bath called *mikveh*. A little bit like what your baptism probably was."

Robert nodded slowly. "That seems no small undertaking."

Leo grinned. "And for men… well. There's one more requirement."

Robert raised an eyebrow. "Oh? What would that be?"

Leo's smile widened. "Circumcision."

Robert blinked, his mind not quite grasping the unfamiliar term. He asked for an explanation. Leo clarified.

"Surely you don't mean that! Seriously?"

"Yes. Full commitment. Nonnegotiable!"

Robert flinched for a moment, realizing Leo was

serious. Then: "I'm afraid I'll be keeping my… coverage, thank you kindly, my friend."

Leo burst into laughter. "I don't blame you!"

Robert cracked a grin, shaking his head. "If you're trying to keep me from converting to your faith, that will work! My word, what kind of welcoming is that!?"

"The kind that separates tourists from the truly convinced," Leo said, eyes twinkling.

"No wonder you Jews don't proselytize!"

They shared a laugh. Real and unguarded. The kind that comes not just from crass male humor, but from the warmth of being seen, listened to, understood, and accepted.

Nearby in the second-class area, just out of their view, Lawrence Beesley and Benjamin Hart exchanged knowing glances. Hidden by a darkened walkway and tucked quietly around the corner, they kept their amusement to themselves. Barely.

Lawrence stifled a chuckle behind his knuckles while Benjamin whispered something under his breath that made them both quietly grin. Lawrence placed his hand against the wall to steady himself.

Neither man said much, but both were relieved to see Robert finally coming out of his shell. It was a side of him they hadn't seen before. Not in the library, nor in any of their other interactions with him. Perhaps it was the wine, or perhaps it was the friendship. Maybe a bit of both. Either way, it was good to see. Deciding to give the two men some privacy, Benjamin and Lawrence went off to play a round of cards in the Smoke Room.

Completely unaware of this, Robert and Leo both stood in silence for a while; placing the braided candle on one of the stairs. The sounds of the *Titanic's* engines, distant yet constant, hummed through the air like the heartbeat of the world. Robert had forgotten what a relaxing calm felt like. His mind was often racing from the overlay of thoughts he struggled to sort out in his mind.

He took a deep breath, feeling something stir inside him, something he couldn't quite place. The *Titanic*, the greatest ship ever built, might carry him through the Atlantic, but in that moment, amidst the sounds of the sea and the scent of the spices, he felt a deeper journey beginning. Stars sharp against the cold black, Robert stared up at the sky for a moment before articulating what was on his mind.

"I read something odd earlier in a book I have," he said, pulling his coat tighter. "A man said you can feel ice long before you see it. The temperature drops faster the closer you are to it. Almost like… heat is running away from it. He described it as negative heat and mentioned something about energy loss. You can calculate how close ice is by how fast the air gets colder."

Leo chuckled. "You sound as though you've been reading from a scientific textbook. Or borrowing a thermometer from the ship's doctor."

"Neither. It's in a novel of all things. The writer says that cold is just negative heat. Something that travels and dissipates, like light. That it could be measured. Even predicted. You can feel it… if you know what to look for."

"That's not something I've heard before," Leo said with a faint smile. "And yet here we are. Trusting hand-drawn charts and stars more than our own skin."

"Maybe I'm just reading ahead in a story that feels a little too familiar," Robert said. "But what I can't stop thinking about is that it's been right about a lot of what I've observed so far."

Leo glanced up, thoughtful. "I always thought cold just meant your clothes weren't thick enough."

"Perhaps," Robert replied. "Or it means something's getting too close."

Leo studied him a moment, unsure where the conversation was heading. "You seem quite taken with this book. You can't seem to shake its hold on you."

"No, I can't. Every page reads like it's a warning in advance."

"So that's what you've been concerned about. What's the name of this book you've been reading?"

Robert pulled it from his satchel and held the cover up to one of the deck lights. "I haven't read what happens next, but apparently the ship in the book sinks with great loss of life."

Leo exhaled slowly. Puzzled by the author's name on the cover, he didn't let on that he had noticed it. "Well, that title, *Futility*, certainly is a grim one. And you're sure of this? Robert, books can be wrong in some places even when they're right in others. That's why we keep the good ones close," Leo said as he held up his *Union Prayer Book*. "Let's hope your author got the ending wrong."

Robert watched Leo gather his belongings before disappearing into the dark. He then turned back to the sea and whispered into the wind, "So do I, Leo… so do I."

Clutching the novel under his arm, he gripped the railing tight.

"Please, God, if you are real… Please let me be very wrong about this."

The night was growing colder. Before heading back inside to the warmth and safety of the ship, Robert lingered a moment longer at the rail. Allowing the ship's superstructure to shield him from the wind, he tried to grasp the vastness of the sea. The nothingness beyond the lights. Only black water stretching as far as the eye could see.

Later, in the solitude of his cabin, he lay on his bed with a single lamplight on and his journal on his knees. He needed privacy to think and to write.

'The sea has turned strangely calm tonight, as if resting before something. I read in Futility where the officer and the main character, John Rowland, discuss ice that was not seen, but sensed. The cold intensifies as you approach. It says, "Cold is negative heat and can be treated like radiant energy..." How odd that such an abstract theory from an obscure novel feels truer now than it did on the page. The air bites harder the farther I walk from warmth. It almost feels... directional. Exactly as that obscure novel described. A cold presence, not just ambient, but actively expanding, drawing the warmth from the air around it. And the ship, this colossal vessel, cuts through it, seemingly oblivious. Is it just the Atlantic night, or is something hidden?'

The next morning, after breakfast, the dining saloons for first and second class were arranged for Sunday church services. In the Second-Class Dining Saloon, between two sideboards, a cushioned bench was pulled out from beneath the upright piano. The fall-board was lifted, and a steward began testing the keys one by one, making sure each note rang true. A small stack of sheet music was placed neatly on the ledge.

Robert considered staying to listen. Some of the tunes were familiar from the old hymnal he had back home. Being British, a few were unknown to him but still comforting to hear. The gentle rise and fall of notes on the piano offered a momentary peace.

Then a particular melody caught his attention. A hymn he partially recognized, but he couldn't quite place it at first.

Robert stood up to walk toward the piano for a glimpse of the song's name.

However, before he got close enough to read it, the

man finished the song, and the final line struck like a cold wave. "... *for those in peril on the sea.*"

Robert knew he couldn't stay, couldn't bear to hear another note. It felt too direct, too personal; a chilling echo of his own fears brought to life in song. He quietly and hurriedly stepped out from the room, needing to escape the invisible weight of the words, the unsettling feeling that the ship itself was singing its own somber prophecy.

The words echoed in his ears, a chilling premonition that felt suddenly, terrifyingly real. *'For those in peril on the sea.'* The melody, once comforting, now felt like a lament, a solemn pronouncement. He found himself walking faster, needing to escape the invisible grasp of the song, the unsettling sense that he was being spoken to directly, personally, by the very forces he had been trying to rationalize away. And could not.

Sunday Late Afternoon—5:30 PM—Near Sunset

The deck lights of the ship cast a soft glow against the encroaching night. A hush had settled over much of the area. Inside the Third-Class General Room, voices rose in quiet song. Distinct from the clamor of the day, rich with meaning.

Robert made his way cautiously across the Aft Well Deck toward the doors, uncertain if he should enter the space where Leo had invited him. Inside, a handful of passengers had gathered. Men with hats and a few women seated together nearby. Leo stood near a small table, *Union Prayer Book* in hand. The Hebrew was unfamiliar to Robert, but the cadence soothed him.

One of the men, already mid-prayer, paused to greet him warmly. "Welcome, friend! If you would like to leave your hat on as a sign of respect during our prayers, you may do so."

Important prayers about peace, protection, and others were sung softly in Hebrew or Aramaic and then followed by English. Strangely familiar in their longing.

Robert stood quietly in the back next to his friend. Leo explained that the other Jews were very orthodox in their observances, so none of their prayers would be said in English. "But their order of prayer is the same as what I use anyway. Participate in as much as you're comfortable." Leo held his *Union Prayer Book* in front of Robert so he could follow along in the translation.

"Also," Leo whispered gently, "at any point, it's very important to add your own personal prayers as well."

The opening lines of each prayer were said aloud. Then the main text was recited in whispers before the concluding lines of each prayer were voiced clearly for all to hear. Leo pointed to the English text each time the leader chanted in Hebrew. There was structure, but also a flexibility that Robert had noticed. Toward the end, the tone turned toward gratitude. When it had ended, Leo caught Robert's eye with a quiet smile.

"That was *Ma'ariv*. Our evening service. It was shorter than back home due to us not having a minyan currently. That's a quorum of at least ten adult male Jews for certain prayers. Which is probably for the best because another group needs this space for their community prayers in a moment," said Leo.

Before Robert could respond, his attention was caught by movement just outside the doorway. Two Muslim men, one older and one younger, had waited outside before entering. They now began unrolling their prayer rugs in a quieter corner of the room. They checked the time and the compass on a chain. One of them glanced up and nodded courteously to Robert as he slipped off his shoes.

Robert turned to Leo, lowering his voice. "What are they doing?"

"This is how Muslims pray. It's called *Maghrib* in Arabic," Leo answered respectfully. "Their tradition calls for it after sunset. Ours may begin as the sun *begins* to set. Different languages, different customs, but the same pull toward the divine. They face Mecca, their holiest city, just as we face our holiest city, Jerusalem when we pray."

Just then, a young man passing by scoffed audibly. "What's that then? Some heathen show?"

Robert tensed. "They're not hurting anyone," he said calmly. "Just praying like we all do but in their own way. Please leave them alone."

As Robert turned to leave, the echoes of Hebrew still fresh in his mind, a man loitering near the stairwell gave him a look with a mixture of confusion and contempt.

"If you're not a Jew or a Muslim," the man muttered, "why associate with those vermin? Don't you know those Jews killed Christ?"

Robert stopped mid-step. He turned slowly. An inner rage began building within him. Noticing the small leather-bound book with "*New Testament*" on the cover in the man's hand, Robert asked, "Do you truly believe Jesus died for your sins?"

The man frowned. "Of course. The New Testament says so. You should read it sometime."

Robert chose his words carefully, remembering the boastful man from first class on the *Nomadic* a few days prior and more recently. "I already have," Robert said evenly. "My late father and his brother taught me Greek so I could read it in the original without a translation. Now, since you're convinced the Jews killed Jesus, even though the Gospels say it was the Romans, maybe you should be thanking the people who you think made that possible. Unless Jesus didn't die for your sins after all?"

A stunned silence fell. Robert's voice didn't rise. "If Jesus were aboard tonight, he'd be in *shul* with them. Not in church with us. They are still speaking his language after all. Read Luke Chapter 4 carefully. When he returns from the wilderness, see where Jesus went to worship God every week? I'd rather be there. And I'm not even Jewish."

The man opened his mouth, then closed it, turning away without another word.

Just then, a third-class woman nearby who was young, plainly dressed, with a small wooden cross around her neck, glanced up and said quietly with an Irish lilt, "Chapter 4, verses sixteen through twenty. Amen… I know that is true. That was part of my devotional reading this morning." She held up a small book with strips of paper sticking out. Bookmarks.

Robert gave her a grateful nod and started to walk away. He hadn't planned on defending anyone tonight, but somehow, it felt like the most natural thing he could've done. Before he could walk away, the older Muslim man, who had already begun praying, stepped gently in front of him. His English was accented but clear.

"Friend, you spoke with honor," he said. "May I please give you a blessing?"

Robert, not expecting this, took a step forward and nodded his head. Then, with reverent dignity, the man placed both hands on Robert's shoulders.

"May Allah bless you with peace, safety, happiness, and a long, satisfied life."

Robert blinked, surprised, moved. Unable to hold back the tears filling his eyes, he instinctively lifted his own hands and placed them lightly over the man's, his fingers slipping gently into his palms.

"Thank you," Robert whispered. "May all of that be for you and for everyone you love as well."

The man bowed his head slightly, then returned quietly to his companion.

Leo, having watched it all, stepped closer and said five Hebrew words with quiet reverence.

Robert turned toward him. "What does that mean?"

"Blessed are You, God, who listens to prayer," Leo translated.

The Christian woman stepped nearer and placed her hand over her cross. "Thank you, Lord God," she said calmly, "for allowing us to witness this sacred moment. Sir, an Irish blessing my grandparents used to pray: *'May love and laughter light your days and warm your heart and home. May good and faithful friends be yours wherever you may roam.'*"

"May all of that be for you as well, ma'am. I'm glad to see you today." Robert lingered a few moments longer, watching as the two men continued their prayer. Their verses rose in Arabic, movements fluid and reverent. Prostrating forward, their foreheads gently touched the rugs. Then, with a quiet farewell to Leo and the woman, he made his way out to the Second-Class Dining Saloon.

He arrived just in time. The lay-led Christian service had begun, with perhaps a dozen passengers seated in rows. Some held the Anglican *Book of Common Prayer*; others had their Bibles open. Each person offered a song or a short reading. One of the men stood and walked toward the middle of the room to recite a section from Psalm 107.

The British translation was a bit different, but Robert easily recognized the text. It was almost the same as what Leo had said earlier. Closing the Bible, the reader concluded, "The Word of the Lord." Most replied, "Thanks be to God."

Robert chose to remain silent while listening. Surprised to hear part of the same psalm so soon after reading it during the Jewish prayers, his mind returned to the novel.

A woman who looked very similar to Robert's mother walked over to the piano and announced a hymn number. Then came the song. The notes of *Nearer, My God, to Thee* swelled through the room. Robert was very familiar with the lyrics. It was the last song he heard when he decided to stop going to church. The words caught unexpectedly in his throat. His voice wavered as he tried to steady it.

Three languages. Three prayers. Three very different, yet also similar faiths. He had not intended to witness any of them, let alone all in the same day. But he had. As the hymn ended and passengers slowly filed out, Robert stayed behind for a moment longer. He reached into a pocket of his satchel and pulled out his journal.

'Three types of prayers. Three longings. Perhaps three names but maybe just one God. Or maybe the same search that wears many faces. If a sermon had ever been given about the S.S. Titan, *would it have really made any difference? Or is it already too late?'*

Outside, the sea remained calm. Too calm. The stars above blinked in quiet witness, indifferent. Inside, Robert closed his journal and tucked it away. The prayers had ended. The songs had faded. But something lingered. An ache, a question, a hush before the storm. *Titanic* pressed onward. And Robert, now more than ever, felt the weight of what might lie directly ahead.

5

HIDDEN WITHIN THE DARKNESS...

Restless and unable to sleep, Robert lingered in the Second-Class Library with his copy of *Futility*. The soft hum of the engines vibrated through the deck beneath his feet. The library attendant, Thomas Kelland, a young fellow of only 19, wouldn't leave as long as any passengers were around. The man went over the inventory of the bookshelves, documenting who had borrowed which books and what had been returned.

Robert hadn't expected to stay so late, but the quiet conversation and dim amber lighting had lulled him into a strange sense of peace. That peace would too soon be shattered. A flicker of thought crossed his mind about the last time he'd been at sea this late at night on the *Mauretania*.

He had stood out on the boat deck in the chill, listening to a deck steward explain the meaning of the lookout bells, pointing toward the black outline of the crow's nest. It had been an idle curiosity then, a harmless bit of seafaring knowledge. He never imagined he'd hear that signal himself. He just finished reading the end of chapter 6.

'*... a shout from the crow's-nest split the air. "Ice!" yelled the lookout, "ice ahead. Iceberg. Right under the bows..."*'

The rest of the chapter didn't interest him much. But it was the opening of the next chapter that caught his attention.

'*Forty-five thousand tons—dead-weight—rushing through the fog at the rate of fifty feet a second, had hurled itself at an iceberg. Had the impact been received by a perpendicular wall, the elastic resistance of bending plates and frames would have overcome the momentum with no more damage to the passengers than a severe shaking up… She would have backed off and, slightly down by the head, finished the voyage at reduced speed to rebuild on insurance money and benefit, largely, in the end, by the consequent advertising of her indestructibility. But a low beach, possibly formed by the recent overturning of the berg, received the* Titan, *and with her keel cutting the ice like the steel runner of an ice-boat, and her great weight resting on the starboard bilge, she rose out of the sea, higher and higher—until the propellers in the stern were half exposed…'*

Robert flipped the page absentmindedly, but a chill prickled the back of his neck; a sensation independent of the library's warmth. The air around him suddenly felt colder, as if the very words on the page had manifested a draft. He shifted in his seat, glancing around. No one else remained in the library. Even the ticking of the wall clock seemed loud now, its rhythm uneven in his ears, or perhaps it was his own pulse intruding on the sound.

His palms had gone damp without his noticing, and he wiped them on his trousers. Only the soft flicker of the electric lamps on the reading desks and the steady thrum of the engines below; a sound he had come to rely on as the ship's heartbeat.

He tried to shake off the feeling, chalking it up to exhaustion and an overactive imagination fueled by the story.

It's just a novel, he told himself, but the conviction felt thin and brittle.

Then he heard it.

Through the thick steel and wood, above the constant thrum of the ship, he faintly detected three sharp rings on the bell in the lookout post on the foremast. The sound was distant, muffled, but utterly distinct.

From what someone had explained to him when he sailed on the *Mauretania*, a single ring on the bell conveyed an alert of something to the ship's right side. Two rings meant an alert for the left side. But three signaled an urgent warning of something directly in front of them.

His breath caught. Suddenly, he remembered the image of the *Lusitania* after the rogue wave. A photograph clipped from the *Times*. Closing his eyes, he saw the image clearly in his mind.

It was the main reason he was so hesitant to cross the ocean in the first place. But if Freud was the only one who could help him, he had to take that chance. Robert had been so focused on making it to Vienna for help that he hadn't thought of it in weeks. But now it surfaced with brutal clarity: the bridge badly battered, railings twisted like wire, officers standing amid the wreckage with expressions that didn't match the scale of the damage. Not panic or grief. Just stunned silence. As if they hadn't yet understood what had happened.

He had stared at that photo for a long time back then, wondering how a wave could do such a thing. *Lusitania* still arrived in New York, but her command center was covered in thick canvas. Permanent impressions in her foredeck. The entire bridge had been shoved back two whole inches. The glass shattered by the wave had been 75 feet above the waterline.

Robert had wondered if the sea had moods, if it could choose when to punish. Now, he wondered who it chose.

Titanic was traveling just under top speed, a fact that now hammered in his chest with sudden, alarming rhythm. The deck beneath him felt steady, confident, and almost arrogant.

And yet the bell had rung. Three times.

Something directly ahead.

The sea didn't care for their stories. It wrote its own.

Meanwhile, on the Navigation Bridge, First Officer William Murdoch, shortly after taking over command as Captain Smith retired for the night, suddenly heard the call screamed into the phone from the crow's nest, his voice tight with alarm: "Iceberg right ahead!"

But Murdoch had just barely made out the dark shape directly in front of them. He shouted to the helmsman in the wheelhouse directly behind him, "Hard to starboard!"

Robert Hichens spun the helm hand-over-hand so fast he slammed it hard against the bronze telemeter.

"Hard over, sir!" he called back at the top of his voice.

Everyone in the ship's command center knew they wouldn't be able to stop in time. During the ship's sea trials, it took half a mile and 3 minutes, 15 seconds to stop. The berg was less than a quarter mile in front of them. It was growing larger by the second.

Up in the crow's nest, the lookouts muttered, "What's taking so long? What are they bloody doing down there?" Reginald Lee and Fredrick Fleet's desperate whispers seemed to hang on the frigid air, unheard by those who could act.

The iceberg was now plainly visible. Looming, massive, and impossibly close. A silent, dark wall rising from the black sea.

A faint, sharp scent seemed to hang in the air. It was salty, cold, and faintly metallic. It was in Murdoch's nostrils as he gripped the railing, his breath frosting the air.

"Is it hard over?!" he barked, his voice edged with a desperate plea.

"It is hard over, yes sir!" came the insistent reply.

Hichens kept the helm pressed hard against the mechanism.

Murdoch was losing hope, his face grim in the dim light of the bridge. "Come on, you… turn… please turn!"

Seconds later, realizing it was too late, he rushed to the lever and triggered the mechanism to seal the watertight doors. While doing so, he also activated the emergency alarm to the stokers below—a jarring, metallic clang that reverberated through the ship's lowest decks.

Back in the library, Robert suddenly felt the engines lurch, then slow; the very floor beneath him vibrating with a new, unsettling tremor. The familiar, deep hum that had been the *Titanic's* heartbeat began to fade, replaced by a subtle deceleration that sent a shiver through him.

The telegraph clanged loudly. Its order changed from "All Ahead Full" to "Full Astern."

That message alone signaled an emergency. And to brace for collision. A ship of this size didn't simply stop in the middle of the Atlantic without reason.

Far below, the stokers frantically closed all the dampers, reduced steam pressure to 100 PSI, and then reversed the twin reciprocating engines in a desperate attempt to stop the ship.

But the turbine for the center propeller, only capable of forward motion, now idled uselessly.

The massive machinery fought physics with all the might it could muster, but it was too late.

Titanic was 450 miles from Canada, and the ocean beneath her was more than two and a half miles deep; far too deep to drop the anchors.

It wasn't violent, but it was profoundly *wrong*. The shift in motion was unmistakable, like a gigantic creature recoiling from something unseen. Robert didn't yet know precisely what was happening. But he was deeply unsettled. The pit of his stomach churned with a nameless dread.

Moments later, the *Titanic* struck the iceberg.

But Robert never heard the impact. Nor did he feel it.

Just as it happened, he closed the novel and placed it beside his journal on the table, shrugging into his coat. He wanted fresh air, and the Second-Class Promenade seemed like the perfect place for a late-night breath and a moment to reflect.

Rather than take the stairs, he opted for the lift, hoping the brief ride would clear his head. At this late hour the lift attendant, 17-year-old Reginald J. Pacey, was off duty and likely in bed by now.

It moved upward at its usual smooth speed, but something about it felt… off. A subtle tremor ran through the walls of the small enclosure. The light overhead flickered, casting jagged shadows like cracks across the rich wood-paneled interior. Then, with a sudden, sickening jolt, the humming stopped. Silence. A second stretched into forever. The blackness itself felt freezing and absolute, enclosing Robert in a tiny, suspended tomb.

For a single, breathless second, the lift hung still. No motion. No sound. Just blackness, but a coffin of wood and steel suspended in silence. Robert's heart pounded against his ribs, a frantic drum in the oppressive quiet. His breath hitched in his throat.

Just as quickly, the light returned, glaring and sudden. The lift jolted once more, struggling, and then the doors groaned open with an unnerving shudder.

He stepped out into the corridor, his anxiety spiking for reasons he couldn't place, a primal alarm blaring in his mind. At first, he turned instinctively toward the Port-Side Promenade. When he stepped outside, a frigid wind greeted him, and he buttoned his coat tighter. The stars were sharp and brilliant above; a diamond dust scattered across a velvet sky. The sea looked as calm as glass, reflecting the celestial fire.

Everything seemed normal… eerily normal, a deceptive tranquility that felt more unsettling than chaos. A few other passengers were out too, peering over the railings or rubbing their arms. No sign of anything unusual on this side of the ship.

He began walking, drawn by some unspoken urge, following the curve of the ship toward the aft and around toward the starboard side.

Then he finally saw it.

The iceberg!

Robert's eyes widened as if trying to fit the mountain of ice into them, his mind struggling to process the sheer, impossible scale. "No… how could it…?" he whispered, his voice thin against the vastness of the night.

It loomed beside the ship, slipping away into the darkness like a ghost. He watched it glide past, a silent, monstrous leviathan of ancient ice. Easily over a hundred feet high, it towered above the boat deck, an impossible, gleaming sapphire mountain in the starlight, reflecting the ship's deck lights in sharp glimmers of icy blue and gray. It turned slowly in the black water as if recoiling from the impact, its mass so immense it seemed to dwarf even the mighty *Titanic*. Great chunks of ice, sharp and angular, broke off and tumbled into the sea with heavy splashes that vanished into the night, like fragments of a shattered dream.

Not only that, but the berg had thin streams of water flowing down it, like it had just recently flipped in the water before the collision.

'*… possibly formed by the recent overturning of the berg, received the* Titan…'

Just as it was described in *Futility!*

A chill colder than the berg itself ran down his spine. It was the chill of dawning horror. Was he hallucinating again? Was this shock or madness? Had the story slipped from the page into his mind or into the sea itself? Or was this really happening?

It matched *Futility's* description. Sapphire, glistening, unnatural. He stood in shock, the scene before him echoing words he had read only moments ago.

Robert stood frozen, the berg receding into the dark like a secret too vast to hold. The air around him felt thinner now, as if the night itself had exhaled. Somewhere below, the engines groaned in confusion. Above, the stars blinked indifferently. And his hands trembled not from wind, but from something deeper. He had read the future. And now, that future had just begun.

And suddenly, it wasn't just fiction anymore. It was real, terrifyingly real; a prophecy made manifest before his eyes. A cold dread, far deeper than the frigid air, seeped into his bones, seizing him. His mind reeled, struggling to reconcile the impossible coincidence, the sheer audacity of this fictional warning come true. Every rational defense he'd built, every logical dismissal, and every comforting thought suddenly crumbled away, leaving him exposed to the stark, terrifying truth. This wasn't a story he was reading; it was a reality he was now living.

The faint shudder beneath his feet lingered longer than he expected, a continuous, low vibration that pulsed through the deck. The hum of *Titanic's* mighty engines, recently softened, then ceased altogether, leaving a profound, unnatural silence. For the first time since leaving Queenstown, the ship's steady rhythm faltered and then died. Robert stood still, gripping the railing, knuckles white, eyes locked on the jagged mass as it drifted into the haze astern.

The soft, shimmering, ice-blue glow of the floating mountain. The stillness of the night, broken only by the gentle lapping of waves against the silent hull. The way the ship now trembled beneath his feet. As if it was somehow… injured. Bleeding.

He swallowed hard, his breath curling into a thick cloud in the frigid air. Looking out over the ocean, there was nothing. No other ships, no signs of life beyond the *Titanic's* own receding lights. Just an endless, indifferent sea, vast and terrifying in its emptiness.

Robert gripped the railing as the scene before him blurred with the words he had read. *Futility* wasn't a novel now. It was a warning in advance. And no one had listened.

And now he was living it!

Looking behind, he noticed that the wake behind the *Titanic* was beginning to fade into a smooth calm, the churned water settling as the ship lost momentum. The engines were now slowing to a stop, their mighty power silenced. Little did he know that those engines would never run again.

Robert didn't know it then, but the brief impact had set in motion a rapid chain of events, already unspooling toward an unthinkable end. An end foretold.

He turned and bolted toward the staircase, unsure if he suffered another hallucination or not; he didn't trust the lift tonight. Taking the steps two at a time, he hurried back to the Second-Class Library. He had to get the novel and his journal. He had to document this to make sense of the impossible.

Bursting into the library, he grabbed both from the table, nearly knocking over one of the chairs in his haste.

He checked his pocket watch. 11:55 p.m. The time felt impossibly compressed, the last twenty minutes a lifetime.

Robert stepped out of the Second-Class Library, the faint hum of conversation and the soft shuffle of a few passengers fading behind him. He pulled the neatly folded map from his coat pocket, his hands trembling slightly. By the electric light, he traced the lines and compartments with his finger, finding his current position and mentally charting a route toward the forward Well Deck.

He saw it for himself. He was sure of it this time. An iceberg had passed by on the ship's starboard side. If the ship had been damaged, the impact would be somewhere ahead, in the bow. He followed the map's guiding lines down the stairs to E Deck and found the sign that read "Scotland Road," the long passageway that stretched nearly the length of the ship. It was on the port side, but he could make it to the bow and look around outside. If he made it that far.

Most passengers had gone to bed by 11. The corridor was coming alive with murmurs and hurried footsteps as stewards moved between compartments, quietly reassuring nervous passengers. The *casualness* of their reassurances now felt like a cruel joke to Robert. He hurried forward, keeping to the side where he could avoid drawing attention to himself. Occasionally, he glanced at the various posted signs and the map to ensure he wasn't wandering into any restricted areas. He couldn't afford to be detained or questioned.

On the way, Robert quickly stepped aside around a corner as a few crew members approached. He caught part of the exchange from a young stewardess with concern in her voice.

"Violet, I know you were on the *Olympic* when the collision happened. But this ship is much safer."

A man interjected brusquely. "What's this? Ah, Miss Jessop again." His tone was edged with irritation. "There's nothing to worry about. That shudder was nothing more than a thrown propeller blade. This ship's construction is quite sound."

Nonsense, Robert thought.

The man's voice hardened. "And remember what I said earlier, Miss Jessop. If I see that rosary again outside your apron, I'll seize it and throw it overboard. Are we clear?"

Robert scraped his fingernails into the wood paneling of the wall. He never denied the religious rights of others only so long as they did not intrude on the wellbeing of those who practiced a different one or none at all. To deny a woman her faith, in this hour of all hours. It sickened him. He couldn't hear her reply, but it seemed enough for the man.

"Very good. Now be a good example to the passengers. Have them dress warmly, see to their lifebelts. Tell them this is only a precaution."

As the group ascended the nearby stairs, Robert muttered under his breath, "We'll see about that," before continuing down the long corridor.

He was feeling a bit out of breath when he noticed the First-Class Entrance that gave access to the bottom of the main grand staircase. He walked past it so as not to be seen by stewards attending to the first-class passengers. He couldn't afford to get in trouble this time; not now, not when every second might count.

Finally, reaching the forward general area for third-class passengers, he located the stairs that would take him up to the access doors outside. The sign above one of the doors read "Forward Well Deck." This was it. He opened the thick steel door and stepped outside into the chilly night air. Robert had to close his eyes for a moment due to the cold, which prevented him from seeing the chunks of ice directly in front of him. He stepped out and froze.

A sharp crunch. Ice. Just like stepping on a cube in his kitchen back home. It glittered across the deck like shattered glass beneath the electric lamps. Just like the chunks he saw falling off the iceberg when he stepped onto the boat deck. Dark, jagged chunks of ice lay strewn across the wooden planks. Some of the third-class passengers who were awakened by the noise were kicking the ice around, having fun. So he wasn't imagining it after all! Robert noticed some of the night owls in First Class had come outside to see what was going on. He had reached down to pick up one of the pieces of ice.

A few crew members hurried past him with tense urgency, disappearing down the forward stairs to inspect the damage below the waterline. Robert remained still, but his senses were heightened. Beneath his feet, he could hear a low, ominous hiss of air rushing up from the cargo holds, a chilling sound that spoke of displacement, of an unseen force filling the spaces below. The heavy canvas covers of the two hatches near where he stood, once stretched taut over the openings, now bulged and shifted, rising and falling like giant, uneasy breaths. The *Titan*… no… *Titanic*… breathed! Slowly, uneasily, as if waking into a nightmare, its lungs filling with the icy Atlantic, drowning it.

It was warm inside the ship as his grip tightened around the folded map in his other hand. This ship was said to be unsinkable. Yet here, on the Forward Well Deck, beneath the stars and silence, a strange unease rose from below his feet. Slowly, he turned to glance up at the crow's nest. The two lookouts were speaking. He couldn't make out the words, but he could've sworn he heard one of them say, "I think we hit it."

Then the shadows moved. It seemed the men were leaving the post.

Robert looked down again, his eyes catching on a splintered chunk of ice laying near the rail. Then he got an idea.

Walking toward one of the covered cargo hatches, his feet felt the warm air being pushed from below as it escaped. The canvas was pushing the air down onto his feet. Placing the chunk of ice next to the hatch, he watched as the warm air began melting the ice. At first, the melting water pooled in place, then flowed forward. His eyes widened.

The deck… didn't feel level anymore. Not drastically, not enough to alarm the average passenger but there was a subtle slant beneath his shoes, just enough to feel profoundly wrong.

The ship had stopped.

The iceberg had already drifted far astern, its shape faded into the darkness, a phantom swallowed by the sea. But its passage had been unmistakable; its wound left open upon the deck where Robert now stood, undeniable.

Robert pulled the novel out of his satchel and clutched it in his hand, the cover now cold and slightly damp with condensation. *Futility.* The spine curled slightly where it had pressed against his palm. The timing, its story, the moment, was impossible to ignore.

The warning had been written. And it had not been heeded.

Robert didn't know what would happen next. But he knew the silence wouldn't last. The story had begun. And this time, he was inside it. He was convinced that he was on the real *steamship Titan!*

From somewhere else above, voices echoed down. Perhaps Captain Smith or Thomas Andrews assessing the situation. Though Robert couldn't make out the exact words, the grave expressions on the faces of the nearby crewmen and their hushed, urgent tones told him all he needed to know.

Leo. Robert wasn't able to recall what cabin he'd be in or on what deck. There was no time to look around for him, no way to warn him directly. Many of the single men down there likely wouldn't even understand English, let alone grasp the fantastical, yet terrifying, nature of his discovery. And he couldn't afford to get caught in there, a second-class passenger in a restricted zone. The last thing he needed was to get locked up in the brig on a sinking ship, robbed of any chance to help or even to save himself. His heart ached with the impossible weight of this knowledge, this urgent truth he couldn't share.

Hiding the novel as he returned to E Deck and found Scotland Road, Robert stepped around a nearby corner to keep from being seen for a moment. Suddenly understanding the magnitude of the situation, he scoured the pages of his journal over the past week, frantic with a desperate hope to find some logical flaw.

In *Futility*, the *Titan* was traveling in the North Atlantic during the month of April. In Chapter 2: '*... for, though it was April, the salt air was chilly...*' Just like the *Titanic*, it was the largest ship in the world. The first line in the entire book: *'She was the largest craft afloat and the greatest of the works of men.' S.S. Titan* and *R.M.S. Titanic* were both of similar length. The *Titan* was 800 feet long, but the width was not stated. *Titanic's* length was just over 882 feet, while the beam width was 92 feet and 6 inches.

Their tonnage was similar: 45,000 tons for the *Titan* and 46,329 tons for the *Titanic*.

Both ships had the same type of steam-powered triple expansion reciprocating engines, watertight compartments with doors that could be closed either manually or automatically in less than a minute to restrict flooding, triple screw propulsion, and the most upsetting fact of all.

"Oh damn," he whispered, the expletive feeling utterly inadequate.

Both ships carried only so few lifeboats as would satisfy the current maritime laws, which were now horribly outdated. If so, with only 16 lifeboats on board, with 4 smaller collapsible ones, there were not enough boats for half the people on the *Titanic*! The *Titan* at least had 24.

Robert's hands trembled as he turned the pages, the paper rustling like dry leaves. The weight of the book in his hand suddenly felt like an anchor, as if he were holding something not meant to exist, something that defied the natural order.

This wasn't just a coincidence. It couldn't be. But if it wasn't, then what was it? Another realization… the author! Looking at the cover: Morgan Robertson. Like a reverse image of Robert Morganson. Everything he had read in *Futility* so far had happened. Robert was too afraid to read any more of the book. He refused to. He couldn't bear to learn the rest of the ending prematurely. In his satchel, his fingers tightened around the pocket that held the pages of *Futility*. The words echoed in his mind, not a whisper, but a shout: *Futility has been foretold.*

He knew that the wealthier passengers would have access to the lifeboats before anyone else, by virtue of their position and their perceived importance. His chances of survival as a single man traveling alone in second class were not the best. Nor were they the worst. Suddenly… "Oh God!" the people he'd met. His mind raced, a montage of faces flashing before his eyes.

Lawrence Beasley. Where was he? Eva and her mother, Ester Hart, who knew something was wrong. And Leo

Zimmermann! What about the honeymoon couple from dinner? The elderly woman who had offered him tea? Would any of them survive this? Would he? Suddenly, the deck no longer felt level. It was like a slight slant forward, an undeniable slope pulling him toward the bow.

Through a grated hatchway, Robert glimpsed men in heavy coats and caps inspecting the bulkheads near the mailroom. The hiss of water echoed faintly from somewhere beyond, a chilling, insidious sound. He edged closer when a voice sounding very calm yet burdened with a terrible weight drifted up the corridor.

"It's all the first five compartments, Mr. Andrews," the crewman said, his voice strained. "They're already flooded. At least fourteen feet above the keel in the first ten minutes."

Thomas Andrews was *Titanic's* chief designer. His pale face, illuminated by an electric lamp, looked grim, etched with a dawning horror that mirrored Robert's own.

"She is designed to float with at most four flooded," Andrews murmured, his voice barely a whisper, filled with the crushing weight of his calculations. "Not five."

Robert's breath caught, a cold knot forming in his stomach. The implications were catastrophic.

Further along the corridor, as he tried to make his way back to Second Class, Robert's sharp ears caught the voice of Thomas Andrews again, emerging from a stairwell that led up from the flooded compartments. Andrews spoke in hushed tones to an officer, his usual calm now weighted with quiet urgency. Robert stayed quiet around the corner to keep from being noticed, pressing himself into the shadows.

"She will hold for the moment," Andrews said, his voice flat, devoid of hope. "The pumps are presently draining water in Boiler Room 5, but water is rising rapidly in all the forward holds. We can't reach the forepeak to drain it. The bulkheads should keep us afloat… but only if we can stem the flooding in Boiler Room 6. At the most, she can float with any two or three compartments compromised. She could even survive with all four of the first compartments gone. But not five. Not five. I must return to the chartroom and confer with the captain regarding calculations to ascertain our remaining time."

The officer nodded gravely and hurried off. Robert lingered in the shadows, heart pounding. Looking around to be sure he was hidden from sight; he pulled the map out and found the starboard side view. He knew the ship had three forward cargo holds. So that's three compartments. What other two?

The forward most would have machinery for raising and lowering the anchors, plus others for the mooring lines. That makes four. And the fifth?

Robert saw the only other compartment it could have been. The location of Boiler Room 6 was directly under the forward funnel behind the bridge. The berg damaged that much?! If the ship could survive four flooded compartments… but not five… then he had found the steel walls that formed the bulkheads. Most didn't extend far above the waterline.

Robert never considered himself to be very religious. But if he could survive the night, if he ever saw daylight again… Fighting back tears, a sudden, desperate prayer forming in his throat, he made another note in his journal. Steadying his dominant hand to keep it legible, he wrote: *'Futility has been foretold! If God truly exists, perhaps coincidence is His cruelest disguise!'* He scrawled the words with a desperate urgency, as if the act of writing could somehow make sense of the chaos. But Robert knew it could not.

He closed the journal for a moment, staring at its worn

leather cover. His mouth was dry, tongue thick, as if the act of writing had drained him. Somewhere far forward, the faint, steady hiss of water carried through the steel, a sound so soft he wondered if he were imagining it.

He quickly put the novel and his journal away in his satchel, stuffing them deep inside. Suddenly, while tucking the map back into his coat pocket, he heard it. Water. Inside the ship. Directly below him, unmistakable. A cold, wet lapping that hadn't been there moments ago. He saw a grated hatchway across the hall, the metal dark and ominous. Forcing himself to walk over to it, he got down on his knees so he could look through it, and he saw water rising up, dark green and foaming, reflecting the dim electric light! He needed to get back to Second Class. He needed to get to a lifeboat, any lifeboat.

A cold dread, numbing and complete, crept over him as he hurried back toward the second-class areas. The steady march of both time and water would not wait.

It was a long walk back through Scotland Road to access the Second-Class Stairs. Silence. No alarms. No shouting. No widespread panic. Not yet. But deep down, he now knew. It was only a matter of time. The main question now was: how much time did anyone really have? And what could he do with it?

He hurried to his cabin to grab the cork-filled life jacket and await instructions. He wasn’t sure how, when, or even if he would die. Only that the story was already written. Perhaps even the ending; one he had decided not to read, but one he would never escape. And this time, it wasn’t fiction.

He stopped just outside the cabin door, the sudden quiet of the corridor amplifying the distant, groaning sounds of the ship. A moment of breathless stillness, a suspended gasp of air.

He pushed open the door, stepped inside, and, without hesitation, reached for the cork-filled life jacket, a grotesque, buoyant promise of a fighting chance, or at least a cleaner end. The coarse cork felt rough against his fingers. Then a bitter thought crossed his mind, a fleeting, desperate attempt at gallows humor: if he was going to *freeze* to death that night, at least he wouldn't *drown* first!

Standing in the quiet of his cabin, he knew that the night had only just begun.

6

COLLATERAL DAMAGE!

In the absence of the engines being operational, a hollow silence filled Robert's cabin. It was a stark contrast to the gentle, rhythmic hum he had grown accustomed to over the past few days, a sound that had been the very breath of the mighty ship. The space no longer felt warm or comforting. Only still and unnervingly quiet, permeated by a growing chill. Even the residual warmth from the steam pipes seemed to fade, leaving behind a cold, metallic tang in the air.

He stood in front of the fold-out basin, holding the thick silver chain of his pocket watch above the water. Robert had filled it almost halfway, just enough to create a miniature, irrefutable level. Laying his watch next to the faucet, at first, the chain had hung perfectly still, a plumb bob of certainty. Then, half an hour later, when he checked, it leaned just slightly. A few degrees off vertical, but enough to prove it. The reflection of the chain, once a straight line, now angled to the right.

Was he hallucinating it? No. He was really seeing this. This was no delusion!

A sickening lurch settled in his stomach, a dread far colder than the unheated washroom, far deeper than any fear of drowning. The *Titanic* was listing. Sinking. And he saw the irrefutable proof in the few inches of silver and still water, a silent witness to an unthinkable truth. But who would believe him—a quiet, paranoid man clutching a strange novel—before it was too late?

Watching the chain closely, Robert noticed another

link, then another, easing further into the water, a relentless, slow descent, like the ship. "Oh God... please no," he whispered, the words choked and raspy in the sudden, profound silence. The room was silent, but Robert could hear his heart beat loudly between his ears.

Gripping the wooden frame of the cabinet, he stared at his reflection in the mirror for a moment longer, his own eyes wide with a desperate, dawning horror. He wound the chain back around the watch and slipped it into his pocket, the solid weight of it a futile comfort. Looking at a glass bottle of water on the shelf, he saw the water within was not perfectly level either. Despite the perfect stillness of the room, the water moved slightly.

He didn't even bother to drain the basin. He saw no point now; the water outside was already doing that job.

Nearby, his journal lay open on the desk. He had scribbled a few notes after the impact, a desperate attempt to capture the initial shock. He picked it up and held a pen over a blank page. But now words failed him completely. What could he write? What language, what combination of letters and ink, could capture the slow, agonizing unraveling of a supposedly invincible ship?

The futility of it all was overwhelming. A fitting name for that small book. All he could think of writing was: *'The book knew... that book knew!'*

After closing his journal and being sure the novel was securely tucked deep within a side pocket of his satchel, he grabbed his passport and all his money, and stepped out of the cabin, wrapping his coat tight around him.

Seeing his boarding ticket lying on the bed, he considered leaving it there. What was the point? Then again... if he was documenting... evidence... it might prove useful. It had his name on it after all. Robert grabbed the ticket and tucked it into his passport.

He held the life jacket in his hand, a bulky, cork-filled monstrosity, unsure if he should put it on or simply keep it close, as if its mere proximity could offer any protection. It felt more like a costume for a play he never wished to perform.

The corridor felt different now. Quieter and tenser. As if the ship was holding its breath. But beneath that unnatural silence, Robert could detect a new symphony of distress: the low groan of lifeboat davits being swung out along the starboard deck, a mournful, metallic screech against the night. Ropes creaking against pulleys like strained sinews. The sharp, urgent blast of an officer's whistle cutting through the thick, cold air. Muffled voices drifted from open cabin doors, and hurried footsteps echoed on the polished floors.

"... they said water's up to E Deck forward. Boiler rooms, too..."

"SH! Don't say that so bloody loud. You want to start a panic?!"

Robert kept walking hurriedly. The cold night hit him as he stepped onto the lower Second-Class Promenade. The stars above shone with perfect clarity, but the darkness below felt bottomless. He moved slowly, unsure if his legs were shaking from the cold or the truth.

They were sinking. He knew it before any other passenger could.

Walking around the lower Second-Class Promenade, Robert thought about the fragments of hurried voices he had heard from the crew rushing below decks.

"She's taken on too many compartments. The weight of the water in the bow is pulling her down by the head. Flood intake is nearly 400 tons a minute. Water is already beginning to spill over the tops of the compartments," one fireman explained to another as they passed.

Robert's heart tightened. He didn't fully understand the mechanics of a ship's construction, but the urgency in their tone told him more than enough. *Titanic*, this marvel of engineering, was fighting a losing battle against the sea.

Stepping toward the railing, he peered into the vast darkness, hearing the strain of the ropes tightening to raise the lifeboats off their settings so they could be lowered down the sides of the ship. The icy air bit through his coat, but he barely noticed.

Robert felt an unfamiliar weight press on his chest. The statistics from that crumpled newspaper photo of *Olympic's* collision with *HMS Hawke* flashed through his mind. The *Olympic* survived that impact… but this was different. They were much too far from land. More than a few hundred miles anyway. The sea was relentless, and this ship's fate was already sealed. Esther Hart was right after all. *Titanic* would never reach New York nor endure long enough to see another sunrise.

He gripped the railing, staring into the black sea that stretched endlessly ahead. Somewhere below, water was racing into the ship. Robert, wrapped in cork and silence, felt the weight of a truth too vast to speak: the *Titanic* was dying. And he was one of the few who already knew it.

Had Esther read *Futility* also? Robert wished he would have asked her about it or even shown her the book, but he thought it best to keep it a secret. Maybe he was wrong to hide it.

He clutched the railing tighter now, its smooth surface cold beneath his fingers. Soon there would be no warmth on the ship as *Titanic's* bow dipped ever so slightly. The sea, once calm and majestic, now seemed cold and predatory.

Nearby, Lawrence Beesley, the quiet schoolteacher, stood with a watchful gaze. Robert approached him, sensing a shared unease.

"Lawrence," Robert began hesitantly, "I overheard the crew… Five compartments flooded. That's… beyond what the ship was built to withstand."

Beesley's expression tightened. "Yes. I heard the same. The forward compartments act like watertight cells, but water can spill over the tops of the bulkheads if too many are breached. They only go up to E Deck, which is ten or so feet above the waterline. It's like filling sections of an ice tray. Eventually, the weight pulls everything down."

The simplicity of the analogy struck Robert with chilling clarity.

"I met a Jewish passenger in Third Class. He said they have a prayer for travelers. They ask God to calm the waters and guide us to a safe haven… like in Psalm 107."

Beesley gave a solemn nod. "Then perhaps, my friend, we'll need more than engineering tonight."

The two men agreed that they should split up to try and find any lifeboats that would allow men to board. Robert felt the weight of the novel pressing on him, yet he couldn't tear himself away from the ship that had promised to conquer the sea. If this was the end, he would bear witness to it.

The ship groaned beneath Robert's feet as he made his way toward the boat deck. The subtle tilt of the floor was becoming more pronounced, though most passengers remained blissfully unaware of the true danger. As he ascended, the temperature dropped. The night air was bitter, as the stars glistened above like distant, indifferent watchers.

Near the davits, Second Officer Charles Lightoller was shouting orders: "Women and children first! Captain's orders!" The crew worked swiftly to ready the lifeboats. Passengers hesitated, reluctant to leave the great vessel for the fragile crafts swaying in the blackness below. Some clung to hope, others to disbelief.

"This ship can't sink," Robert overheard a gentleman mutter.

"She's made of steel," Robert replied quietly. "I know that she can, and she will."

He lingered, torn between the growing panic around him and the strange pull to stay aboard. From the starboard side, he saw a lifeboat being lowered, filled with women and children wrapped in blankets. A steward, with a calm that seemed practiced, guided a young mother and her daughter toward the lifeboats, assuring her, "Not to worry, madam. This is merely a precaution."

Robert glanced back toward the lower decks. From somewhere deep within the bowels of the ship, he heard the rhythmic thudding of pumps and the occasional clang of metal against metal. The firemen and engineers were still fighting, desperately trying to keep the water at bay.

Leo. He had to find Leo. But how could he? Looking at the lifeboats and seeing how most refused to get into them, Robert felt the pressing need to hurry into the third-class areas to try and find his friend. He had to be fast.

Hurrying back inside, he ran down the staircase that would bring him to Scotland Road.

Descending lower, a fireman, blackened with soot and streaked with sweat, staggered past. His eyes were wide, his breathing labored.

"Boiler Room 5's gone. Water's pouring into the coal bunker," he muttered to someone before disappearing up the stairs.

Robert's stomach tightened. The low hum of the ship's engines had ceased, leaving a creepy silence, broken only by the distant strains of music from the Second-Class Lounge. Someone was playing a light waltz, as if to calm the nerves of those who remained. Yet beneath the melody, Robert could hear the *Titanic* herself groaning. Her steel frame shifting as the weight of the sea pressed further into her wounded hull.

As he approached the entrance to Scotland Road, he turned toward the porthole and saw the ocean climbing higher just below the glass. The sea was no longer a distant force; it was creeping upward, relentless and unstoppable.

He thought of Leo Zimmermann's words from earlier, the *Jewish Traveler's Prayer* and Psalm 107 from the chapel service earlier that night: "*Then they cry unto the Lord in their trouble, and He bringeth them out of their distresses. He maketh the storm a calm, so that the waves thereof are still.*"

The irony of the verse struck him. There would be no calm tonight. Only the vast, cold Atlantic and the sound of human voices rising in fear and desperation.

A shiver raced down his spine, though he wasn't sure if it was the cold or something deeper like an ache of disbelief. He already knew. He had seen the truth for himself. He had already been to the forward Well Deck, seeing the ice scattered. Seeing the small pieces slipping just slightly forward, and hearing the terrible groan of air forced from the depths below as the sea claimed another corridor, continuing to drown the giant.

The night air was frigid, but the chill that gripped Robert came not from the wind. It was something worse. Like standing at the edge of a freshly dug grave.

He lowered his arm over the other side of the rail, then, leaning against it for balance, grasped the metal with numb fingers. Looking down, he saw the water gently brushing the side far below. The bow would be undeniably lower in the water. No longer a distant theory. No longer a question.

Robert heard the faint sound of water being pumped

out the side of the ship somewhere behind him. Looking far below, he could see a stream of water being ejected from the ship. The pumps were on. The ship was truly sinking! They could not stop it, but they could at least slow it down to buy some time. If just minutes only.

Above him, muffled voices called orders. Officers directing passengers to starboard, crewmen struggling with lifeboat davits, but it all faded into a dull roar. Robert could only stare into the abyss ahead, where the horizon had vanished, and the stars above were reflected, not in calm waters but in a black void swallowing everything.

In Robert's mind, this was the beginning of the end. What he didn't know yet was that it was actually the end of the beginning.

Still gripping the railing, he looked up. Above him, crewmen worked with a sense of urgency to uncover the lifeboats and prepare to swing them over the side of the ship for loading, hanging them high above the sea. Their voices echoed oddly in the stillness. He turned his face to the wind and let the cold sting his skin. He needed to feel awake.

It was then he noticed something odd. The stars at the horizon were no longer aligned with the railing. Robert crouched down to position his eyes level with the railing. To his left, the horizon was just above it. To his right, the horizon was almost to the bottom of the top rail.

The angle had already changed! His stomach dropped. "Oh please no…"

This was no temporary delay, no precaution. The ship was fatally wounded. And all the steel and speed in the world could not change that now.

He rose slowly, the cold biting deeper now; not just into his skin but into his soul. Robert clutched the railing one last time, then turned toward the stairwell. He had to find

Leo. And if the story was already written, then he would meet its ending with open eyes.

When he finally reached the areas for third-class passengers, Robert noticed that something else was different here. The gates. He stumbled over to one of them to try and open it. They were closed and locked!

The corridor was dimly lit and tilting ever so slightly. He could hear water flowing around the lower decks. Exhausted but frantic, Robert called Leo's name through the locked barriers as water crept into the corridor beyond. His voice, hoarse with desperation, seemed to vanish into the groaning of the ship, swallowed by the ominous rush of water from below. He glimpsed blurred figures in the dim light of the Steerage corridors, their faces etched with confusion and fear, a sea of bewildered expressions beyond the iron gates, separated by an unyielding barrier.

When he reached another barrier gate near the third-class section, it was locked also. They all were. A few officers and crewmen stood at the next gate, controlling the growing crowd of third-class passengers. Voices in English, Irish, Italian, and various others blended into an anxious murmur. Robert knew that they could see the water flooding their areas better than he could. Suddenly, he was concerned for all of them.

There, just beneath the stairwell on the other side of the gate, Robert barely spotted him, standing with one hand gripping the railing, watching the crowd.

"Leo!"

He looked up and broke into a smile, tired but warm. He hurried toward the gate where Robert was.

"My friend! What are you doing here?! Are you all right?"

"No, I'm not," Robert said, gripping the bars. "And neither is this ship. They're loading lifeboats already."

Leo nodded. "I thought as much. We can see the water rising in the forward rooms. At this rate it will be entering Scotland Road here on E Deck soon."

"You have to come. I'll get a steward. I'll ask someone to open the gate."

Looking down the hallway, Robert was shocked that the stewards he saw had left. As he searched for help, he spotted an ax in a case on the wall behind him. He stepped away from the gate and walked over to it, a deep anger building inside of him.

"Robert? Wait, what are you…?"

Seeing his reflection in the glass, Robert lifted his foot and kicked hard at the case. Breaking the glass, he reached in and grabbed the ax. With a burning fire in his eyes and rage in his bones, he told Leo to stand back. Robert raised the ax and brought it down hard on the lock. The joints in his hands vibrated up his arms to his shoulders, as the clang echoed loudly through the passageway. He barely scratched the paint. With tears in his eyes, Robert could barely see as he raised the ax and slammed it down hard, missing the lock and rattling the gate violently.

Leo yelled at him to stop, but Robert wasn't listening. Just as Robert was about to raise the ax again, Leo reached through the bars, grabbed the handle firmly, and begged Robert to stop. Finally, Robert looked at his friend.

Leo looked over his shoulder at the people behind him. The mothers with children, the men with worried eyes, and the handful of young women who clutched prayer beads or religious texts. They were all scared. In trying to help them, Robert had unintentionally frightened everyone!

Robert's vision blurred, his throat tightening. He began losing the ability to hold back his tears. "No, no! I'm not leaving this ship without you. There has to be another way."

"I can't leave them," Leo said quietly. "Many of them don't speak a word of English. They don't know which way to go."

Robert shook his head and placed the ax down, hanging it on the black iron gate. He pulled hard on the bars, knowing they would not give. "But you'll never get out in time."

"Maybe not. But if I can help even a few of them find their way, it's something."

Robert paused. Then, reaching into his coat, he pulled out the folded map; the one he'd carried since boarding. It was dog-eared from use, with lines drawn in pen where he'd marked staircases, passages, and crew corridors. He pressed it through the gate into Leo's hand.

"Then take this," he said. "It's not perfect, but it'll get you to the boat deck if the path clears. Show it to the others. Use it. Maybe there's still a way out. Look for stairways near the engine room bulkhead. There's a narrow passage… see here? Look for access ladders leading up."

Leo accepted the map and quickly looked over it, his eyes scanning the markings. His fingers trembled, just a little.

"You marked every stairway, every turn… You made notes here as well?"

"I got turned around a few times," Robert said, almost apologetically. "Didn't want to get lost again."

Leo smiled faintly and nodded. "Thank you, my friend."

He then raised an eyebrow. "You've been carrying that small book, *Futility*, around since the start, haven't you?"

Robert blinked, surprised by the shift in tone. "Yes… why?"

Leo shook his head with a small chuckle. "If you ever meet the man who wrote that cursed thing… do me a favor, would you?"

"Anything."

"Give him a good, strong kick in the *tuchus*!"

Robert laughed. A real, surprised chuckle. "Leo, I don't know Hebrew or Yiddish, but I have a good idea what a *tuchus* is!"

Leo's smile softened. "Good. Now go and be sure you live long enough to do it."

The two men hugged with the bars between them. A beat passed. Then Leo said, "You carry words in your journal. Let these also travel with you," as he slipped something into Robert's satchel. "I want you to have it. Just in case."

Robert hesitated. "But that is yours."

Leo's voice was firm. "And this map was yours. But you gave it freely. Let me do the same."

Robert accepted the unknown item slowly, reverently.

"Please… I don't want you to die down here!" he said.

Leo's smile faded, but not from fear. It was something deeper. A resolve shaped by years of hardship and hope alike.

"Then live. That's what you can do for me. Listen carefully: near the end of Deuteronomy, Moses said, 'I set before you this day life and death… blessing and cursing.'" Leo gave a slight smile, his voice steady despite the rising panic around them. The sounds of rushing water were getting louder. "This night, I choose life, Robert. But not for myself. For you. Choose life, my friend… so that you may live."

Their eyes met through the iron bars. Leo's silence told Robert everything.

Robert's throat tightened. "You know, it's strange. When I boarded this ship, I felt like I wanted to disappear from the whole world. Drift quietly into… I don't even know. Tonight I very well could have."

"Then maybe," Leo said, "the *Titanic* gave you a second chance instead."

"Leo, if you can make it to the boat deck… please try! Take the ax also in case you need to break through a locked door." Unable to resist, he hugged Leo again when he noticed that the water had made it to the area where the third-class passengers were locked in.

"*Zei gezunt*," Leo said as he grabbed the ax before hurrying down the stairs to try to guide people to safety while the sound of rushing water grew louder. A beacon of selfless courage amidst the gathering doom. Robert made his way back toward the lifeboats in a daze. He could still hear Leo's voice echoing in his mind… so that you may live…

As Robert climbed the stairs back toward the lifeboats, the sound of the ship straining along with rushing water echoed near him like a memory he couldn't outrun. The map was gone. The ax was gone. Leo was gone. Into the depths, into the crowd, into the story. But his words remained, etched into Robert's chest. "Choose life. So that you may live."

Robert burst onto the Second-Class Deck into a blur of shouting voices, crying children, and clattering shoes, as people tried to find a way to escape. A desperate, surging tide of humanity. He stumbled across the deck. Looking forward, he saw a streak of white light shoot high into the night sky. Then it erupted. Rockets! There was only one reason to launch rockets at sea. Now, everyone knew.

Someone running by had shoved him out of their way, causing him to fall. With his breath fogging in the frigid air as he struggled to get back on his feet, his eyes darted between the growing crowd and the towering shadows of *Titanic's* funnels. He was near the fourth one now. Its colossal bulk began rising like a monument against the indifferent stars.

The deck beneath his feet had begun to tilt ever so slightly forward, a relentless, undeniable incline toward the bow. Underneath him, he heard the sound of furniture scraping as whole rooms of it began to slide and fall over. Subtle, but unmistakable. Robert could feel it in his stomach and in his legs, a disorienting pull. His stomach sank. The ship was bowing to the sea, a slow, agonizing descent.

He didn't want to join it in its icy embrace. But would it let him go?

He hesitated, heart pounding, scanning the chaos. He had emerged on the starboard side of the Boat Deck where every lifeboat in that row was already swung out and lowered into the darkness. They were gone.

"The boats are gone!" Robert heard a young woman say. The man she was with tried to guide her away from the crowd.

Robert's mind reeled. He hurried around to the port side, and there was one left, a lone shape against the night sky, still resting on its davits and filling fast. People were fighting to get into it, a desperate rush of bodies. Unable to make his way through the surging crowd, Robert realized that all the remaining lifeboats in the Second-Class Promenade area were going to be full before he could even get close!

"Oh shit!" Robert, never one for foul language, didn't mind breaking his rule this time.

He had run out of time! Or had he?

Nearly giving up, a cold despair beginning to creep in, Robert's eyes darted upward. He walked up onto the raised platform surrounding the fourth funnel that towered over the aft end of the ship. Then, stepping up onto the rails, he looked forward, his gaze sweeping across the vast expanse of the Boat Deck. Noticing that there were another couple of lifeboats far forward, near the bridge, not yet loaded, Robert got an idea. It would be a desperate, reckless gamble. Another railing ran along the outer edge at the back of the Boat Deck he was on, with a small access ladder connecting to the First-Class A Deck Promenade below. Its roof now sloping forward with the rest of the ship. As he hurried to the edge near the aft mast, the dense crowd of people, now pushing and shoving, kept Robert from reaching the small access ladder. He had to go over.

Robert grabbed the handrail. The cold metal stung his bare fingers. He swung one leg over the edge, guiding the other, forcing himself to steady his trembling body against the ship's increasing tilt. He could feel the stern rising. His satchel bumped awkwardly at his side as he began to climb down the framework as carefully as he could, each rung a precarious step into the abyss, a dizzying drop to the deck below. He slipped once due to his foot skidding on the slick metal. His heart jumped into his throat, a gasp caught in his lungs, but he caught himself just in time. His arms were burning with effort and his muscles were screaming. He hung from the railing like a rag. Then, gritting his teeth against the bitter cold and the paralyzing fear, he let go and dropped the last several feet to the deck below, landing hard, the impact jarring through his bones, his knees buckling.

His shoes skidded slightly on the increasing slant, the forward slope now undeniable even on A Deck. He fell hard to one knee, using his hands to push himself back up, his palms stinging. Robert hurried forward, a new urgency propelling him toward the rising water in front of him.

A chill air tore past, carrying with it the ominous groan of the great ship's hull, a sound of immense steel twisting and tearing. From somewhere up ahead, he could hear an officer shouting with urgency in every syllable, the commands swallowed partially by the wind. Stopping partway, Robert heard a man say to someone, "Stay here; an officer on this side is letting men on." Robert knew he had to try. He struggled to recall from memory which lifeboat it likely was. Perhaps the one at the very front of A Deck. Boat Four? It had to be.

He ran. Past shuttered windows, the dark glass reflecting his own desperate, strained face. He heard glass and ceramic breaking somewhere inside. Past a few passengers clinging to railings above him, their silhouettes etched against the stars. The A Deck Promenade was mostly empty. The chaos was concentrated further aft. The slope was working against him now, a constant, downhill battle, like the ship itself was trying to drag him down with it, resisting his every step. Looking out over the side, Robert could see the dark ocean getting closer the further forward he hurried, the waterline creeping steadily upward.

Residual steam hissed from vents along the side of the funnel closest to him, a mournful sigh. He caught a glimpse of the forward expansion joint directly above him, stretched to its limit, nearly breaking, showing the immense strain on the ship. The rubber seal was peeling off, exposing the raw, groaning steel beneath. The ship was going to break apart!

But Robert didn't stop. Not yet. Not until he reached the cluster of people gathered near the A Deck windows, huddled together in the dim light. Near what he hoped was Boat Four. Then, at last, he saw the ropes attached to the lifeboat that had been lowered from the top, its wooden hull now level with this deck. They had let some men get in. Hope surged through him, hot and desperate.

A deckhand spotted him from the lifeboat through the window and banged hard on the white-painted steel. "You! Get over here!" His voice was urgent.

Robert stumbled to the frame, throwing himself forward. Looking to his right, the Atlantic had invaded the A Deck Promenade and crept closer. The speed of the sinking was increasing with every moment.

An officer, his face drawn and grim, glanced at him. Noticing his soaked coat, his bleeding hand, he nodded once, curtly, before turning his attention back to the crowd.

"Tell me, can you row, sir?" the officer asked, his voice sharp but direct.

Robert nodded, breathless, his chest heaving. "Yes. Yes, sir, I can."

"Right then. Please hurry, but be careful. We're loading now."

Robert had thought he would have taken the stairs located at the bow up to the boat deck again. But this boat had been lowed to the A Deck Promenade. Yet the windows were closed and crewmen were struggling to open them. As each of the only few that could be opened were ready, passengers hurriedly climbed through them to escape the ship. The water approaching their feet providing the necessary motivation.

Robert was able to climb from the deck and up to the side of the lifeboat, his hands finding their grip on the cold, wet wood. He squeezed himself through the narrow opening just after a group of passengers was ushered in ahead of him.

Robert collapsed into the boat, hands shaking, breath ragged, the rough wood digging into his back. He was in! The cold night air still bit at him, but he was in a lifeboat. He didn't whisper the words so much as beg them, a desperate plea to an unseen force, echoing Leo's final command.

Beneath him, the sea claimed the ship. Above him, the stars watched. Between the two, a lifeboat rocked. Robert carried no sermon, no prophecy, but only the echo of a friend's voice and the memory of a map traded in faith. This was not an escape. It was permission. No, it was a command.

"CHOOSE LIFE..."

7

DEATH OF A TITAN

Terrible groans could be heard. Deep echoes of metal straining beneath the surface, loud enough to pierce the air and the cries around them. Robert had barely sat down in Lifeboat 4 when he heard it. He flinched, a sickening lurch twisting in his stomach, as if his own body were being torn apart. The long, reinforced bow, designed to break through large waves, had already been swallowed by the sea. It was dragging the rest of the ship down with every passing second, a massive, unseen hand pulling at her heart.

Robert turned in his seat, peering past the heads and shoulders packed around him. What had once been solid steel, the foredeck, where passengers had strolled just hours earlier, was rapidly vanishing beneath the Atlantic. The forward Well Deck plunged first, water spilling over the edge onto the wooden planks, swallowing the cargo cranes and winches… Then the forward mast. The *Titanic* was diving by the head; her proud nameplate already disappeared under the sea, a monument to human hubris.

Robert gripped the gunwale as icy spray stung his face. The falls still hung from the davits. No longer instruments of rescue, but limp threads disconnected from hope. The ship's bridge had completely gone under. Now, the freezing water poured into the ventilation shafts.

They were still attached to the ropes hanging from the davit. As the *Titanic* sank, it began to yank on the lifeboat. Just as it lurched forward, Robert caught sight of something sliding off the roof of the officers' quarters. A canvas-sided raft, half-secured, half-forgotten. People were attempting to use oars to slide the collapsible off the roof at the base of the forward funnel and down onto the Boat Deck.

One of the officers called out at the top of his lungs. "Hold it… HOLD IT!"

The oars broke, and it tumbled awkwardly, striking the deck hard with a hollow thud after flipping upside down and landing right on top of someone! For a moment, it lay still.

Then movement!

Someone's arm reached out beneath the raft, trapped as the freezing water rose around them, their body pinned by the inverted hull. Several people hurried to the upturned craft, trying to flip it over.

Robert gasped, leaning forward, but the lifeboat was already drifting. The sea surged, lifting the raft and the man with it, until both vanished into the chaos.

He didn't know who it was, but he would later learn it was one of the wireless operators, Harold Bride. The image seared itself into his mind: survival not as triumph, but as accident.

A lifeboat meant to save had nearly killed. And still, the ship groaned in front of them, collapsing inward like a wounded beast.

Moments later, the guide wires securing the forward funnel strained and snapped overhead. They sounded like gunshots in the chaos. First, only one broke. Then another. Suddenly, in rapid succession, all of them gave way, slashing through the air and striking the water like giant whips.

Realizing what was about to happen next, one of the crewmen shouted, "Cut us loose! Now!"

"I need a knife!" came the reply. The words had barely left the man's mouth when the first funnel broke free.

Looking above them, Robert saw it fall. The twisted rigging and steel frame tumbling like a wounded beast, an unthinkable act. This colossal symbol of human ingenuity, now nothing but a weapon, ripped free, crashing down with a guttural roar to the starboard side directly on top of numerous people caught in the freezing water trying to swim to one of the lifeboats.

With a deafening crash, it silenced the screams for just a moment, a grotesque punctuation mark on the disaster. A massive wave of water surged up as it hit, drowning lights, bodies, and the last breath of the mighty liner's former elegance. Leaving nothing but churned foam and unseen horror.

Where the funnel once stood proudly with the other three, a massive, gaping hole now marked its absence. A deep chasm into the bottom of the ship as untold tons of water raced in faster than ever. The ship's sinking speed increased dramatically, pulled down by the immense weight, swallowed by the enormous, exposed wound. Anyone nearby was forced to run en masse to the back of the ship.

Robert flinched, shielding his face. The lantern beside him swung wildly. Debris. Splinters of wood and twisted metal rained around the lifeboat. He didn't realize he was shouting until someone gripped his shoulder to steady him.

"We're clear! The falls are cut! Row now, row!"

He looked back once through stinging eyes. Where the funnel had stood, there was only smoke and sparks, a raw wound in the ship's back. Water poured into the gaping hole like a black waterfall.

And still, she sank. Faster now, with a renewed,

sickening urgency. At that moment Robert recalled some of the details of the *Titan's* destruction.

'Amid the roar of escaping steam, and the bee-like buzzing of nearly three thousand human voices, raised in agonized screams and callings from within the inclosing walls, and the whistling of air through hundreds of open deadlights as the water, entering the holes of the crushed and riven starboard side, expelled it. The Titan moved slowly… and launched herself into the sea… a dying monster, groaning with her death-wound… by the roaring of steam from her iron lungs.

This ceased in time, leaving behind it the… whistling of air; and when this too was suddenly hushed, and the ensuing silence broken by dull, booming reports—as from bursting compartments—Rowland knew… that the invincible Titan, with nearly all of her people… was beneath the surface of the sea.'

Although Robert didn't pull the novel out at that moment, he could see every detail of the cover design. The multi-funneled ship sinking into the waves. Three funnels, but perhaps the foremost one had already broken free and crashed down.

Is this what was now happening to the *Titanic*?

Anyone in a lifeboat close enough to the ship could see water pouring through the intake vents and the others spewing water out onto the people still stranded. The ventilation system was pulling water in, which sped up the sinking.

Safe, for the moment, in the bobbing lifeboat. It rocked beneath Robert, the cold biting deep into his skin, a pervasive chill that settled in his bones. The further they drifted, the smaller the *Titanic* seemed, receding into the darkness, a diminishing giant. But she was still there, her stern towering high over the ocean, her bow swallowed by the sea. Somehow, her power, clearly fading, remained, a formidable silhouette against the glimmering stars. "She can't last much longer," someone whispered, the words hanging heavy in the frigid air.

Another set of guide wires, the ones for the second funnel, snapped free. As the second funnel fell, black smoke continued to emit but mixed with a fountain of bright sparks shooting into the sky as it toppled over.

A strange quiet settled over the boat, interrupted only by the splash of oars, the rhythmic creak of the oarlocks, and the ragged breaths of those packed inside. No one else spoke. No one could. They just watched helpless, mesmerized as the impossible unfolded before their eyes.

Then the ship lurched, a sickening, final shudder that rippled through the water, as it rose even faster, a death throe.

The bow was gone now, swallowed into the sea, the stern rising higher with each passing minute. It was an angle no vessel was meant to take. The decks were tilting into a nightmare staircase, lights flickering like candles in a draft. Somewhere deep inside the hull, something boomed. A hollow, metallic concussion that carried across the water and into Robert's bones.

A sharp gasp rippled through the boat, a collective intake of breath. Someone whispered something, maybe a prayer or a curse, but Robert couldn't focus on the words, only the overwhelming image before him. He gripped the cold edge of his seat, his fingers aching from the pain of constriction.

The people on the stern of the ship were packed close, a single mass against the railings. From this distance, they seemed almost still, but he knew they were moving, clinging, climbing, some simply frozen in place. The white arcs of their arms caught the light before vanishing into shadow. The stern, refusing to sink, continued to rise, defiant in its final moments; the angle shocking, impossibly steep. The propellers, massive blades of gleaming bronze, were now completely out of the water, catching the starlight and reflecting it in an eerie, metallic sheen as they dripped freezing water.

Robert thought about what he had just recently read in *Futility* before the evacuation began, the words flashing in his mind with terrifying clarity: '*… she rose out of the sea, higher and higher—until the propellers in the stern were half exposed…*' It was almost exactly how it was described. The precision of the words chilled him to his core. The main difference was the *Titanic* continued to sink on an almost perfectly even keel. Unlike the *Titan* that fell onto her side.

Somewhere deep inside the monstrous hull, metal groaned very deep and low, like the death wail of some enormous animal, a final, tortured cry. The ship's lights flickered again, dancing erratically, and dimmed even more. Struggling. Now, even the emergency lights were failing, one by one. The *Titanic* was dying, her very nervous system shutting down as if her soul was preparing to leave.

As the stern rose higher into the sky, a black, impossibly angled tower against the stars, Robert instinctively reached for his pocket watch; its chain still looped around his fingers, a familiar comfort. The luminous dial flickered in the dimming light, revealing the time: **2:14 a.m**. He knew the *Titanic* hit the iceberg shortly before midnight. If he could see the watch, he could know how long the ship had lasted and how long it had fought. But for how much longer would it last?

And yet… something still breathed.

From the fourth funnel, a massive, towering object where it stood, a faint trail of light gray smoke curled up into the night air. It was thin, ghostly, and almost unnoticed in the shadows of the dying lights. It wasn't the thick, coal-fired billows of days past, but a softer haze, like the dying breath of a hearth deep within the First-Class Smoking Room, a final, lingering warmth from a vanished world. Maybe some embers still smoldered there; abandoned, irrelevant, yet stubbornly, miraculously alive. A flicker of refinement, sizzling in the bones of a dying beast.

Robert blinked, scrubbing his eyes with the back of his hand. Was it real, or just the haze of tears and cold in his eyes, a trick of his exhausted mind? Either way, he couldn't look away. *Titanic*, vibrant in life, proud even in death, had sighed a final, wistful exhalation. That faint smoke rose gently into the heavens and *Titanic's* very breath was gone.

Then, without warning, a blinding electrical surge. The ship's lights flared in a final, desperate gasp, the incandescent bulbs burning with a furious, impossible brilliance. For a brief moment, *Titanic* looked almost alive, glowing against the black sky, her final breath caught in an eerie, silver shimmer, illuminating every rivet, every deck. Almost as if she could somehow rise back up to the surface like "*Venus from the Sea*." Then, absolute darkness. The lights didn't fade. They shone brightly for just a moment, a defiant farewell, and finally snapped out for eternity, plunging the ship into a profound, suffocating blackness.

A collective cry, sharp and raw, rose from the water. A pure, unadulterated terror from those still clinging to the wreckage, now stripped of any comforting light. The ship, now just a black shape against the stars, was nothing more than a colossal silhouette, merging with the oppressive night.

Robert gasped at the sudden, complete loss of sight, and in that moment, his grip failed, his fingers numb with cold and shock. The watch, his only anchor to time and reality, slipped from his fingers. A sudden burst of desperate movement. His heart leapt into his throat, and he snatched at it midair, instinctively. Unable to see, he heard his watch bounce from the side of the lifeboat, a metallic tinkle, and the faint silver shimmer, a tiny, fleeting beacon in the starlight over the icy water. His hand grasped for the watch, plunging blindly, but it was too late.

The watch was in the water, slowed just slightly by the water's resistance. Robert grasped it, his fingers closing around the cold metal, and the cold shock felt like thousands of needles tearing his skin, a brief, horrifying taste of the ocean's vicious bite, a glimpse into the terror of the thousands who would succumb to it. His grip beginning to fail again, his fingers stiffening, he concentrated on bringing the watch back to the air, pulling it from the frigid depths. The freezing Atlantic reached his elbow. Robert barely got his watch back into the lifeboat before he dropped it again between his knees, unable to hold it properly.

Lowering his head and straining his ears, he could barely hear the faint ticking. Then, abruptly, the ticking stopped. It was only a short moment in time, but the Atlantic's grip was cruel. It stabbed through his arm like ice-tipped needles, slicing to the bone and radiating outwards. The pain traveled up the rest of his arm and gripped his shoulder like a vise, finally invading the top half of his back and chest, a searing agony.

Robert had experienced only a very brief sample of the agony that nearly 1,500 people would never escape. Hell was not a fiery torment; it was being trapped in liquid ice!

He found his watch with his dry hand, lifting it carefully. Too late. The water had seeped into the delicate mechanisms. The hands of the watch shuddered… twitched… then stilled. When he finally managed to see it with his dry hand, illuminated by the boat's lantern, the time read 2:15 a.m. A mere five minutes before *Titanic's* official end, the watch would never move forward again.

Robert clenched it tightly in his trembling palm, the cold metal digging into his skin, his chest heaving, his breath visible in the frigid air, each gasp a painful effort. Time hadn't just stopped. It had drowned. He hadn't lost the watch but time had, in a very real way, stopped for *Titanic*.

Robert got it back into his pocket and refused to reach for it again until they were rescued, as if acknowledging its final, grim pronouncement.

Then came the most horrifying sound of all, a sound that would haunt his nightmares for the rest of his life.

It was a very deep, gut-wrenching crack, followed by an earsplitting tearing of metal. *Titanic* actually broke apart; her very spine and ribs sounding like they were being crushed, pulverized in a catastrophic symphony of destruction! The sound resonated through the air, through the water, through the very hull of their lifeboat, and into Robert's bones.

His breath caught, a strangled sound in his throat. Even at this distance, he felt the immense force of it, a deep, powerful vibration in the air, rattling his joints. He wanted to throw up. He actually tried but couldn't.

A moment later, something erupted inside the ship. A quick, blinding flash of white, then another deafening crack. The sound alone felt powerful enough to split the entire sea in half, or to break the very firmament above.

It wasn't just heard, it was felt. A deep shudder through the water beneath the boat, a vibration in the oar handles. The sound carried an impossible weight, the voice of steel and rivets tearing apart.

Then, at last, silence. An absolute, profound silence that felt heavier, colder, than any sound.

Unable to hear his own breath, feeling as if his heart had stopped with his watch, Robert thought he'd gone deaf, his world plunged into a sensory void.

Then he saw it. The black shadow was falling! The stern, impossibly vertical, was slamming back into the water like an enormous skyscraper falling off its foundation, crashing down with a tremendous splash.

Robert flinched as a noticeable wave, dark and powerful, rushed outward, pushing their lifeboat further away from the sinking site as if to keep them safe, to spare them the final, gruesome sight. Those in the freezing water, those who had jumped earlier, screamed as the wave swallowed them whole, a fleeting, horrifying vision of desperate arms flailing before being engulfed.

Some resurfaced, coughing water, gasping for air. Others didn't. Many were crushed instantly by the bottom of the stern as it plunged, a gruesome, unimaginable end.

And then, inconceivably, defying all logic, the stern, having righted itself partially, began to rise again, its broken back now visible.

"No… NO!" The word escaped from Robert's throat before he could stop it, a raw, anguished cry of his own, a desperate plea for the suffering to end. In another lifeboat close by, illuminated dimly by a distant flare, he saw the outline of a bawling child standing up, impossibly small and vulnerable, arms outstretched toward the receding black mass, calling for someone, 'Mama!' perhaps, or 'Papa,' a word that pierced the night with all the aching innocence of a life not yet old enough to understand death. A sound that tore at his heart, a pure, innocent wail of inconsolable grief.

Reaching with both hands toward the dead *titan*, the child's desperate plea was a stark reminder of all that was lost, all that could not be saved, and the countless lives extinguished in the icy depths. Robert would have given anything he could to comfort that child, to offer a word of solace, or to hold them in his arms for as long as they needed. But he couldn't comfort anyone, not even himself, paralyzed as he was by the enormity of the suffering, the scale of the tragedy. All he could do was watch, helpless, adrift in a sea of despair.

Titanic, or what was left of her, was somehow balancing mostly upright for a terrifying moment, an enormous, slanted, black tower against the stars, impossibly poised on the brink. It was the last image many in the lifeboats would ever again see of the great ship. Looking at the small kerosene lamp on the aft mast, flickering valiantly, Robert could see the stern slowly turning, pivoting toward their direction, as if to give everyone a final, lingering look before giving in completely to the sea.

With a final rumble, the steel plating, nearly an inch thick, tore open like parchment as the giant slid beneath the waves. The mast light, the final fragment of *Titanic's* warmth, was now extinguished. The wails were all that remained.

Robert couldn't move. Couldn't get a full breath, his lungs constricted with horror. He nearly fell out of the boat in shock, leaning dangerously over the gunwale. He wasn't aware of it, but someone, a strong hand, had reached out to grab the back of his coat and pull him further inside, away from the edge, saving him from his own trance.

The cries sliced through the night like a knife, cutting open the very soul. Hundreds of voices calling out, begging, dying, their pleas held in the still air, echoing across the vast, empty sea.

His stomach cramped, twisting with nausea. His mind was now unable to continue processing anything that was happening, overwhelmed by the sheer, unbridled horror.

Someone in their boat, he wasn't sure, possibly an older woman, hopefully wrapped in a coat, covered her ears with trembling hands and sobbed uncontrollably, whispering, "Make it stop… please… dear God, make it stop…" Robert swallowed hard, his throat tight and raw. He tried to look away. He needed to escape the auditory torment. But he couldn't. The sounds were everywhere, inescapable, seeping into his very being.

Titanic, the real *Titan*, was gone. And yet that night was never so full of loss or of silence. *Futility foretold*… had actually happened! Only Robert had seen the warnings before it happened. But he said nothing, afraid he had gone mad again. But he was right after all. The stars above them, eternally silent to this day.

The pain-filled screams filling the night air were by far the worst sound Robert had ever heard in his life. Much worse than hearing the mighty *Titanic's* decks and hull shatter like glass during its final plunge to the bottom, worse than the tearing metal, worse than the falling funnel. He could still hear the distant, muffled implosion of the stern after it broke from the bow and descended beneath the lifeboats into the crushing pressure of the ocean's depths, two and a half miles below, a sound of compressed air violently expelled, of steel crumpling like tissue paper.

No onc at the time, not even the most brilliant minds, could have fathomed that it would be seventy-three years before anyone would find the wreck and see it with their own eyes, a long-broken monument to an age long since gone.

There was a single lantern in the lifeboat, providing a faint, flickering glow that barely cut through the oppressive darkness. Shivering violently in the bitter cold, his arm still aching from the frigid shock, Robert opened his satchel and pulled out his journal and pen, desperately trying to trap his thoughts on paper before they were swallowed by grief, by madness. The screams… the endless screams. He wrote, forcing his hand to move. Almost none of them were drowning. They were all freezing to death! The realization was a new, agonizing layer of horror.

'If knowledge is power, he scribbled, his hand trembling, *'then applied knowledge with proper wisdom is more powerful. But what of ignored knowledge? Of ignored warnings?'*

His arm brushed against the worn outline of *Futility* tucked beside the small book Leo had slipped into his satchel. Their trim sizes were identical. He looked out into the profound darkness, straining to hear over the wails, trying to distinguish individual voices from the chorus of agony. One of those screams… could it be Leo Zimmermann? His heart ached with a desperate, futile hope.

His hands trembled not from the cold, but from profound anguish, from the crushing weight of what he knew, what he had witnessed, and what he had failed to prevent. The tears on his face froze solid, icy tracks on his cheeks.

The voices were thinning now. One by one each faded into silence, the ocean reclaiming them, pulling them into its cold, indifferent embrace. The raw, desperate cries turned into whimpers, then gasps, then nothing. And then, finally, an unnatural, terrible silence descended over the vast expanse of water. And then someone in the lifeboat spoke up. Soft at first their voice was thin with emotion, then louder, gaining strength: "We have to go back. We have to."

A heated debate followed, voices rising and falling in the frigid air, arguments clashing. Some passengers argued frantically against it, their faces pale with terror, afraid of being swamped by desperate swimmers, their own raw fear overriding any sense of compassion. Self-preservation, stark and brutal, won out for many.

"We'll be overturned! We'll all die!" one woman shrieked. But others, including Robert, insisted. A deep conviction rose within Robert, silencing his own trembling fear. "Please, sir. If we don't try," Robert said through chattering teeth, his voice barely steady, his gaze fixed on the officer in charge, "then we are no better than the ones who built that ship without enough lifeboats." The words felt raw, undeniable, and like a moral challenge in the face of unimaginable horror.

The quartermaster, Robert would later learn his name was Walter Perkis, agreed. His face was grim. In the darkness, Robert and a few others volunteered to row, their hands numb but their resolve firm. The single lantern from their boat was passed carefully to Fifth Officer Lowe in Lifeboat Fourteen, who had tied up to them and was organizing a daring rescue attempt, a solitary beacon of humanity in the vast darkness. Lifeboats Four, Ten, Twelve, and Collapsible D were secured together, creating a makeshift raft, a small island of hope.

No one else dared attempt such a thing that night. Only Lowe, driven by a fierce sense of duty and compassion.

The transfer was perilous. People leaned from boat to boat in the icy blackness, stepping over the yawning abyss with only oars and gloved hands to steady them, the fear of falling into the freezing water palpable.

Robert carefully climbed into Lifeboat Fourteen with Perkis, his heart pounding not from fear for himself, but from the immense weight of what they were doing, the lives they might save, or the horrors they would soon witness. His arm still hurt, a dull, throbbing ache, from the shock of pulling his watch out of the freezing ocean, which was unusually calm for the North Atlantic.

And then they rowed. The oars dipped into the glassy water, pulling them back toward the site of the disaster. Officer Lowe called out to anyone who might hear his voice. "Is anyone alive out there? Can anyone hear me?" He called louder. Repeating the same questions.

Each creak of the oars was like a heartbeat, a slow, laborious rhythm in the silence. Robert scanned the water, eyes burning from the cold and the strain. Shapes emerged from the darkness. Mostly bodies. Unmoving. Floating grimly, their faces pale in the faint lantern light. Some were holding onto floating wreckage, their grip tenuous. One of them was still holding her dead baby.

They began grabbing the nearest bodies to check them. "These are dead, sir."

"Well make sure they are." Now, even Lowe couldn't hold back his tears. "We waited too long… blast it all," he said softly, as he looked out over the still waters with the floating bodies. He was on the verge of losing his composure. Then he shouted again, more from sadness.

"Is there anyone alive out there?! Can anyone hear me?!" But then, a sound. A weak cough, a faint cry, a desperate gasp.

"Over there! We passed one!" Robert spoke up, his voice hoarse, pointing with a trembling hand.

Lowe turned to look behind him as he lifted the lantern high, its beam cutting a path through the gloom. "Come about!" he shouted, his voice commanding, as the people prepared to backtrack, oars digging in.

Edging closer, they called to the young Chinese man who had barely managed to keep most of his body out of the freezing water by balancing on a couple of wooden deck chairs. He was soaked to the bone.

Officer Lowe called out to him, but the man responded in a language they didn't understand. A sudden rush of adrenaline flooded Robert with a burst of energy. "Officer, it will take at least two men to get him into the boat safely before he loses his balance," Robert said, speaking up.

"Yes, quite possibly. Here, get close to me sir and help me get him in before he's lost."

They pulled him from the sea, his body heavy. His hands were blue, his lips nearly frozen shut. A thin layer of ice had formed in his soaked hair. Robert noticed that a pair of lifebelts were secured to the other side of the two deck chairs, adding buoyancy. It was the only way the Chinese man was able to escape hypothermia.

Lowe laid the man down on one of the side benches in the boat and ordered Robert to get him dried as quickly as possible. When the blanket became too damp, Robert took off his coat to dry the rest of the man. The cold air hurt his joints. The man's skin felt like ice.

Another survivor, a young woman, was floating on some wreckage, barely conscious, her eyes unfocused. Somehow she had either swum over or stayed with a crewman on the same piece of wreckage. He was dead. She was blowing with all her remaining strength into his whistle. Robert helped pull her up, whispering reassurances to keep her awake, to keep her clinging to life, as he helped someone wrap her in a dry blanket.

Each person they brought into the boat was dried as quickly as possible.

A bit later, the lifeboat creaked as Robert leaned forward, reaching out across the icy black water with one of the lanterns in one hand and his other gripping the edge. Shadows danced across the waves, turning corpses into ghosts and silence into suspense.

"There!" someone cried from the bow. They thought

they saw someone moving. Robert set the lantern on the bench and leaned over the side, heart racing, hands burning from the cold as he grasped the lifebelt. With help from another man, they heaved the body over the edge. Water sloshed into the boat as the weight shifted.

The figure was young. Brown hair slicked against his forehead. His eyes were closed. His cap. *Leo's cap!?* It had floated just beside him in the water, snagged by the side of the lifeboat.

Robert's breath caught. The cap was identical. The face…

"Leo? LEO?!" he asked, trembling and crying.

But there was no answer. The man's lips were blue, and when Robert touched his face, the skin was ice. Dead for minutes. Maybe longer.

"It's not him," someone said, gently pulling the cap away and showing the name inside as part of maritime protocol before setting it aside.

Robert nodded, but not with certainty. The shadows of the night had a cruel way of blurring truth. They carefully returned the body to the water to keep enough room for others still alive.

For the rest of the night, he said nothing. Not about the man. Not about the cap. He just sat in silence, staring at the ice-glazed brim resting on the boat's floor, wondering if he'd just watched fate slip away from him for good. Only a handful could be saved. But it was something. Far better than none.

Eventually, the last of the cries ceased altogether. The sea was silent again.

Robert stared out at the stillness. The water was as smooth as glass, unnaturally calm, as though it also mourned the dead in reverent stillness, a mirror reflecting the uncounted souls beneath. He glanced at the lantern light reflecting in the ocean and realized they were now adrift in a floating cemetery! A cemetery without coffins or grave markers, only the endless depths below.

Robert didn't know what time it was. He didn't ask. He didn't want to know. Time, for him, had stopped with his watch.

He sat down carefully in the lifeboat, his entire body shaking uncontrollably. Both of his forearms were soaked to the skin, numb with cold, clinging to his satchel and the faint, flickering hope that somehow they had done the right thing, that their small act of courage had mattered.

He had hoped, desperately, that they would find Leo alive. But out of so many people, swallowed by the ocean in minutes? Robert began, at last, to accept the terrible, crushing truth: he had seen Leo for the last time. He tried to hold onto any possibility that his friend had made it into a lifeboat, clinging to it like a drowning man. But Robert knew he had escaped in one of the last boats to leave.

Out of fifteen hundred souls, they had saved but a few. A handful. But Leo was not among them. The cap still lay before Robert, an icy, tangible reminder of loss, and with it, one of the last fragile threads of hope began to unravel, dissolving into the cold, silent night.

On their way back to the others, they met up with Perkins and Lightoller in Lifeboats Twelve and Fourteen. They were informed that Collapsible B had overturned during the evacuation and there were people balancing on the upturned boat. Lowe turned to Robert and asked him if he was capable of making another rescue attempt for those on the overturned boat. Robert nodded insistently and quickly grabbed one of the oars. Everyone on the overturned boat was saved.

The ocean, once alive with screams, was now as silent

as the watch in Robert's pocket, its ticking drowned, like the voices that would never rise again.

He didn't sleep. None of them did, not truly. The sea remained impossibly still, the stars too bright, and the silence too complete. Robert sat hunched over, shivering and clutching his satchel like a child clings to the last remnant of a vanished home, his limbs stiff with cold and something deeper—the grief calcified into his bones.

The cap still lay before him, and he couldn't bring himself to move it. Time no longer mattered. The world before had ended, and the one ahead was unknown, if it even existed at all.

During the evacuation, Robert knew that distress calls had been sent out. Other ships had to have gotten the signals. He told himself that. He had to believe it.

Somewhere out there, the *Carpathia* was coming. But rescue would not mean deliverance. Survival was no triumph. It was a burden they all would carry ashore.

8

RESCUED!

Absolutely frozen. Time itself seemed to have stopped cold for everyone in the lifeboats, a dreadful pause after the chaos of the night. A faint glow on the horizon stirred whispers across the clustered boats, cutting through the chilling silence that had followed the *Titanic*'s disappearance.

At first, Robert thought it was a trick of the lantern or the eyes. Some cruel illusion conjured by sheer exhaustion and the crushing weight of grief. But the glow flickered and slowly intensified. A soft, golden blush against the inky, endless sea, rising imperceptibly above the waves like the answer to a prayer no one dared to speak aloud.

Sunrise? No. Better… much better. A ship! Then, a brilliant white rocket, like a rising star born of desperate hope, launched from the distant vessel and flashed above, bursting to cast a bright flash of light for a moment, revealing the faint outline of a small steamer.

"It's a rescue ship," someone murmured, the words barely audible, fragile.

Though profoundly relieved, no one in that lifeboat cheered. No one clapped. Just silence, save for the chilling sound of water slapping against the hull, and the occasional groan of frozen wood. Even hope, like their limbs, had gone numb in the long, horrifying night.

Some people in another lifeboat, further away, were indeed cheering, their voices thin across the water. Looking over to them, Robert saw makeshift torches being lit. Anything to signal their presence. One woman had her fancy, feathered hat aflame, standing on her seat, waving it in wide arches. A small, defiant beacon trying to signal the distant rescue ship, a desperate dance of light and shadow. A tiny amount of warmth returning in more ways than one.

Exhausted, every muscle aching, Robert lifted his head slowly, blinking against the sharp, cold breeze. The tiny orange lights of the approaching steamer, visible above its distant hull, looked like stars descending to touch the waters, a piece of heaven coming to retrieve them. He held his satchel close, the worn leather a familiar comfort against his trembling hands, his arms aching with the effort, and watched the tiny rescue ship carefully approach with every agonizing, drawn-out minute, its progress painfully slow. People in other lifeboats began waving the lanterns and setting some of their paper or cloth possessions on fire. Even their money.

By the time the *Carpathia* reached them, navigating cautiously through the still-unseen danger, the lifeboats had begun to drift apart slightly, pulled by subtle currents. Calls were exchanged across the water; voices cracked with fatigue, hoarse from shouting, and stiff from frostbite. A few rope ladders, thick and dark against the ship's hull, were lowered down each side of the steamer, swaying gently, and sailors reached out over the edge, their faces grim but welcoming, to help the first survivors aboard.

Ropes with lanterns attached were lowered from a few of the *Carpathia's* davits to secure the nearest lifeboats to the ship, guiding them into position. It was still pre-dawn dark, the approaching ship a shadowy behemoth. Robert reached to help secure the lifeboat, but his fingers wouldn't close. They were as stiff as iron from the cold, unresponsive, and refusing to obey. Once secured, the lifeboat was guided closer to the rope ladder, its rough fibers looking impossibly daunting. Robert hesitated, a wave of profound weariness washing over him.

The cold had made his limbs ache and throb, a deep, persistent pain that settled in his bones. He had never been so cold in his life. He moved carefully, slowly, passing the lantern, nearly out of fuel, back to the man who had rowed beside him, a silent exchange of thanks. Then, with a monumental effort, he tightened the strap of his satchel across his shoulder, its weight familiar.

He could feel the outline of the small, cloth-wrapped item that Leo had put into his satchel, and the hard cover of that small prophetic book pressed against the worn leather, a constant, physical reminder of the night's impossible prophecy. Robert made sure his journal was securely inside, nestled between them.

Crewmen were stationed at the large doors opened in the side of the ship, their forms silhouetted against the internal lights of the *Carpathia*. They called down to tell people to climb the ladders one at a time, their voices surprisingly calm.

On either side of him, Robert noticed the sick and injured being lifted in sling chairs. Small children were put in canvas bags and hauled up via ropes attached to the davits.

After the women and children had made it up, a slow, painstaking process of lifting and pulling, Robert gripped the ladder, his numb fingers barely closing around the rough rope, as he began the agonizing climb, each movement an act of will.

Step by step. Each rung was a small victory against the crushing exhaustion.

Every inch raised him further from the freezing nightmare they had survived and closer to a reality that he wasn't sure he was ready to face. A reality where the *Titanic* was gone, shattered, and submerged.

Where Leo would also likely be gone, swallowed by the indifferent sea. Where everything that had once seemed impossible, unthinkable, had now… happened, reshaping his world in an instant.

As he hauled himself aboard the *Carpathia's* deck, with the help of two crewmen grabbing him by the arms to help him the rest of the way, the warm air hit him like a physical wave. Not comforting just startling. His skin burned from the sudden shift in temperature, a painful prickling sensation, and for a moment, he felt dizzy, the world tilting precariously. Barely making it onto the deck, he stumbled forward a few steps and then fell, his energy utterly gone.

He couldn't move and simply lay there, shivering uncontrollably. Someone told him, gently but firmly, that he needed to make space for others attempting to board. Robert, barely conscious, lay down on his side and rolled himself out of the way, a small, pathetic bundle of cold exhaustion.

A man rushed up to check his vitals, his touch professional and swift. A ship's doctor? Or just someone with warm hands and a profound will to help? Robert nearly blacked out as someone covered him with a thick, warm blanket, its unexpected weight a sudden, overwhelming comfort.

Blankets. Coffee. Bread. Soup. All heated and steaming, brought to him by kind, anonymous hands. Questions were asked in hushed tones. Names were recorded, meticulously, on any scraps of paper people could find. Faces scanned with desperate hope. Cries of reunion with sharp, joyous bursts of sound that pierced the general quiet, and wrenching sobs of those realizing no one was left to meet them, their families gone forever. Robert heard it all, a muffled symphony of survival and loss.

He found a quiet place near the stern rail, away from the immediate chaos of boarding, and sank down onto the deck, eyes fixed on the darkness behind them, searching. Somewhere out there, below two and a half miles of crushing water, rested the remains of the largest ship in the world. The dream that couldn't sink was now a shattered reality. Far beyond recovery.

He opened his journal, his trembling hands struggling with the clasp, held it near one of the deck lights, paused, the blank page waiting, and then barely managed to write just one word, his pen scratching faintly: *'Rescued!'*

The *Carpathia's* deck bustled with movement around him, survivors being led away, and crewmen tending to the injured, but it all felt strangely distant to Robert, as if he were watching a play unfold from behind a thick pane of glass. He'd been given a blanket, a tin cup of something hot, and a place to sit, to exist. But he couldn't drink, the liquid feeling foreign on his tongue. He couldn't speak, his throat too tight, too raw. Only watch. He held the cup only to warm his hands.

Around him, others huddled close together. Some weeping openly, their faces buried in their hands, others silent, staring blankly ahead, their minds still trapped in the horror. One woman, her face streaked with tears, stared endlessly at an empty lifeboat still bobbing in the water off the port side, as though willing it to give up a missing face, a lost loved one.

Time passed. Robert didn't know how long, each moment stretching into an eternity. The stars above faded one by one, swallowed by the creeping, relentless light of dawn, bringing with it the harsh reality of the new day.

And then came the gasps. Another horrifying realization, dawning with the sun.

Someone near the railing pointed, a trembling finger extended into the emerging light. Others stood to look, their movements slow and hesitant. Robert rose slowly, gripping the cold metal rail for balance, his body stiff, and turned toward the horizon, dread coiling in his stomach.

Suddenly, everyone understood why and how the Atlantic was a perfectly flat calm, undisturbed by waves or swells. The very reason for the clear, cold night.

The ice. It was everywhere! A vast, silent graveyard that had waited in the dark.

Great slabs of it. Pale blue and jagged, luminous in the dawn, floated like silent sentinels around the *Carpathia*, grim reminders of the night's tragedy. Massive bergs, some taller than buildings, loomed in the distance, their peaks touched with the first fiery orange blush of sunrise, appearing almost ethereal, deceptively beautiful. Blocking the surrounding waves of the ocean outside the ice field.

Smaller chunks, like scattered teeth, bumped gently against the hull, a soft, sickening sound, like bones tapping on a coffin lid. Surrounding them also was an immense expanse of flat, unbroken sheet ice, stretching to the horizon.

Robert's breath caught, a cold knot in his chest. The sheer amount of ice surrounding them was staggering, incomprehensible. Some of it glistened beautifully in the morning sun. Shimmering with diamond-like facets. But there was nothing beautiful about what it had caused just beyond it, where the *Titanic* lay. Which one of these silent, colossal killers did the *Titanic* strike? Suddenly, a line from *Futility* flooded his mind, chilling him anew: '*... that in case of an end-on collision with an iceberg—the only thing afloat that she* *could not conquer…*' The words, once a literary curiosity, were now a terrifying prophecy.

He wasn't the only one thinking it. A man beside him muttered, his voice hoarse, "What would we have done if this ship hit one of those before reaching us?" The terrifying thought hung in the air, a silent question that permitted no answer.

The *Carpathia* navigated carefully, almost reverently, through the frozen danger, her twin propellers churning slowly, her crew posting extra lookouts along every deck, their faces strained. Survivors watched in silence, a collective understanding dawning. Some shivered, wrapping their blankets tighter. Some crossed themselves, murmuring prayers. A woman wrapped her head in a scarf and bowed low, placing her forehead onto the deck in silent, profound prayer, perhaps for the lost, perhaps for their miraculous survival.

A few began to cry again. Not from fear, but from the terrible, raw weight of daylight and what it now revealed: the precise, deadly landscape that had claimed their rescue ship. Here was the merciless gauntlet the *Titanic* had charged into at nearly full speed in the dark, confident in its own invincibility.

Robert pulled out his journal again, his fingers stiff, and turned to the page from earlier, still damp. Beneath the word *'Rescued!'* he added, his pen scratching furiously: '*We are alive. But that water is grave-cold. Hell is not some fiery torment; it's being trapped in a dark, freezing ocean.*' He felt the words deeply, viscerally.

He closed the journal gently and clutched it to his chest as the sun broke fully over the Atlantic, painting bright orange and red fire across the vast, shimmering sea of ice, a beautiful, cruel irony.

Later, once Robert had regained a fraction of his

strength, once the broth had somewhat thawed the chill from his bones, someone told him the chilling truth, the numbers that quantified the unimaginable loss. The number of those who had died the night before.

He literally dropped the journal from his hands, the leather-bound book thudding softly on the deck, the sound lost in the general murmur of the ship.

"Only 705 souls in the boats? Is that all!?" Robert couldn't believe it, his voice a choked whisper of disbelief. "There were accommodations for at least 1,200! More than 2,000 on board!" Less than a third of the people on the *Titanic* survived the night. Never before had so many people perished outside of wartime in a single, peaceful disaster.

Robert, his heart pounding with a desperate, futile hope, asked if a young man named Leo Zimmermann was on the survivors list. A crewman of the *Carpathia*, his face etched with sympathy, delivered the devastating news. "I am very sorry, sir. We have compiled a list of all those who were rescued, and that name does not appear on it."

Picking up his journal, Robert walked away without saying a word, the weight of the book heavy in his hand. Heavier still was the knowledge it contained. It was not a sadness he felt. But a blinding rage, cold and consuming, festering in his gut. For all the shipbuilders' pride, for all the passengers' dreams or all the grand proclamations of unsinkability, this was the true, horrific cost: over a thousand voices silenced, a floating palace turned into a vast, watery tomb.

And he was still here. Still holding the book that saw it coming, the book that warned, ignored, now a testament to a monstrous oversight. The idea that a young man who worked his entire life, saving every last coin to buy a boarding pass on a ship to a better life, who prayed every day, thanking God for what little scraps he had, asking for a safe journey, not only for himself but for everyone. That such a person could be extinguished so cruelly, so senselessly, was an unbearable affront.

Robert stood near the stern rail, looking out at the glittering, deceptive calm of the ocean, knowing that a man as good, honest, and kind as Leo had suffered a horrible death, swallowed by the cold along with countless others. The injustice of it all festered inside him, a burning coal. Why him? Why had he, who had questioned God and who had doubted, survived when countless believers, humble souls like Leo, had perished in such unspeakable agony?

He pulled out the small item Leo had dropped into his satchel. The prayer book! Its delicate, almost fragile, leather binding felt impossibly light in his hands. Why would Leo give him that?

He opened it, finding a petition before starting out on a journey, the words seeming to mock him in their earnest hope: '*O God, our Creator and Sustainer, unto Thee my thoughts turn in this hour of parting. Thou directest all my ways, and Thy providence watches over me on both land and sea. May it be Thy will that, going in peace, I may reach my goal in peace. O gracious Father, consider the eager yearnings of my soul. May no ill befall me, so that the sadness of my parting from my dear ones may not be changed for them to grief. Strengthen my soul that I may feel that Thou art keeping them under the shadow of Thy wings. Blessed art Thou, O God, who dost guide my going out and coming in for evermore. Amen.*'

The prayer book's fragile pages fluttered in the cold breeze, a gentle sigh, as Robert reread the words Leo had likely prayed the night before the voyage, perhaps even on the deck of the very ship that killed him: '*May no ill befall me, so that the sadness of my parting from my dear ones may not be changed for them to grief.*' That same breeze now threatened to carry those very words to oblivion, just as it had carried so many lives, so many hopes, into the abyss.

Robert found a small, folded slip of paper tucked into the book, his fingers fumbling with it. Below the company's insignia with the name *S.S. Titanic*, at the top it said, *'Morning of April 14*[th]*, 1912.'* Underneath it, a simple, profound statement: *'Another lovely schmooze with Robert Morganson. Praised are you, Eternal One, Ruler of the Universe, who gives us good friends in love.'* It was Leo's handwriting, his final, unexpected gift. His initials, *'L.Z.,'* were written at the bottom right corner.

As Robert's grip tightened on the small piece of paper, Leo's voice echoed in his mind, clear as if he were standing beside him. He remembered their first conversation with the railing between them, a world ago, when Robert had questioned the very need for prayers on a ship as magnificent as the *Titanic*.

"Well, they certainly couldn't hurt," Leo had said with a warm, gentle smile, his eyes twinkling. "There's a Yiddish proverb that says, 'Man plans, and God laughs!'"

Robert could still see the hope in Leo's eyes, the quiet determination of a young man who had worked tirelessly to save enough for a ticket to America. Not for wealth or fame, but for freedom. For a future where he could observe his faith openly without fear. Where he could one day send help for others and bring them out of the poverty and persecution they faced in Europe to a land of opportunity.

As he turned the pages of the *Union Prayer Book*, Robert's eyes fell on a passage Leo must have cherished, one that seemed to mock the current reality: *'Into Thy hand I commit my spirit; Thou hast redeemed me, O Lord God of truth.'*

Redeemed? He scoffed, a bitter, hollow sound. What truth was there in this? What mercy was there in allowing so many good people, so many faithful souls, to die in freezing darkness while rich cowards like Ismay found their way into lifeboats and preserved their lives? The cries of the dying still echoed in Robert's ears, fading into the endless black waves, an unceasing torment. How could a just God allow such suffering, especially for people like Leo and all the others who prayed with such unwavering faith?

Robert's grip tightened on the satchel, the books within pressing against his side. He could still hear the cries of those left behind in the water, fading into the darkness, forever trapped in his memory. He could still see the faces of all those people just like Leo, hopeful, humble souls who had trusted in God and were swallowed by the sea. Denied not only life but even a simple grave. If God had truly heard those prayers… why had so many perished? Why had Robert, who did not care to believe in God, and who doubted and questioned, survived when better, more devout people had been lost?

Looking a couple of pages later, his eyes landed on a text called *'A Prayer in Time of Trouble.'* It did not give him peace. Seeing those words, hollow and meaningless in the face of such devastation, did the complete opposite. Robert clutched at the pages and nearly tore them out, his knuckles white. "Man plans… And you laugh? You really think this is funny?!" Robert growled, his voice raw with fury, a guttural sound torn from his soul. He looked in his satchel to see his journal and the novel, the twin witnesses to his despair.

Then he got an idea, a terrible, desperate impulse. "Why don't you laugh at this then?" He shoved the *Union Prayer Book* back in with the others, bundling them together in the satchel, and walked purposefully over to the railing, his breath coming in ragged gasps. "Perhaps the sea should claim these relics. My journal that recorded the truth. This novel that warned about the future. And the prayers you ignored!"

Robert gripped the railing of the *Carpathia*, the cold metal pressing into his palms, the ship sitting in the very same waters where the *Titanic* had slipped away, where so many had vanished, where all hope had died. He let out a slow, shuddering breath and tilted his head forward, eyes burning, refusing to blink, refusing to release the pain. But when he finally did blink, his tears fell freely, unchecked.

One by one, they slipped from his lashes, catching the dim morning light before disappearing into the dark swells below. Gone, as quickly as the hands he had reached for in the lifeboat. As quickly as the voices that had called out in the night, only to fade into silence.

His own tears now joined the countless others from the night before, a solitary contribution to the vast ocean, lost to the same waves that had swallowed their cries, their final breaths. His tears became part of the Atlantic, lost among the waves. Just like them. Robert stepped up onto the lowest part of the railing; his decision was made.

Esther Hart and Lawrence Beesley, who had been discreetly watching Robert from a distance, saw the profound agony in his face as he walked over to the rail, the way his body was shaking. Neither of them could hear every word he had said, but his posture and his furious gestures were unmistakable. So, as they saw Robert climb onto the railing, their fear was immediate and sickening that he was about to jump.

"Oh God, please no… Robert, stop!" Esther called to him, her voice shrill with sudden terror, but he didn't acknowledge her plea, lost in his private torment. She and Lawrence rushed to him as fast as they could run across the deck. Robert stood precariously on the lowest rung of the rail, the salt air stinging his face as if the ocean itself were mocking him, joining in the cosmic laughter.

Blinded by rage and grief, he held the satchel over the rail, its weight a physical manifestation of his despair. He was so angry, so consumed, he couldn't hear the pounding footsteps running toward him or the desperate cries of his friends. He held his satchel with the books over the edge, poised… to drop them. Until a firm hand, strong and unyielding, seized his arm. "Please stop! What are you doing, Robert?!"

Robert turned to see Lawrence Beesley, his face pale and drawn but steady, his grip surprisingly firm. Behind him stood Esther Hart, clutching little Eva in her arms, her own eyes wide with fear and concern.

Robert's voice shook, raw with emotion. "This should not have happened! This… this prayer book, these words, meant the world to him, but they are meaningless to the sea, and they are meaningless to me now as well! I don't believe a single word of them!"

It became clear. Robert hadn't been climbing to jump. Only to throw something over. A wave of relief washed over Esther, quickly replaced by a profound sadness for his pain. She stepped closer, her eyes full of quiet strength. A gentle but firm resolve.

"No, Robert. Those words meant everything to him. I know you're not Jewish; neither am I, but my husband, Benjamin, was. However, they can still mean something to all of us… and to everyone else who needs to know what really happened. They are not meaningless."

Robert's hand trembled, still holding the satchel suspended over the water. Beesley spoke softly, urgently. "Robert, please listen to me. If you cast those books into the sea, you will destroy all that evidence. The truth of everyone who perished that night, of the warnings given and ignored. It will be lost forever."

Esther stepped closer, reaching a hand out to touch his arm. "I know this pain feels unbearable. But what you carry, Robert, is irreplaceable. That novel… your written words… they need to be preserved. What if you later choose to tell someone what happened, and no one believes you because you dropped them into the ocean? Because you destroyed the proof?"

Robert only had one question for Lawrence, a desperate plea for understanding: "But if the Almighty really heard Leo's prayers, why did he not answer them!?" But it was Esther who helped him understand, her voice gentle but unwavering. "God did answer Leo's prayers, Robert. Just as he heard my prayers asking that my husband live. But God doesn't always say yes. Sometimes the answer is no."

Robert's breath caught, a sudden, sharp intake. For the first time, a different perspective opened in his mind. He realized if he let go, if he cast these precious, painful artifacts into the waves, the memories of those who had prayed and perished, of the injustice and the truth, would be lost, too. If he cast these books into the depths, would he forever silence the memories of those who perished? Or would he be surrendering to the very "*Futility*" he so desperately fought to escape? He had to fight for the truth, for memory, for them.

Slowly, his arm relaxed, but not enough to drop the satchel. Instead, he placed the strap securely over his shoulder, as if holding the very souls of the dead within. And as he pulled it back over the railing to safety, he stepped back onto the deck. Still holding the cold rail, Robert sank to his knees, his body trembling, his sobs wracking the early morning silence, each one a deep, guttural sound torn from his chest, heaving with the force of his grief, a release long overdue.

Lawrence, Esther, and her daughter Eva joined him, a silent huddle of survivors amidst the vast, indifferent sea, sharing the weight of their collective sorrow. And still, the sea burned with morning light… as if daring them to believe that any of it had truly happened, that such beauty could exist alongside such horror.

The tiny Cunarder, being 558 feet long, was a much smaller passenger and cargo ship than the *Titanic* had been, a stark comparison. While the *Titanic* had two main masts and four enormous funnels, symbols of its overwhelming power, in contrast, the *Carpathia* had four modest masts still capable of being rigged with thick canvas sails, very much like an argosy. The ship had a single smoke funnel, painted red with thin black lines signaling its ownership by the Cunard company, rising modestly in the middle of the masts.

It was such a stark contrast, as if this lone funnel was a solitary witness to the greatest maritime tragedy during peacetime that would be retold by countless people for many generations, an event that was now indelibly changing world history, writing itself into the annals of time.

Exhausted from the long, freezing hours in the lifeboat, but with a new, fragile sense of resolve, Robert sought a quiet place outside, where the early morning sun, climbing higher, provided some warmth and solitude, a small corner of peace.

With little strength left, he sank onto the deck like a child, leaning against a bulkhead, and pulled all three books from his satchel, their familiar weight a comfort. Looking over them, his journal demanded attention first. The words flowing as smoothly as his pen on the paper, a conduit for his thoughts: *'Courage, virtue, struggling to do what is right. People want to believe that we're always in control. That we can aid loved ones in any crisis. Yet there are times, like this, when life mocks our hubris. That's when we learn true humility, and that the greatest of our strengths is this simple insistence to survive. Self-knowledge is a rare and sustaining prize, hard-won and elusive. The strongest people are those who know not only when to ask for help but also when to accept help when offered by those who care. Arrogance and hubris (Greek:* ὕβρις*) can blind a person, denying them the power of living fully and truthfully.'*

Nearby, Esther and Lawrence were speaking with Captain Rostron and one of his officers on duty, their voices hushed.

"Has he ever behaved like this before? Is he traveling alone?" Esther explained that Robert was a very reserved person, that he often read books, and that he wrote more often than he conversed with people.

"Indeed, he clearly requires close observation. We could place him in the ship's brig if necessary. He appears distraught. If he becomes a danger to himself or others, we may need to confine him for everyone's safety," the crewman explained, his gaze lingering on Robert.

Lawrence disagreed immediately, stepping forward. "No, sir. We misunderstood his intentions. He's not a suicide risk. He was overcome, sir. Grief and shock, nothing more."

Esther added her observation, her voice firm. "He had a dear friend traveling in third class. The poor young man did not survive. He feels this loss deeply."

Captain Rostron expressed his sympathies, his face softening slightly, and asked his crewman to be sure someone was watching Robert closely, and that if there was any other rash behavior, they would put him in the brig for his own well-being. He was to be watched until they docked in New York.

Around them, survivors huddled in borrowed blankets, their faces pale and gaunt, etched with the trauma of the night. Few were accepting the hot soups and tea or fresh bread, their appetites gone. Robert caught snippets of their conversations, fragments of loss and disbelief that drifted on the salt air, each one a shard of the shared nightmare.

"My husband, he put me in the lifeboat and stepped back," a woman wept softly, her words choked with tears. "He told me he'd meet me in New York."

"The ship did not merely sink," another voice insisted, a man with haunted eyes. "She broke asunder. I saw it myself. But I fear they will never believe us. They'll say it was impossible."

Robert hesitated. He'd heard it, too. Felt the deep, sickening shudder as the *Titanic's* spine snapped like a tree branch and her stern rose skyward. But the experts, those who had designed her, those who built her, those who had proclaimed her unsinkable would never admit such a thing could happen. It would shatter their carefully constructed world.

Looking out at the ocean, knowing *Titanic* lay over two miles beneath them, broken into pieces, far beyond human reach, Robert wondered if anything recognizable would last long at those crushing depths, in that perpetual darkness.

In *Futility*, the *Titan* had also broken apart. He imagined both ships, so alike in their hubris, their names nearly twins, lying together in the freezing black silence of the deep. Perhaps side by side, their sterns pointing to the surface like twin tombstones. Perhaps staring across the darkness at one another, their wreckage entwined in some grim, eternal union. Neither would ever see daylight again.

Both had been *titans*, in name and in outcome.

How, in all the world, had Morgan Robertson gotten the name so right? How had he foreseen this? Robert stared at the horizon, the question gnawing at him, a restless, urgent need for answers. He had to know. Somehow, he would find Morgan and ask him himself.

'Truth can drown as easily as people in dark waters.' He scribbled the thought quickly, urgently, in a separate line of his journal, a new conviction solidifying within him.

Lawrence Beesley, who had carefully watched Robert from a short distance, ever the attentive schoolmaster, moved closer and read over his shoulder, his eyes scanning the words. "Do you truly believe they will attempt to conceal this? The breaking apart of the ship?"

Robert glanced at him, his gaze hardened. "I know they will. The world wants heroes, villains, and tragedy. Not our inconvenient truths. Not proof of their own fallibility."

Beesley nodded solemnly, his expression grave. "Then it is our duty to speak. To remember. To bear witness. The time will come when all of us who have survived this ordeal will have passed on. The truth must be recounted, Robert. For those who were lost and for those of us who remain. Otherwise, history itself will sink with the *Titanic*, buried beneath layers of convenience and denial."

Robert began to cry again, silent tears now, but just as profound. "Lawrence, I can't… I just can't do this. It's far too much. The weight of it… it's unbearable."

Lawrence sat down on the deck next to Robert, a comforting presence. "You can, and you must. For anyone who will listen. Keep writing, my friend. Until that journal of yours can't hold even one more drop of ink. After that, start another one. Write. For the rest of your life."

Robert flipped to a fresh page, taking a deep,

shuddering breath, and continued writing, his pen moving with renewed purpose. He began listing fragments of memory, desperate to capture them before they faded. Not just the famous or the powerful, but the forgotten voices of second-class passengers, like himself, and the countless souls from Steerage: *'The Irishman prayed aloud as the sea rose around him, his voice strong and clear until the last. The young steward who removed his own life jacket to put it on a shivering child, knowing what his fate would be. The firemen who stayed below, keeping the lights burning until the very end, a final act of defiant duty. The quiet mothers who hummed lullabies to their infants in the lifeboats, even as their hearts broke for those left behind. The countless, anonymous faces in the third-class corridors, bewildered and afraid, trapped behind locked gates.'*

After all the survivors had been picked up and some of the lifeboats retrieved that the *Carpathia* could carry, secured to her rigging, the ship began preparations to leave the scene. However, one of the boats never made it to them. Collapsible A was never found. It had been one of the last boats to escape the sinking ship, reportedly swamped with people. There had been people in it, clinging desperately.

There was no sign of it anywhere, lost in the vast, indifferent sea. So, with over 700 people needing more medical attention than what was available, the difficult decision was made to return to New York and call off the search for Collapsible A and any other possible survivors.

Robert couldn't help but wonder: what if Leo had made it out in time, only to be lost adrift in that collapsible raft? What was the point of continued agony, of seeing daylight one last time, only to perish unseen? People noticed that they had to abandon numerous lifeboats from the *Titanic*, cutting them loose.

Now, floating empty in the Atlantic, their purpose

accomplished, their human cargo safely transferred, they were mere flotsam. There wasn't nearly enough room on the small vessel to salvage them all. Attempting to tow them would not only slow the *Carpathia* and delay urgent medical care, but also likely destroy the boats along the way.

Captain Rostron, a man now burdened by the weight of so many lives, understood that he needed to get the survivors to New York as quickly and as safely as possible. Once they were certain all the survivors had been brought on board, the ship's twin propellers began turning with a steady hum for the urgent return to New York.

As the *Carpathia* began vibrating slightly before pressing forward through the waves, a gentle but insistent movement, Robert felt the burden of those stories settle heavily on his shoulders, a weight he now willingly accepted.

Morgan's *Futility* had been a warning. One the world had ignored, to its peril. But this was no fiction. This was brutally, unequivocally real.

Robert turned to Lawrence, his voice stronger now, less despairing. "Do you suppose, if enough of us speak plainly, the world might listen? Truly listen this time?"

His friend's eyes were distant, haunted by the night's images, but he held Robert's gaze. Ever the schoolmaster, ever the truth-seeker, he said quietly, "The world has a tendency to forget, Robert. We allowed ourselves to believe these vessels were unsinkable, that we had conquered the sea, and that progress was beyond reproach. Clearly, we were mistaken. But the written word endures. Those who seek the truth will find it. But only if we preserve it for them. Only if we speak."

Robert gripped his pen and pressed on, the rhythm of

his writing a new pulse in his veins. Lawrence silently read the words as Robert wrote them; a shared commitment.

'The written word is all that stands between memory and oblivion. Without books as our anchors, we're cast adrift, neither teaching nor learning. They're windows on the past, mirrors on the present, and prisms reflecting all potential futures. Books are our lighthouses, erected in the Dark Sea of Time.'

Breathing a sigh of relief, a fragile sense of peace settling over him, Lawrence discreetly signaled to a nearby crewman, then made a gesture toward Robert. A subtle nod, signaling that he was calm and rational now, no longer a potential danger to himself.

Feeling better rested, thinking he was being left alone and not realizing he was being watched, Robert stood up for a moment and noticed a particular iceberg nearby, still about 100 feet high above the waterline. But not quite as dark, no longer as menacing, as it had been the night before.

He couldn't help but focus on a distinct smudge of red and black paint at its base directly above the waterline. A deep, dark scar. Once again, with a sickening jolt of recognition, Robert had seen the very iceberg once again that mortally wounded the great ship.

Surprisingly, the thought in his mind was not of revenge, but of balance: apparently the *Titanic* had also badly damaged the iceberg. Other than the survivors and the empty lifeboats, this was all that remained of the once mighty ship above the water. That also would soon disappear as the iceberg continued to melt away, taking the faint evidence with it, erasing its mark from the world.

He had barely begun his monumental task, and already, the weight of remembrance felt impossible to bear, an endless ocean of stories. Still, the *Carpathia* hurried forward. Carrying them toward the world that was just learning about the *Titanic* sinking but had not yet heard their stories, the raw, unfiltered truth. Robert decided, with a quiet, burning resolve, to tell anyone who would listen.

Robert took out Leo's *Union Prayer Book*, its leather cover softened by the sea, pressing it atop his written record. Standing well away from the railing this time, no longer battling despair, he gazed toward the vast ice field that now marked the final resting place of so many, a beautiful, deadly memorial. "Leo… I'm sorry… I'm so sorry. I really miss you, my friend," he whispered, the words carried on the wind, a private lament.

Lawrence Beesley noticed Robert nearby and approached him to offer comfort or to simply be available. Hearing Robert's apology to Leo had deeply moved him. He stood beside Robert to place his hand on a shoulder.

"A man's faith is often tested in the darkest waters. Don't let this be lost."

Robert nodded in agreement as he pressed the small book tight, as though it might warm his frozen soul, a possibly futile but necessary gesture. He was beyond crying now. Drained of tears and everything else but a profound, aching silence.

Later, the engine's hum was steady, a soft, reassuring rhythm beneath Robert's feet. It was so different from the trembling thunder he remembered from *Titanic's* boilers, a sound that now conjured only images of horror.

Up on deck, bundled in an overcoat someone had handed him, its wool rough but warm, Robert stood by the rail, watching crewmen adjust spars and lines. Remnants from earlier voyages, much older ways of seafaring.

One of the sailors, a grizzled man with kind eyes, noticed his interest. "She was built for steam," the man said, motioning toward the lone funnel, its red and black gleaming in the growing light, "but she still wears her rigging like an old sea dog clinging to his whiskers. We rarely use it now, but it still works if need be should we lose steam and power. A nod to the past."

Robert nodded, eyes tracing the ropes up into the vast, gray sky, contemplating the blend of old and new.

"What would you call a ship like that?" he asked, a thought stirring in his mind.

"Well, this here is still a steamer, so probably an argosy, if you're feeling poetic," the sailor replied, a faint smile touching his lips. "A merchant vessel, usually with sails. Carrying mostly cargo." The sailor paused, looking out at the glittering sea. "Romantic word. Brings to mind treasure fleets and long-forgotten ports, adventures across the globe."

Robert repeated the word quietly, letting it settle on his tongue. "Argosy. The *Titanic* didn't have any sails," he added softly, stating the obvious, yet sensing a deeper meaning.

"No," the sailor said, his voice tinged with a quiet knowing. "She didn't need them. Like so many others out there today, people thought she was too grand for the old ways. Too modern, too fast." He shrugged, a gesture of resignation. "But the sea doesn't care how modern you are. It doesn't care about grandness. It just is."

"No, sir. It sure doesn't. Thank you for teaching me," Robert said, a new layer of understanding settling within him.

Robert introduced himself, then gave the man a grateful handshake before stepping away.

Drawn toward the quiet belowdecks, he found the reading room while seeking a place for contemplation. Recalling a line from the second chapter in Robertson's novel, he pulled it out and found it: *'On deck, sailors set the triangular sails on the two masts to add their propulsion to the momentum…'*

Returning the novel to its pocket with the other books, he clutched them, their presence a tangible reminder of his new burden. He rested his back against the wall in a corner near a staircase leading below deck, a quieter, more sheltered space. The satchel was strapped to his side like a life preserver for his very soul.

While still leaning his back against one wall, he used the other wall joined at the corner to brace his side, finding a measure of physical and emotional stability. "So, the mighty *Titan* was more like an argosy then," Robert whispered to himself, the irony not lost on him. He closed his eyes. Not to sleep, but to steady the tremble in his breath, to center himself against the emotional aftershocks. The gentle, almost imperceptible pitching of the *Carpathia* was nothing like the *Titanic's* proud, steady glide; it moved with a creak and groan, a tired vessel carrying the enormous weight of a night terror no one had yet fully awakened from. Truth be told, most never would.

From where he sat, Robert could hear the muffled sobs of other survivors. Some muffled in sleeves, a desperate attempt at privacy, others echoing openly across the decks, raw with pain. He heard someone softly call a name that would never answer, a plaintive, mournful sound. He heard a woman humming a lullaby to her child, a low, steady melody, perhaps to quiet her child, or perhaps, also, to calm herself.

Suddenly, he heard the soft cries of a child lying bundled in a blanket on one of the larger chairs near the hallway. Robert got up to get a closer look. It was the child he saw from the lifeboat! He heard the child clearly now. "Mamaí, Daidí!" Suddenly Robert understood. Although he didn't understand *Gaelic*, he realized that this little boy had lost both of his parents. He was calling out for both of them in the lifeboat the night before as the *Titanic* broke apart.

Upon learning that the child spoke some English but not much, Robert attempted to communicate with him. Seeing the child was holding a photo, Robert pointed to the two people in the photo with him. He pointed to the woman in the photo. "Mamaí?" The boy nodded, eyes welling. When Robert pointed to the man in the photo, the little boy whispered, "Daidi," pointing out toward the ocean.

Robert gestured to himself and said his first name twice. Slowly, the boy caught on. He whispered his own name. Robert repeated the boy's name to be sure. The child nodded. Then Robert pulled out the stationery he got while on the *Titanic* to write his name and the child's name.

Robert wrote a number next to his name: 27. His age. Writing a question mark next to the boy's name, he handed the pen to the child and tapped on the question mark. Putting the pen down, the boy held up four fingers in one hand and two fingers on the other.

Robert touched the tip of each finger held up and counted from one to six, then he stopped and held up the same number. The little boy nodded again, and Robert wrote the number 6 next to the child's name. A name and an age. That was enough for now. A bridge had been built.

Robert began to show his own tears while the boy wiped his face again. He made motions with his hands for the little boy to climb into his lap, and he held the child. Finally able to attempt to comfort him.

In that moment Robert thought about the first time he heard Leo sing a melody. He still didn't understand what the words meant in English, nor could he recall each of the foreign words, but he began softly singing what he remembered, using one of his hands to rhythmically pat the little boy on his back to the rhythm. Robert cried with the child to show that he also lost someone he cared about. The boy fell asleep in his arms. Suddenly, Robert decided to find out what those comforting words meant.

Nearby, two members of the ship's crew were deeply moved by the interaction. "That there is a very good man," one of them said as the other nodded.

Walking around some of the hallways while carrying the little boy, Robert came across a room with the children survivors. Boys and girls ranging from under a year old to the age of 14.

Considering leaving the little boy with the rest, Robert thought better. The little one had already lost his parents and didn't understand much English. So Robert would watch over this child until they reached land. He had hoped that there would be immediate family at the pier who could legally claim the boy and raise him.

"God, if you can hear this prayer, please, let there be some form of family waiting at the docks in New York who can take this little one into their home and raise him. Brothers, sisters, cousins, an aunt and uncle, just anyone who can bring him to their home so he won't be in an orphanage. Don't do this for me, but for this little one. Please."

It was the first prayer that Robert could recall not saying for himself. Not demanding or even wanting anything for himself, but a humble request for another person so that their suffering could be lessened if possible.

Robert pulled the small prayer book from his satchel again, this time not to condemn it, not to question its validity, but to understand it, to seek solace within its pages. The leather binding still smelled faintly of seawater and old ink, a poignant mix of the tragedy and

Leo's enduring spirit. He traced his finger along the words Leo had written on the folded piece of paper he had tucked into the book, a message almost sent from beyond the grave. *'Praised are you, God, who gives us good friends in love.'*

He hadn't realized until now how much Leo had seen in him. Much more than Robert ever saw in himself. Not just as he was, an anxious, solitary man, but the man he could become: a keeper of stories, a voice for the lost. But, in order to accomplish that, Robert would have to heal from his new trauma, a long, arduous journey that had just begun.

The warmth of the rising sun touched his skin, golden and silent, a promise of a new day. It brought no immediate answers, no sudden revelation from the Divine, but it brought light.

He opened his notes and turned to a blank page, the crisp paper awaiting his words. His hand ached, but he wrote anyway, pushing through the physical discomfort, compelled by an inner force.

'April 17th. I'm now on board the Carpathia. *How or why, I do not yet know. Maybe I never will. Perhaps to remember. Perhaps to write. Perhaps because someone must speak the names of the dead and ensure the living never forget. Leo Zimmermann. He prayed. He hoped. He believed. He patiently taught me. I did not do any of those for him. He listened when I did not. He was my friend.*

He stopped for a moment and let the ink dry, staring at the fresh words, a silent testament. Then, without looking up, he wrote a single final line, a solemn vow: *I must carry this forward. Not just for him, but for all of them. This must not be their true ending.*

Robert closed the book and placed it gently back in his satchel alongside the *Union Prayer Book* and *Futility*. These were not relics to be cast into the deep. They were, in that moment, the only true memorials to those who had no grave but the sea, their only voice.

From somewhere behind him, a steward's voice, clear and strong, called out, "Landfall by tomorrow, everyone. We'll see New York soon."

Even once he got to New York, Robert would still be very far from home. But at least he would be on solid earth again.

The small ship gave a noticeable shudder and a tremble. In a panic, Robert looked around for a life jacket. The crewman explained that the *Carpathia* had pushed her equipment far beyond what she was designed for in order to reach the *Titanic* as soon as possible. The small twin engines and other equipment would need a detailed examination before taking another voyage.

Standing up for a moment, his legs still a little unsteady, Robert looked out the nearest window and across the endless water. First, he looked behind the ship to the final resting place of the *Titanic*, a vast, empty expanse that contained unspeakable horrors, then toward the distant horizon that would one day bring him to land. Dry land.

But before that, he would make a solemn promise. He whispered it softly, almost afraid to say it aloud, as if the very air might reject such a monumental task, a lifelong burden: "Everyone, I will tell your story. I promise. I will carry your stories forward for all of you. You will not be forgotten. Your lives, your hopes, your struggles, and your ends. I swear to you that they will not be forgotten beneath the waves."

He remembered his friend's voice very gentle and assured saying, "*The truly rich are those who enjoy all they already have.*" Robert wasn't there yet, not fully, not spiritually. But maybe he could be someday. He would try. Financially, he was very wealthy compared to many others. But not in the way that mattered most, not in the richness of spirit and connection that Leo had once possessed.

Thinking of a mantra, a guiding principle, Robert pulled out his now leather-bound written testament and wrote it, the words a beacon in the darkness: *'Gratitude is the best medication for your attitude.'*

And for the first time since the *Titanic* slipped beneath the waves, he felt the faintest ember of purpose flicker in his chest. Fragile, yes, but undeniably alive, a pilot light in the vast darkness that had threatened to consume him.

CARPATHIA CARRIED them toward the shore.

And now, he carried something, too.

The truth, memories, and need to speak for those lost.

The *Carpathia* pressed on.

And now, so would he.

The *Carpathia* kept its course.

Robert, at long last, had found his!

9

A NIGHT TO ALWAYS REMEMBER

Thursday, April 18th
Hudson River—New York City

Not even the drizzle could mask the heaviness of sorrows in the air. Almost no one spoke as the ship approached the harbor. Gentle rain fell steadily along the eastern seaboard. Manhattan was soaked, as if the sky itself wept in mourning. By now, the world had begun to grasp the true scale of the tragedy, and a hushed reverence seemed to hang over the entire harbor.

Robert stood motionless on the deck, allowing the cold rain to soak through his clothes and his skin, as if the falling water could somehow cleanse the grief that clung to him. The chill in the air was sharp but oddly comforting and numbing, in the way that grief sometimes is. He kept a close watch on the small child, who was also out in the rain looking east toward the vast ocean. Speaking the Irish language, Robert understood the child was praying, so he gave the little boy some privacy to do so.

Finally, the rain let up and gently faded. When the child became quiet, Robert walked up and crouched down next to him. The little boy asked to be picked up again. Robert pulled out a small blanket from under his coat to dry the child before wrapping him in it and then picking him back up. The boy was heavy, but Robert never complained.

His satchel was tucked under his coat, preserving the precious books from the downpour. His tears had dissolved into the rain, indistinguishable from the grief falling from the sky. Even he wasn't sure which drops of water were the tears or rain.

When he looked up, she was already waiting there to welcome him. Standing directly ahead of him in the distance, slowly revealing her frame, her right arm stretched over her head, rising from the harbor mist like a silent, solemn sentinel, stood Lady Liberty. She was enduring, and a beacon of promise now shadowed by tragedy. Seeing actual land once again, even a small island of it, provided a sense of relief.

Less than ten years prior, a bronze plaque was set up inside the pedestal. Robert had memorized the words of Emma Lazarus' poem, "New Colossus" almost perfectly:

'Not like the brazen giant of Greek fame,
With conquering limbs astride from land to land;
Here at our sea-washed, sunset gates shall stand
A mighty woman with a torch, whose flame
Is the imprisoned lightning, and her name
Mother of Exiles. From her beacon-hand
Glows world-wide welcome; her mild eyes command
The air-bridged harbor that twin cities frame.
"Keep, ancient lands, your storied pomp!" cries she
With silent lips. "Give me your tired, your poor,
Your huddled masses yearning to breathe free,
The wretched refuse of your teeming shore.
Send these, the homeless, tempest-tost to me,
I lift my lamp beside the golden door!"'

As the rescue ship made her careful, deliberate way up the Hudson, a profound silence fell. Numerous passenger liners and other vessels, their own lights dimmed in recognition, had respectfully given plenty of space, their crews standing at attention on deck, some saluting, others bowing, creating a somber but respectful greeting for the rescue ship. Though the clock would soon strike 9:30 p.m., the atmosphere was one of timeless sorrow.

Many were puzzled at first when the *Carpathia* bypassed their own company pier to make a short pause at White Star's Pier 59 nearby, carefully offloading the empty lifeboats. They were ghastly, poignant reminders of the horror. It was not simply returning someone else's property, but a maritime method of attempting to comfort the bereaved. Then, once done, they backtracked to Cunard's own Pier 54. This arrival was a stark, public declaration of the lives saved and the lives lost.

During the final approach for the dock, crewmen announced that *Carpathia's* passengers would disembark first. Then the *Titanic* survivors would be allowed to leave. Though Robert had rested most of the time aboard, he still felt drained. The kind of tired that sleep couldn't fix.

"Robert!? Is that you?"

He turned and was surprised to see Molly Brown marching right up and wrapping him in a firm hug.

"A hell of a trip, wasn't it?" she said, her voice low but steady. "But we made it. And that means something."

"Most of us didn't, though, Molly. Less than a third, actually."

"Yes," she said softly. "It's awful. A lot of good people are gone. Far too many. People you and I both knew. And who is this handsome little fella?"

Robert explained the situation.

She gave them both a once-over. "You boys look like you've been dragged across the Atlantic by your shoelaces. Listen, I'm organizing help. Food, shelter, and a few dollars in pockets. For everyone in second and third class. No one will get ignored this time. Whatever we can gather for the ones who need it most. Including this sweet guy."

Robert remembered not depositing his money with the

purser once he had boarded the *Titanic*. He had hardly thought about it during the evacuation or since.

Then, noticing that Robert's demeanor had noticeably improved, with that indomitable fire in her eyes, she added, "Come on, sonny, we've still got a country to walk back into."

Seeing that the *Carpathia* was approaching the pier and they were preparing the mooring lines to secure the ship, Robert gave a weary smile.

"No argument there, Molly. I'm ready to feel solid earth again."

The pier was flooding with reporters. Flashes of magnesium bulbs flared, pens scratched on pads, and voices volleyed questions faster than answers could catch breath. Molly Brown stood tall beneath her umbrella, fielding each inquiry with the poise of a seasoned general. An officer had given her his coat, which clung to her in the drizzle, but her presence was fire itself.

"Mrs. Brown, over here. Mrs. Brown, you came through!"

"Well, the *Titanic* wasn't unsinkable, but I sure am!"

Two reporters stood on opposite sides of her, writing notes. "How do you feel about the White Star?"

"In Leville, Colorado, where I come from, Ismay would be hung up on the nearest tree."

"Did you lose much?"

The question angered Robert. Even after a tragedy like this, possessions were the focus. Not the people.

"Much of what I owned is at the bottom of the sea. But don't mention it. Don't you know the real shame is that many of those lifeboats left half empty!"

"Mrs. Brown, what are your plans?"

"I'm thinking of running for the Senate. I survived this; I could survive politics! But first, we'll get every soul housed. And I want names remembered, not just numbers," she said, lifting a gloved hand. She motioned over to Robert, who handed her the little boy. "Thank you, Robert. Now look here, everyone. There are a lot of children who lost their parents like this cutie. They more than anyone else need to be tended to first. *Titanic* was grandeur sure. But those souls lost were sacred. I'm accepting help from anyone to assist the survivors, beginning with him!"

Robert stepped away and watched from a distance, half-sheltered beneath the overhang of a customs awning. The drizzle patterned his overcoat, and each drop seemed to strike not only fabric but also thought. His satchel was against his side, not for safekeeping, but for gravity. A tether.

He'd looked. Scanned. Waited. But no one came for Leo.

Not a brother. Not a cousin. No distant relative waving a sign. Nothing. Only the silence where names should've been called aloud.

It wasn't negligence. It was erasure. And Robert felt it like a knife against his ribs.

At the edge of the crowd, two other reporters were passing by, shuffling notes. Robert overheard one reporter ask a man for a last name, but he couldn't catch it.

"Don't see him on the survivor list."

"Who'd he travel with?"

"Solo, Third Class. Probably didn't make it. Awful."

They moved on. Brief. Efficient. Already forgotten. How many more would get that cold note for the official records?

"Far too many," Robert said to himself as he leaned against the iron railing near the warehouse wall. Behind him, the backdrop of Manhattan blurred in rain-streaked outlines as another downpour arrived. He wasn't part of the interviews. He wasn't part of the headlines. Just one man keeping watch. Not for rescue, but for memory.

He pulled out Leo's prayer book not to show, just to hold. The crowd pulsed around him: steam, boots, names called aloud, papers shuffled, rain falling. And in the middle of it all, his silence was louder than everything.

Sunday, April 21st—United States Senate Inquiry
Day Three of Testimony into the Loss of Titanic

Quietly sitting near the back, Robert kept his leather-bound journal resting on his knee. He had filled many of its pages with observations from the voyage, moments stolen from time. And now, with the ghosts of the abyss pressing in on him, he turned to its blank pages once more. The Senate chamber felt cold, yet nothing could compare to the icy darkness of the North Atlantic, a chill that had seeped into his very bones. His body, still aching with exhaustion, felt heavy on the polished wooden bench. He was acutely aware of the lingering scent of salt and death that seemed to cling to him, even in this grand, formal space.

With his journal in hand, he made notes in the gallery of the Senate hearing room, surrounded by reporters and grieving family members. Looking around them, the distinctions between classes that were so clearly segregated on the *Titanic*, those barriers now gone, seemed almost ironic in the face of such universal loss. The realization that only 700 people survived while almost 1,500 did not felt heavier now than ever before, a crushing weight on his chest. Robert thought about Leo and the young mother with her child in Steerage. He gripped the worn edges of his leather journal, its pages now filling with scattered, fragmented memories from that traumatic night.

He had barely survived the sinking of the *Titanic*, but here, in this grand chamber, with its scent of aged paper and solemn wood, he was more like an observer of history than an active participant. A silent witness to a truth he longed to shout aloud. The high ceilings seemed to amplify every whispered word, every rustle of clothing. It seemed that no one from the second-class survivors was allowed to give their testimony, their voices deemed less important than those of the wealthy, silenced by unspoken decrees.

He gripped the worn edges of his leather journal, its pages now filling with scattered, fragmented memories from that traumatic night. Since Robert was not allowed to speak, he would write. No one could stop that. *'We're all soil and soul. The only difference is whether we focus on the "i" or the "u."'*

Mrs. Elizabeth Lines, a surviving passenger from First Class, took her seat before the panel. Her composure was steady, though her eyes betrayed the weight of what she had witnessed.

Senator William Alden Smith, who was a Republican senator for Michigan, had previously investigated railroad safety issues and had sponsored many of the safety and operating regulations passed by Congress to govern the operations of the American rail industry. He realized the need for rapid action if a US inquiry was to be possible before the surviving passengers and crew dispersed and returned home.

"Mrs. Lines," Senator Smith began, "you mentioned overhearing a conversation between Bruce Ismay and Captain Edward Smith on the Sunday afternoon of the 14th. Would you please recount that exchange for the official record?"

Elizabeth took a breath, folding her hands in her lap.

"Yes. I was having tea with my daughter, Mary, in the First-Class Reception Room. It was shortly after lunch was served. The afternoon was quiet. Most of the gentlemen had retired to the smoking room or were strolling the Promenade Deck. From where I sat, I could not help but overhear Mr. Ismay and Captain Smith conversing nearby."

She paused, glancing at the senators.

"I did not intend to eavesdrop on them, but as their words carried within hearing of my table, I felt… uneasy."

"Uneasy? In what manner, Madam?" Senator Smith prompted.

"Mr. Ismay was pressing the captain to increase the ship's speed. He spoke of the unused boilers and the possibility of arriving in New York a day early by beating the *Olympic*'s record to impress the press, as he put it. He saw it as a grand opportunity to demonstrate the power and elegance of the *Titanic*."

There was a murmur among the spectators. Robert shook his head in disbelief. He was right to be concerned after all.

"And what was Captain Smith's response to that?" the senator inquired.

Elizabeth's eyes softened as she recalled the captain's measured demeanor.

"Captain Smith refused. He was calm but firm. I remember his words distinctly: 'There is no need to fire the last of the boilers. The safety procedures exist for a reason. I will adhere to them without exception. While this is my final crossing until we return home to Southampton, I remain the captain of this vessel.'"

She hesitated, then added, "Mr. Ismay seemed displeased, but he eventually conceded. He extinguished his cigarette and said, 'You and your fine officers know what is best for us all. I will respect your decision, Captain.' It is evident to me that Mr. Ismay meant his apology."

A senator leaned forward. "Did you believe Mr. Ismay's sincerity?"

Elizabeth hesitated. "At the time, yes. Captain Smith accepted the apology, though he made it clear that any further discussion about the ship's operation would need to go through him first. Yet… there was something in Mr. Ismay's tone, a subtle frustration that lingered."

The senators exchanged glances.

"Mrs. Lines, you also made mention of the boilers. Would you kindly elaborate on what you observed?"

Elizabeth nodded.

"Yes, Senator. Captain Smith was aware of the recent coal strike and chose to conserve fuel by leaving the final four furnaces in Boiler Room Six unlit. He also probably considered the strain on the men working below, where the heat reached unbearable temperatures. We all knew that *Titanic* was already making excellent time. Captain Smith said there was no need to push the engines further, especially with an ice field ahead."

A different senator interjected, "And yet, there were rumors circulating among the passengers that the crew intended to attempt to break the *Olympic's* record. Were you aware of these rumors?"

"I heard whispers among the various people," Elizabeth admitted. "But Captain Smith, with over forty years at sea, always advocated for caution. That's why so many wanted to sail on ships he commanded. Some of the crew that didn't survive explained that Captain Smith ordered a more southern route to avoid the ice. No one could have known how far south the ice had drifted that year."

She lowered her gaze for a moment before continuing. It's exactly what Robert had heard from the steward in Second Class.

"I remember feeling an odd sense of unease after eavesdropping on their conversation. I dismissed it at the time. After all, the *Titanic* was said to be unsinkable."

A heavy silence filled the chamber.

'Just like the *Titan*'... Robert thought to himself silently.

"Mrs. Lines," Senator Smith said gravely, "your testimony has proven invaluable in our understanding of the decisions made aboard the *Titanic*. We thank you for your courage, madam. You may step down now."

The heavy wooden benches creaked as spectators shifted uncomfortably, some leaning forward in anticipation as the next witness took the stand. J. Bruce Ismay, chairman of the White Star Line, approached them with noticeable unease. The weight of the world seemed to rest on his shoulders as he raised his right hand to take the oath.

From where Robert sat, he could see the pale, gaunt figure of Ismay, his complexion sallow, his eyes shadowed by what could only be sleepless nights. The man whose name had, in the public mind, become a byword for cowardice seemed very diminished, his grand stature somehow shrunken by the weight of public scorn. Yet, as Ismay spoke, his voice thin and reedy, Robert saw something more. A man burdened by the immense weight of choices made in the darkest of hours, perhaps even a haunted one.

Seated before the panel, Senator William Alden Smith wasted no time.

"Mr. Ismay, you have just heard the testimony provided by Mrs. Elizabeth Lines concerning your conversation with

Captain Smith on the afternoon of the 14th of April. Do you take issue with her account?"

Ismay cleared his throat. "No, Senator, I do not dispute that a conversation took place. However, I believe Mrs. Lines may have misunderstood my intentions."

"Then, for the official record, you would do well to clarify your intentions," the senator pressed.

Robert's pulse quickened. He remembered the rumors circulating among the second-class passengers that Ismay had urged the captain to push the engines to their limits in hopes of arriving in New York ahead of schedule.

Elizabeth Lines' Testimony had only confirmed what Robert had long suspected. Ismay had sought glory for the White Star Line, while Captain Smith had resisted. And yet, that iceberg cared nothing for ambition or caution.

As Ismay's trembling voice echoed through the chamber, Robert's eyes narrowed. He could almost hear Captain Smith's steady, authoritative tone, refusing to compromise the safety of those aboard. "Mr. Ismay, listen to me. There are safety procedures for good reasons. I will adhere to them at all times. Without exception."

Robert imagined the quiet tension between the two men in the opulent reception Room. He pictured Elizabeth Lines, pretending to sip her tea while discreetly absorbing every word. How powerless she must have felt, knowing she could never speak out until the ship was at the bottom of the ocean.

Ismay shifted in his seat, a picture of discomfort, though Robert sensed it was more self-pity than genuine remorse. "My inquiries about the ship's speed and the unused boilers were not made to pressure Captain Smith. I am a man of business, yes, but I have the utmost respect for the sea and those who command her vessels. My questions were born out of curiosity, not coercion. I was on the ship only as a passenger."

Murmurs rippled through the chamber, some of indignation, others perhaps of sympathy for a fallen titan. Robert's jaw clenched. *Curiosity? Coercion?* The words felt hollow, a flimsy veil over a desperate need for glory. He remembered the faint, desperate screams in the water and the sheer, unimaginable cold. Ismay spoke of respect for the sea, but what respect was there in tempting it with such arrogance?

Robert could almost hear Captain Smith's steady, authoritative tone, refusing to compromise the safety of those aboard. Robert could understand the quiet tension between the two men sitting in an area where passengers could overhear them.

He pictured Elizabeth Lines, pretending to sip her tea while discreetly absorbing every word, her unease palpable even then. How powerless she must have felt, knowing she could never speak out until the ship was at the bottom of the ocean. Senator Smith leaned forward. "Is it not the case that you expressed a desire for the *Titanic* to arrive in New York ahead of schedule in order to impress the reporters?"

Ismay hesitated. "Well, I… I may have expressed hope that the *Titanic* would demonstrate her capabilities. She was the pride of the White Star Line. But I would never ever compromise the safety of any people on board."

"Yet, you acknowledged the *Titanic's* inability to match the speed of the *Mauretania*. Your primary focus, then, was on surpassing the *Olympics'* record, was it not?"

Ismay's face flushed. "The *Titanic*, as well as the *Olympic*, were built for luxury and stability, not speed. I simply wished for her to perform to her fullest potential.

Captain Smith, a man I trusted implicitly, had the final authority. I deferred to his judgment, as I always had."

Senator Smith's expression remained stern. "And when Captain Smith declined to light the final boilers, what was your reaction at that time?"

Ismay's voice softened. "I accepted his decision, though I confess I was disappointed. It was not out of vanity, Senator, but out of pride in what we had accomplished. The *Titanic* represented the height of British engineering and elegance. I wished for the world to see her in all her glory."

The chamber fell silent as the weight of Ismay's words lingered.

In his journal, Robert scribbled, *'Ismay speaks of pride in engineering. But what of pride in human lives? What of the Steerage souls left to drown and freeze while men of wealth slipped into the lifeboats? The sea does not care for class, nor should our justice.'*

As Ismay continued to defend his actions, Robert's mind drifted to the third-class mother clutching her child, and the people trapped behind the iron gates. He thought of Leo again. His small prayer book and the echo of the people's screams that night still lingered in his ears, louder than any testimony that could be given in this room. While the vocal screams did eventually stop, in Robert's mind they would never end. Robert now knew that hell was not some fiery torment. It was being trapped in freezing water!

"And yet," the senator pressed, "you survived while over fifteen hundred souls perished. You, the chairman of this esteemed company, boarded a lifeboat while women and children remained on deck. How do you respond to that?"

Ismay's voice cracked as he spoke of stepping into the lifeboat. His hands trembled as he gripped the edge of the stand. "I can never justify my actions. I can only speak the truth. I helped others into the lifeboats, and only when I saw that no women or children were present did I step in. I believed I could do no more on that sinking ship." His voice cracked. "I have rightly been condemned as a coward by the world. But I assure you, Senator, I carry the burden of that night with me. And I shall bear it for the rest of my days, long after my soon-to-be resignation as chairman."

The room remained deathly still as Ismay's eyes fell to the floor.

There was more questioning about the safety measures. Copies of the blueprints for *Olympic* were displayed so everyone could see. Everyone was horrified to learn that during that ship's construction, Ismay had ordered the majority of the watertight bulkheads to be lowered to E Deck. Just ten or so feet above the waterline. The decision was to accommodate more luxury for the first-class passengers. The same was done on the *Titanic*.

Although the *Olympic* didn't sink from its collision, it had all the same vulnerabilities as the *Titanic*!

But the most upsetting was learning that the builders had planned for many more lifeboats to be provided than the laws required. It would have been 48. Sufficient for all passengers and crew on board. When pressed for why the number of lifeboats was lowered to only 16, the reply from Ismay was inexcusable. "They'll cause the decks to be too cluttered. There'll be no need for lifeboats on this vessel." It was evident to everyone that the maritime laws needed an emergency, drastic updating.

Ismay then gave his closing statement: "Everybody learns by experience. One thing that I learned when the *Titanic* went down is that the laws relating to the preservation of life are clearly not adequate. They were based, no doubt, on the assumption that these great ocean liners, with their highly developed system of watertight compartments with automatically closing doors, would stay afloat no matter what happened. But experience has now taught us that at present there is no such thing as an unsinkable ship. I admit that I was among those who were deluded on this point."

Senator Smith's tone softened, mostly from sadness, though it carried the weight of judgment. The room tensed as the senator's words struck like a knife: "History will ultimately determine, Mr. Ismay, whether your actions were those of a man solely seeking his own survival or evading his own responsibility."

Robert's breath caught in his throat. If only those who perished like Thomas Andrews, Benjamin Guggenheim, and so many others, passengers and crew, had been given the chance to defend their own actions. And yet here sat Ismay, alive and despised for the rest of his life, condemned not for what he had done but for what he had failed to do.

The chairman rose slowly, shoulders hunched, eyes sunken. For a moment, Robert thought he might collapse under the weight of his own words. But Ismay did not falter. He walked stiffly toward the back of the chamber, a broken man who would never again escape the shadow of that April night. As Ismay stepped down, someone approached Senator Smith and whispered softly in his ear. Robert lowered his head and scribbled in his journal: *'There is a deeper tragedy in survival, for it is not the sea that haunts a man, but the faces of those he did not save.'*

Suddenly the next witness to testify was called up. Robert was very surprised as Lawrence Beesley, a fellow second-class survivor, rose to take the stand. A schoolmaster by trade, he spoke with measured clarity, recounting the ship's slow descent and the chaos on the lifeboat deck. Robert gripped the edges of his journal, wishing he, too, could speak for those lost in the darkness. But in this grand chamber, words were reserved for those deemed worthy of being heard.

The air in the inquiry room felt thick; heavy with unspoken truths and the weight of so many lost souls. The room itself, with its dark wooden panels and tall windows that allowed pale daylight to stream in, seemed like a mausoleum for memories no one wished to ever exhume.

Lawrence Beesley took his seat on the witness stand at the front of the room, a quiet yet commanding presence. The official position, repeated in newspapers and insisted upon by the White Star Line, was that the grand liner had slipped gracefully beneath the waves, intact. But Beesley spoke not from speculation, nor from the carefully constructed illusions of the wealthy, but from the raw, terrible clarity of survival. "Yet, Mr. Beesley, it is our own best experts who designed and constructed that ship to withstand the absolute worst the Atlantic could throw at her. It's clear to me that she sank without breaking apart. Do you accept the facts that have been presented to you?"

"No, sir. That is false. I was there. You were not. I saw her break apart," Beesley said, his voice steady but filled with the tremor of truth. "As the ship's stern rose high into the sky, she split just forward of the third funnel. The sea took her in pieces, not whole as you claim."

The room stirred with uneasy whispers, a ripple of discomfort among those in positions of authority. Men who had never felt the deck shudder beneath their feet or heard the final cries of the dying. They preferred the illusion of a noble ship slipping gracefully beneath the waves, not the brutal, unvarnished reality of steel torn asunder and lives extinguished by hubris.

Robert's grip tightened on his pen as he listened to Lawrence's words. *'Beesley speaks the truth they refuse to hear. I saw it too. I saw the ship rend itself apart, and with it, the lives and dreams of over fifteen hundred souls. Yet they dismiss us. They call it hysteria. But the sea does not lie and neither shall I.'*

As Beesley continued, Robert glanced around the room. Scattered among the crowd were other survivors. Men and women whose eyes carried the same haunted knowledge. Some nodded subtly in agreement; others bowed their heads in silent grief.

As the silence lingered, a cough echoed from the gallery. It was sharp, awkward, and jarring. The spell was broken, and a rustle of discomfort passed through the spectators. A few glanced toward Robert, whose pen had gone still.

Senator Smith folded his hands atop the polished desk, his voice quieter now but no less direct. "Thank you, Mr. Beesley. You may step down."

The next witness, a wireless operator from the *Carpathia*, took the stand. But Robert barely heard his name.

He was no longer in the courtroom. He was back in the lifeboat, arms frozen around his knees, hearing the cries echo across the black sea. The sky had been cloudless. The stars were brilliant. And all the while, that sound, the wailing of the dying, had carried across the waves like a funeral dirge sung by the abyss itself.

A voice snapped him back. "Mr. Morganson?"

Robert looked up. A clerk stood before him with a folded note.

He took it. Inside was a request, handwritten in formal script: *'Please remain after the session. Chairman Smith would like a word.'*

Robert folded the note slowly and slipped it into his coat.

The hearings adjourned moments later with the sharp

rap of a gavel. Reporters rushed to the exits, some already shouting headlines to one another.

But Robert stayed seated, watching as the senators stood and spoke in hushed tones. One of them, Smith himself, caught his gaze and nodded.

The senator approached, his presence steady and direct. "Mr. Morganson, I understand you've kept a journal. Captain Rostron of the *Carpathia* mentioned your observations during your recovery. Would you be willing to submit it for the official record?"

Robert hesitated. The journal had become his confessor, the one place where his rawest thoughts, grief, anger, guilt, and much more had been set down without filter. To hand it over now felt like exposing his soul.

"I suppose I could make a copy for you, sir," he offered.

Smith smiled. "That is a reasonable concession. What you've written may help the public understand more than any testimony could. You're one of the few who've seen both the suffering and the grace of that night."

Robert gave a slow nod.

As the senator turned to leave, he paused and looked back. "And Mr. Morganson, do not ever underestimate the power of a survivor's voice. Whether spoken or written. It is so often the only thing left to speak for those who can't."

"Yes, sir. I'm grateful for your time today." Robert's fingers brushed the edge of the journal. Maybe it was time. Not just to tell the story, but to let the story tell him something back.

As the hearing adjourned for the day, Robert's heart was heavy. He had survived the *Titanic* to bear witness to the truth, and now, through ink and memory, if not his voice, he would ensure that truth would not be forgotten. Robert approached Beesley, who stood by the door, adjusting his simple, modest suit.

"You told them the truth," Robert said softly. "But they will not listen."

Beesley offered a weary smile. "The truth is often drowned before it can reach the shore."

"You spoke with great dignity," Robert said quietly.

Beesley turned, his expression solemn but warm. "Thank you. It is not easy. But I believe it is necessary."

There was a pause between them. Two men who had met in the mostly neglected areas of the same doomed vessel, now standing again on steadier ground, trying to make sense of the aftermath.

"I sometimes wonder," Robert said slowly, "whether recounting it over and over helps us heal or just keeps the wounds from closing."

Beesley considered that for a moment. "Perhaps it does both. But silence would be worse. Silence would be forgetting."

Robert nodded. "I've been asked to submit my journal for the official record."

"A very brave thing to offer."

"Not brave," Robert said, glancing at the folded note in his pocket. "Only what must be done."

Beesley looked him in the eye. "Then do it with honesty. And do not minimize the truth. Let the rawness stay. Let them feel what it meant to listen to the cries and to be one of the many who could not answer them."

That last sentence struck Robert like a bell in his chest. He swallowed hard and extended his hand. "I'm glad you lived."

Beesley shook it firmly. "And I, you."

They parted in the hallway, each disappearing into the soft thunder of reporters and staff. Robert didn't rush. He took his time as he exited the chamber, the weight of history and memory in every step.

Outside, the sky had turned pale with approaching dusk. The chill in the air wasn't nearly as cruel as the one he remembered from that night. But it was enough to draw his coat tighter.

Beesley's words lingered as Robert walked in the cool afternoon air. The streets of New York bustled with life, oblivious to the burden he and the others carried. Everyone was talking about the *Titanic* and the many lives lost. The city moved on, while the ocean's dead remained suspended in time.

Later that evening, in the dim light of his rented room, Robert opened his journal once more. The light of the small lamp on the desk flickered as if stirred by the ghosts of the Atlantic, illuminating the pages he would dedicate to them. Robert counted out the money that had been given to him in compensation. Just as Molly Brown had promised. With that and the money he did not deposit into the safe on the *Titanic*, he knew how much longer he could stay in New York before needing to return home.

'I'm fully convinced that 14 years ago this very event was foretold in this short, forgotten book called Futility. *A novel, of all things. Fiction sooner or later becomes fact. Yet that night we experienced still lives on in those who bear witness. I write these words, not for myself, nor for those living now who refuse to listen, clinging to their comforting lies, but for those yet to come. Generations who deserve to know what really happened. The raw, brutal truth is that the sea itself remembers, even if humanity tries to forget. Those stars above the* Titanic *will never speak, but I will speak for them.'*

He closed the journal and rested it beside his bed, as if guarding the memories within. For most of that night, sleep did not come. It hovered just out of reach, scattered by memories too heavy for dreams. And when at last Robert drifted into uneasy slumber, he dreamed not of ships or storms, but of faces. Andrews, Leo, Esther's trembling hands, vanishing one by one into the starlit dark.

The truth, he now knew, was not something the living always welcomed.

But the dead deserved it.

And he would not stop writing until they had it. For nearly a week now, sleep did not come easily, for in the darkness, he could still hear the groan of splitting metal and the cries that no ocean could silence.

10

THE NIGHT STILL LIVES ON

No detailed plans had been made, but Robert decided to remain in New York temporarily. The money he refused to leave in the safe on the *Titanic* would come in handy, as would the extra funds Molly had made available to her fellow survivors. Something held him there.

He resumed journaling as the world reeled in the aftermath of the *Titanic* disaster. The city's cacophony of the clatter of horse-drawn carts, the distant rumble of the trains, and the ceaseless hum of conversations felt alien and overwhelming after the stark silence of the ocean. His hands still cramped from the ordeal, caught between recovery and obsession, he found himself drawn into every headline and every hearing. He was desperate to understand what had happened and how such a tragedy could be prevented from ever happening again.

He felt a constant tremor beneath his skin, a ghost of the ship's final vibrations. That was nearly the most troubling sensation. Being in a lifeboat and feeling the ship implode from below them. The screams were the worst.

Words poured onto the pages of his journal like a waterfall, his thoughts racing ahead of every pen he held. Anticipating their failures, he had stocked up on spares, ink staining his fingertips like a badge of his new calling. Sleep came only when his hand seized in protest, muscles knotted with exhaustion, his mind too weary to fight the pull of unconsciousness. Even then, his dreams were haunted by the ship, the cries of the dying, and the bitter sting of Atlantic air that seemed to cling to his very breath.

Now, at last, he would pause. Stretching out his aching arm, he scrawled one final reflection before surrendering to rest: *'Time flows forward like a river, carrying us from one moment to the next. But the past, like shadows beneath the water's surface, lingers. Calling us to account for what we have done and left undone.'*

Robert could write no more. So he decided to read. He kept a close watch on the news as both British and American investigations unfolded. The desire for learning was insatiable.

One name stood out. Very familiar from his first crossing: none other than Captain William Thomas Turner of the *Mauretania*. He was a short, stocky man of the Cunard Line, rival to White Star. Turner had been called to testify before Judge Julius Mayer in London, offering his expert opinion on the loss of the *Titanic*. This separate investigation was focused more on improving the safety of ships and deciding if the White Star Line was responsible. Representatives of Cunard also listened in attendance, largely to keep their company from falling under the same scrutiny, since all of their ships also had the same lack of safety precautions… if not worse.

Robert thought back on their brief encounter when he accepted the crewman's invitation to tour part of the ship. Probably as a way to convince Robert to buy a first-class ticket the next time.

Unlike the ever-sociable Captain Smith, Captain Turner had no interest in mingling with passengers or even the crew. He always kept to himself, never out of rudeness, but reflection. Robert had always imagined him a kindred spirit in that way. A fellow man who understood the need to be alone at times. During a very brief exchange with

Turner, Robert did not get the impression the man was being rude to him. Just maintaining professional boundaries.

The transcripts were unusually detailed, especially for newspaper reporting. The sinking had not only shocked the world. It had enraged it. When asked about ship construction, Turner answered flatly, "I do not concern myself with their construction so long as they remain afloat. If they should sink, I endeavor to get out."

Pressed further on what lessons he was able to draw from the tragedy, his bleak response chilled Robert: "With all due respect, Your Honor, I cannot say I have learned the slightest thing from this horrible event. But I'm certain that such tragedies are bound to happen again."

Robert stared at the page, stunned. With most of the pain in his hand and arm gone, he risked writing just a small amount in his journal: *'Great. So this book, so aptly called* 'Futility' *can't happen just once? Does it really have to occur again? When will we ever learn?!'*

He would find out soon enough. Just a few years later, Captain Turner, who had been in command of the *Mauretania*, would be placed in charge of her running mate. Cunard's flagship, the *Lusitania*. And like a cruel echo, a voice from the past returning, she too would go down. Shockingly fast, despite all the recent improvements to her safety. Thankfully, Turner would survive. Unlike Captain Smith. But far too many others would not.

Robert had stopped reading *Futility* shortly after he saw the iceberg. The parallels were too much. Every page felt like a prophecy, and he couldn't bear to know what came next. Now that he was safely on land, he opened the novel again searching for answers, perhaps reassurance, but certainly not what he found.

He turned the pages slowly, reading about how

Rowland rescued a small girl, his prior love interest's daughter, and found safety on the very iceberg that had destroyed the *Titan*. However, shortly after the impact with the *Titanic*, in truth, no one saw that iceberg or any other again until the morning light revealed scattered chunks drifting eerily nearby.

In Chapter 9 Rowland's words were too familiar for Robert: *'Curse them, with their water-tight compartments, and their logging of the lookouts. Twenty-four boats for three thousand people —lashed down with tarred gripe-lashings—thirty men to clear them away, and not an ax on the boat-deck or a sheath-knife on a man… But the whisky was all right. It's all done with now, unless I get ashore—but will I?'*

Then it mentioned the moon rising in the night sky, shining an eerie yet beautiful light on the berg. Rowland's anger was elaborated on the next page: '… *looking into the sky, where a few stars shone faintly in the flood from the moon; "Up there—somewhere—they don't know just where—but somewhere up above, is the Christians' Heaven. Up there… their good God—who has placed Myra's child here—their good God whom they borrowed from the savage, bloodthirsty… that invented him. And down below us—somewhere again—is their hell and their bad god… they invented themselves… Heaven or hell. It is not so… The great mystery is not solved—the human… is not helped in this way. No good, merciful God created this world or its conditions. Whatever may be the… causes at work beyond our mental vision, one fact is indubitably proven—that… mercy, goodness, justice, play no part in the governing scheme. And yet… the core of all religions on earth is the belief in this. Is it? Or is it the cowardly… fear of the unknown —that impels the savage… to throw her babe to a crocodile—that impels the civilized man to endow churches—that has kept in existence from the beginning… soothsayers, medicine-men, priests, and clergymen, all living on the hopes and fears excited by themselves?"'*

Robert understood the doubts and emotions all too

well. He had said similar things to his own relatives. Because if God really cared, why does so much bad happen to good people? Suddenly, Robert began to at last see some of the glaring differences between the novel in his hands and the facts he experienced. But many questions needed answers.

Eventually, they were rescued and brought to London. The public uproar in the novel reminded him of the *Carpathia's* arrival in New York. The crowd's uneasy mixture of awe, grief, and disbelief.

Opening his journal for a moment, Robert wrote at the top of the next page: *'Rowland cursed the heavens. I've done the same. But I wonder, if doubt is a kind of prayer, what does that make me? The* Titan *gave him an iceberg. The* Titanic *gave me a lifeboat. But neither feels like mercy.'*

Then came Chapter 10. And something deep shifted, a sickening lurch in his gut that wasn't from a ship's movement. A man named Meyer, a caricature more than a human character, was introduced: '... *one—the noisiest of all, a corpulent, hook-nosed man with flashing black eyes...*' He circled the phrase '*hook-nosed man,*' then drew a shaky line to the margin and wrote: *'NOT Leo!'*

Robert forced himself to keep reading, each word a punch to his conscience. *'"Father Abraham," he muttered; "this will ruin me."'* His stomach twisted, bile rising hot and acrid. This wasn't just offensive it was personal. This was nothing like the man who had saved his life, not just physically, but in the profound way he reminded Robert that goodness, decency, and peace were still possible no matter where you found yourself in life, nor in what religion you belonged to, or in Robert's case, abstained from.

True, Robert had never known many Jews, at least none he'd been aware of, but Leo and others in Third Class had patiently challenged every ugly, hateful stereotype that Robert had been told growing up, and they did it with quiet dignity and boundless compassion. Was this how Morgan Robertson, the man who had seen the future, truly saw Jewish people? Like Fagin? Like Shylock? Like the lies that had bled into every corner of the continent? The thought alone felt like a bitter betrayal.

Chapters 11 through 13 were even worse. In them, Meyer was portrayed as a greedy, conniving figure. A man who cared more for money than people, who reveled in his vast wealth while others suffered. The same accusation many aboard the *Titanic* had received. Was *that* the future Robertson had foretold rather than the sinking of a ship? Seeing that he'd left his journal open, Robert wrote a few shorthand notes of the chapters he had just read with a question: *'Just because something predicts a tragedy doesn't mean it understands hope. How can a book that predicted so much truth carry such hatred?'*

He closed the novel and looked at the prayer book resting nearby. In that moment, he understood that preserving Leo's legacy was more important than preserving a flawed prophecy. He was shaking. Much more than usual. Robert wasn't able to calm himself. Unable to hold back the storm swirling within, Robert sent a telegram addressed to a quiet listing in a Manhattan writer's directory:

'To Mr. M. Robertson, author of Futility,

I believe we have something in common. I read your book on the Titanic *the night she sank. I'm staying in New York a little longer before returning to the Midwest. May we please meet? I need to speak with you.'*

Signing his name at the bottom had felt absurd. Like reaching through a fog to someone who might not care. But it was necessary.

Two days later, a reply arrived: only a date, time, and

an address with the signature *'Morgan Robertson'* at the bottom. Robert followed it like a court summons. He just had to know.

There were only a few chapters left in the novel. Robert decided it was time to read them and find out how the story ended. Before meeting Morgan.

He carefully analyzed each page, each individual line. He read with growing unease as the protagonist, John Rowland, was brought to London. The novel dragged on. Businessmen concerned more with financial losses for their company that the needless deaths of almost every passenger on their ship. Even the captain survived! Apparently abandoning not only his ship, but also every passenger.

But a very redeeming quality of John Rowland was detailed in Chapter 14: '... *with Myra on his shoulder, he stepped down the gang-plank at a North River dock... he was surrounded... by enthusiastic reporters... and asked for details. He refused to talk, escaped them, and gaining the side streets, soon found himself in crowded Broadway, where he entered the office of the steamship company in whose employ he had been wrecked, and secured from the Titan's passenger-list the address of Mrs. Selfridge—the only woman saved. Then he took a car up Broadway... of a large department store.*

"We're going to see mumma, soon, Myra," he whispered... "and you must go dressed up. It don't matter about me; but you're... a little aristocrat. These old clothes won't do, now." ... In the store, Rowland asked for, and was directed to the children's department...

"This child has been shipwrecked," he said. "I have sixteen dollars and a half to spend on it. Give it a bath, dress its hair, and use up the money on a dress, shoes, and stockings, underclothing, and a hat." The young woman... protested that not much could be done.

"Do your best," said Rowland; "it is all I have. I will wait here."

… later… he emerged from the store with Myra… and was stopped at the corner by a policeman who had seen him come out, and who marveled, doubtless, at such juxtaposition of rags and ribbons.'

John Rowland was arrested. After giving up the last of his money to a child he was not obligated to care for. Having retrieved her daughter, the girl's mother became more enraged at the man who saved the poor girl than before and made his life hell.

While Robert had not exactly rescued the little boy from the *Titanic*, he had tended to the child's needs by watching over him, and he had made sure he got into the hands of people better equipped to take care of him.

Before realizing it, he had already turned to the final page, the book's stiff paper almost sticking to the back cover. The final chapter, number 16, was barely a full page. One large paragraph, in fact. It had barely let go of the back cover with a loud crinkle, as if refusing to give up its final hidden secret. The ending was now revealed.

But that conclusion felt hollow, a jarring and cynical ending that left Robert angered.

Rowland, the man who had survived the disaster, saved the life of his former lover's daughter and bravely stood up to the injustices of the company, rebuilding his life with a grim and solitary determination. Starting as a simple dock lounger, he leveraged his skills, like keen penmanship and a knack for business, to steadily climb the social ladder. He progressed from fishing for scraps and selling whatever he could get his hands on to a small advantage, to a respectable government position within two years. All while shedding the past.

In the final lines of the book, Rowland congratulates himself with the thought, *"'Now, John Rowland, your future is your own. You have merely suffered in the past from a mistaken estimate of the importance of women and whisky.'"*

That was it. Nothing more. It struck Robert as a bitter, almost monstrously callous statement. He lowered the book, the sound of the final pages flapping shut echoing in the quiet room. He thought of Leo and the many other victims, as well as the survivors; of the shared kindness in the face of death, and the profound importance of human connection.

The novel had uncannily predicted a tragedy of staggering proportions, yet its final chapter dismissed the very human bonds and sacrifices that Robert had not only experienced, but also participated in and held so dear. It was as if Morgan Robertson, in his quest to warn of technological folly, had completely forgotten to account for human decency. That was the "unfinished" part of the story, the emotional and moral void that Robert now felt compelled to fill. But how could he? Soon, he would meet with Morgan. A very different feeling of dread bubbled within him. Not of survival now. But of confrontation. Tomorrow would come a reckoning. Robert felt that he would not like the answers.

The next day, sitting alone at a stone table in Central Park, with the warm breeze carrying the scent of damp earth and distant horse manure, the chessboard pattern etched into the surface of the table caught Robert's eye, and he briefly wondered if the man played chess. To most, it looked like a place for battles of wit, strategies laid bare under the open sky. But Robert knew some games were lost before the first move was made, doomed not only by unseen factors but sometimes even clear warnings that no one paid attention to.

His hands clenched his satchel, a nervous energy buzzing through him. Not knowing what Morgan looked like, Robert tried to imagine his face. Maybe rugged, weathered by the sea, perhaps tired from years of unrecognized foresight. Maybe both? His mind buzzed with questions, a swarm of "hows" and "whys" that demanded answers, each one a relentless gnaw in his brain.

He scanned the few figures in the park, his heart quickening with each passing shadow. He didn't even notice the man approaching from his side as he stopped nearby, holding up a telegram as if double-checking its information. The man's gaze landed on the familiar novel in Robert's hands.

The author of *Futility* had finally arrived.

"I see you're reading a book that is familiar to me," the man said calmly, but clearly enough for Robert to hear.

Robert turned, startled.

Finally seeing him, he stood quickly and made sure he pulled only his journal from his satchel, placing it gently next to *Futility*. He left the *Union Prayer Book* tucked away. Hidden.

"You're the one who wrote to me. Said you were on the *Titanic*."

Robert nodded slowly, reaching out. The two men shook hands.

"Morgan Robertson," the man said. "I wrote that book."

"Hello, sir. My name is Robert… Morganson." A nervous laugh escaped before he could stop it.

Morgan refused to hide his smile or his laugh. He breathed in deeply as his eyes drifted down to the journal, then the novel, and back to Robert. He nodded gently. Now that Morgan was here, Robert suddenly had no idea what to say or ask.

"Permit me to be not merely honest, but frank, Robert. I was surprised to receive your telegram," he said, his voice gravelly but not unkind, a deep resonance that vibrated with years of experience. It was Americanized, yes, but something tucked just behind certain consonants, something older from far away, like the distant echo of a harp or flute over a misty loch. He sounded to Robert like a ship's anchor being raised from the deep, making him think of things hidden beneath the surface, pulled up with great effort, heavy truths often submerged and resisting the light.

"At first I thought it was some sort of a prank when I read how you had signed your correspondence. But then I found your name listed among the survivors. You said the story felt like a prophecy. But I never wrote it to predict anything. It came from my time working at sea years ago, mostly as a cabin boy. I wrote it to warn not of what I knew would happen, but of what I thought could someday occur, a chilling possibility born of my own personal observations and naval architecture."

Robert looked down at the two volumes. His own thoughts beside a novel that had haunted him. Robert was mindful not to give any hints to the prayer book.

"And yet everything about it seemed real when I was there," Robert said softly. "Not just the size of the ship, but so many other details. Right down to the name. How could you have known so far in advance?"

Morgan eased himself onto the bench across from Robert, folding his hands in front of the patterned stone. Robert sat in front of him.

"Tell me about it," he said. "About that ship. What happened after you opened my book and experienced its very words?"

Sitting in front of Morgan with the table between them, Robert opened his journal, fingers brushing over familiar pages until he reached the one marked aboard the *Nomadic*, just moments before he saw the *Titanic* for the first time.

His voice was steady as he read the lines aloud. He paused, eyes still on the page, until he heard Morgan repeat it softly.

"We travel not to escape life, but for life not to escape us," the older man said slowly, with thought. "Quite a fitting observation, Robert. Clearly, you escaped the *Titanic*, and I'm very thankful that you did not escape life."

Robert looked up, surprised to find Morgan's gaze not fixed on the book but on him.

"And you honestly were reading this exact copy of my book in the Second-Class Library the night it happened?"

Robert nodded his head.

"Do you recall what page you were on when the collision occurred?"

"I was reading the end of Chapter 6 and the beginning of Chapter 7."

Morgan opened the novel and flipped to the end of Chapter 6, then looked at the first five paragraphs. Now it was Morgan's turn to have chills. "When the *Titan* collided with its own iceberg in my book?! Well, that timing I cannot explain. You don't seem to me to be the kind of person who believes in coincidences."

"No. Honestly, I don't. After all this I don't know what I believe."

"That is quite understandable. How close was the description of the *Titan's* demise to what you experienced?"

"Very different. I stopped reading it after the collision. I only just finished it after we were rescued. The *Titan* seemed to have sunk very fast after falling on its side. But the *Titanic* lasted almost three hours. Also, it sank almost perfectly level."

"Well, Robert, there's something else you carry, even if you don't fully understand it yet. Something the sea gave you back because you were meant to keep it.

Something you don't want certain people to know about."

Morgan paused for a moment, looking up at a pair of birds repairing a nest before he continued. "Even if you didn't know what it was at the time. But, that's why you wrote to me, isn't it? I don't know exactly what else you took from the *Titanic* that night. But do you really understand what you were meant to hold onto?"

"I think I'm finally beginning to," Robert said. "Because something about your book still felt unfinished."

Morgan gave a faint, tired smile as he leaned back.

"Yes. It always did. For over ten years now, actually. I was never happy with how I ended that story. Robert, when I was working on ships, I saw firsthand these new technological marvels. Automatically-closing doors to limit flooding, and wireless telegraphy sending information through the void. Every new ship was built bigger and faster than the last.

I watched the *Lusitania* and *Mauretania*. Those 'Greyhounds of the Atlantic,' as they're now called, slice through the ocean and the Hudson River like silver arrows. Neither quite 800 feet, but close. And then I saw the *Olympic* arrive. Knowing that there were two more being built just like her, but even larger, that was the moment I knew: the world had finally caught up to my fiction."

Morgan paused, his gaze drifting toward the horizon as if watching the past steam by.

"You know, Robert, the first time I saw a four-funneled liner, I didn't believe it was real. It was the *Kaiser Wilhelm der Grosse*. German-built, launched back in '97. Four funnels, not because they were all needed, but because they made her look faster, grander. She wasn't just a ship. She was a statement. Why the Germans refer to their vessels as 'he' I don't know for certain. That design changed everything.

After her, every major line wanted four funnels. It became a symbol of supremacy, not necessity.

That's when I realized that ships weren't just built to cross oceans. They were built to impress, to intimidate, and to promise safety through scale. The *Titan* in my book had four funnels too. Not because she needed them, but because the world had come to believe that more funnels meant more power. More speed, they said. More pride. Too much pride will ruin a man."

Robert nodded slowly, the image of the *Titanic's* silhouette rising in his mind. The four proud stacks against a moonless sky. Then he turned the book over in his hands, studying the cover again. His brow furrowed.

"Morgan, I noticed something odd. The ship on the cover of your book. It only has three funnels. But in your book, the *Titan* is described as having four. Why the difference?"

Morgan gave a quiet chuckle, nodding as if he'd been waiting years for someone to ask.

"Ah, you caught that. Yes, I imagined the *Titan* having four funnels in the text. But my publisher, Milton Mansfield, you may have read his works under his pen name Francis Miltuon, insisted on using this image for the cover. Something they thought looked dramatic enough. They didn't care about accuracy. To them, three funnels was close enough. Most ships of the time had only two or three. Not many had four yet."

Morgan leaned forward slightly, voice lowering.

"But that detail always bothered me. Because the fourth funnel wasn't just for looks. It was symbolic. It represented excess. Vanity. The illusion of invincibility. Ships didn't need four funnels then. *Olympic* and *Titanic*, with their sister ship being built now, apparently don't. But people want them. Just like they wanted to believe they are unsinkable. That's how it is in the shipping business. Everyone attempting to outdo everyone else.

For now, the Americans and British are outdoing the Germans. Soon France will make an attempt, if they haven't started already."

Morgan leaned back in thought. "A few years ago, some fellow from Vienna visited and spoke at some conference. He studies the human mind as a form of science. Said something about the male preoccupation with size and made a rather vulgar comment about men bragging about a certain part of their anatomy to others but, of course, refusing to show the proverbial 'evidence,' if you will. Even I, being a former sailor, chuckled a bit as well as blushed."

Freud! Robert had met him then and agreed to travel to Vienna to get intensive help under the professor's very unorthodox methods. Robert nodded slowly, keeping that detail to himself with the image of the *Titanic's* silhouette rising again in his memory. Four proud stacks against the stars. He could still hear the sounds of the furnishings crashing around inside the ship.

"So even the cover betrayed your warning."

Morgan's eyes met his. "Exactly. Even the warning was dressed up to sell. The publisher owns the copyright. I don't. As such, I had less say."

Robert had to ask the one question that had burned within him since the night of the sinking.

"But how did you ever get the weight and the name of the vessel so right? You didn't call your ship the *Olympian*, but the *Titan*... *Titanic*... how was that even possible?"

"Well, in regard to the weight, I took an educated guess. But as for the name, Robert, before I wrote that book, I had already seen the real steamship *Titan* for myself."

"What? How? Wait… you're telling me the name *Titan* wasn't concocted by you?"

Morgan reached into his coat pocket and pulled out a postcard, yellowed and soft at the edges. He handed it to Robert. It showed a double-stacked steamship, weathered and compact. Morgan tapped the top right corner, revealing a date and a name barely visible. "Not entirely. But I saw in that little ship a ghost of what might someday come.

This tiny thing was built back in '89. Originally called the *TSS Cambria,* she was pulled from service in '91. That same year, a French company the *Compagnie Générale Transatlantique* bought her, converted her, and gave her a new name: *S.S. Titan*. Only 357 tons. Not even close to the behemoth I imagined. But when I saw her, I realized she was more than a ship. She was a seed. Of course, no one remembered her. Not even I would have, had I not stumbled across her in port that day. But the name… the name never left me.

The *Titanic* was not much larger lengthwise or by internal volume. If I were to make a guess, I'm certain that within a couple of decades you would very well see a ship weighing an excess of seventy thousand tons."

Robert could hardly believe it. Everything began to finally make sense. The line between fiction and foresight was not prophecy but pattern recognition.

Robert couldn't fathom a ship that size. "Morgan, do you honestly believe that some shipping companies could build a vessel that massive?"

"Well, if the Americans or British can't, then maybe the French could."

Morgan chuckled as he leaned back on the bench, his weathered fingers tracing the edge of the old postcard. He tapped the edge of it again.

"You know, Robert, like you, I've also crossed the Atlantic on steamer ships. I wasn't always in New York," he said. "I was born in Oswego — small port town on Lake Ontario, up near the Canadian border. North enough to know what cold feels like. I left as a boy with salt in my lungs and just enough sense to chase the horizon."

Robert raised his eyebrows. "Lake Ontario? I was trying to place something in your manner. A certain familiarity with the water."

"Born to it," Morgan said with a faint grin. "Oswego sits right on the lake. The winters come off that water like they're trying to finish something they started. But the sea became my home soon enough." Morgan leaned back, his gaze drifting toward the late afternoon shadows of the park.

"I never expected *Futility* to last. It wasn't exactly a bestseller." He chuckled dryly. "It was barely a seller at all. Most of the time I couldn't give that blasted thing away for free. My publisher listed it for 75 cents. I once saw a copy in a bookstore window in New Jersey marked down to one cent! So little, it seemed, was the worth of my book. A blasted penny."

Robert tilted his head. "Then how did it end up aboard a ship like the *Mauretania*?"

Morgan raised an eyebrow. "Is that where you found this copy? On the *Mauretania*?"

Robert nodded slowly. "In the Second-Class Lounge. Uncatalogued. One of the stewards was cleaning out the inventory and nearly threw it in the trash. He said I could have it at no cost. But I never got to see the books in the First-Class Library there or on the *Titanic*. So I have no idea if there was another on board or not."

Morgan ran a hand through his coarse hair, his expression a mixture of amusement and melancholy.

"Well," he said, "if you ask ten people, you'll get at least eleven stories. Some say I sent out copies myself. Mailed a box to every major shipping line as a gift. Could be true. I might've done that. I've done stranger things."

He held up two fingers. "Others say a passenger once brought it aboard the *Lusitania* and left it behind. The book made the rounds through the crew. Someone must've decided it belonged on a shelf. The kind of quiet rebellion you only see among seamen. How did it end up on the sister ship? God only knows."

He leaned in. "Then there's a story, I don't know if I believe it, about a banker who says he met me in a bookshop in Manhattan, not far from here actually, and bought two copies on a whim. He claimed I looked like a man who had conversed with ghosts."

Robert offered a thin smile. "And which one is true?"

Morgan looked at him evenly. "Maybe all of them. Maybe none. Maybe it was a little bit of each. But what's more important? Is it what you believe to be the truth? Or what you decide to do about it? Books have their own currents. They pass through hands like coins, get lost behind trunks, and are found again in borrowed time. Your copy of my book might've floated through ten lives or even more before it reached the *Titanic*. Books are like wreckage, Robert. They wash up where they will."

"Or get buried in silt until someone stumbles on them."

"Exactly." He smiled thinly. "Of making many books there is no end."

"You're quoting the Bible now?"

"Just part of a line from Ecclesiastes Chapter 12. The part that knows when to stop asking questions. You know your Scripture."

"Not much," Robert murmured. "I thought it was in Proverbs, honestly. I haven't read the Bible in years."

Morgan tapped Robert's journal gently. "Perhaps the author of Ecclesiastes knew the composer of Proverbs. Or if not personally, they could have known of each other at least. But the real question isn't how my book got to you, but why it stayed with you? Of all the passengers, you were possibly the only one who opened it and wrote your opinions down in here."

"So much for my assumptions," Robert said, staring at the photograph. "Even reality had laid the keel for your fiction. Morgan, you didn't really see the future after all. But you perceived the present more keenly than most could. And you understood what could happen next. Thank you for trying to warn us. I'm sorry that no one listened to you."

Morgan's voice was calm, even warm. "But someone did listen, Robert. You did. You kept that journal and recorded your observations in it. No apology is required."

Robert took back his journal for a moment. He turned to one of his final entries before handing it back to Morgan, who read the words out loud, running a finger across each line. Certain words he emphasized slightly or nodded in quiet understanding. Noticing an interesting choice of a certain word, Robert had not only chosen to use it but even underlined it.

'Unfulfilled yearnings live on even within the most contented soul. What might have been. What one day might be if only certain things were different. When life's struggles weigh heavy, the temptation is to only see the happiness of others. But that is utter futility. For each life contains its own burdens. Though they may be forever hidden to all others. Save the one who carries them within.'

Morgan closed the journal and held it for a moment. Before handing it back, he said, "Robert, I must say, you're a much better writer than I am. You should really see about getting this published. Soon."

Robert smiled, humbled by the compliment. He took back his journal and held it for a moment, its pages a record of his past and perhaps a blueprint for his future. He looked at the novel on the table, then back at Morgan. The man who had not really seen but predicted the future and yet had still been misunderstood.

"Morgan," Robert said, his voice soft but firm, "there's another reason I wrote to you. Something about your book... it felt unfinished. Not the warning, but the story. Those final pages, where Rowland celebrated his solitary success and dismissed the idea of human connection, felt so hollow and dishonest after what I witnessed on the *Titanic*. Your book's warning is powerful, but its conclusion is a lie. It told me that in the end, we're all alone. But that's not what I know to be true."

Morgan's tired smile vanished, replaced by an expression of deep introspection. He looked down at his own hands, then back at Robert.

"You're right," he said softly. "Shortly before I wrote *Futility*, I experienced the building corruption of the passenger ship business. Companies put their profit over people. That is why I tried to establish myself as an author. The original ending... it was a product of a younger, more bitter me. John Rowland had struggled to provide for himself but made it in the end to a high-ranking position working for the government. To be honest, I was also without enough money to meet my own needs. Still am actually. That conclusion was something I had hoped to achieve myself.

However, unlike John, I'm still having a hard time getting by. But John was alone in the end. No friends or family. Much like me, but I'm without the money from a good job. There's a new saying going around these days. It hasn't caught on yet, but maybe it will. '*So poor that you don't have a pot to piss in or a window to throw the blasted thing out of.*' My book always needed a final act of redemption, a simple, powerful choosing of human connection over ambition and human achievements. That's why I called it *Futility.* No matter how much effort I put forth, it always felt so futile."

Morgan paused, looking at Robert with new, respectful eyes. "And I've never been able to write it. As much as I tried to. So I had to find someone else. Finally, I know who that man is. You're the one who can write it."

Robert was stunned. "What do you mean?"

"The book was my warning, Robert, but the heart of it, the part that tells us what to do once we've survived, that's your story to tell. Only a survivor can write it."

Robert's hand trembled as he thought of it. "Maybe I didn't survive just to write about the past," he said, his voice soft but firm. "Perhaps I'm meant to help shape the future, to ensure that the lessons learned from the *Titanic* and the *Titan* are both never forgotten, that hubris doesn't claim more lives."

Robert paused, a bold idea taking root. "Morgan, what do you think of reclaiming the copyright from your publisher and trying again by naming yourself as the publisher but with a new title? One that truly reflects the terror and the undeniable reality of what happened? Maybe even increase the size of the *Titan* to 70,000 tons."

"Interesting idea," he said, eyes narrowing in thought, a spark of the old fire returning.

"Then maybe we're both not finished writing after all. However, Milburg's publishing firm went out of business two years after the first print run of my book. I know his address, and I can write to him to see if he will let me have the copyright back. If I can't convince him, I think his wife will. But first," Morgan pulled out a spare copy of *Futility* he kept in his pocket and handed it to Robert with a pen, "what new ending do you think is fitting?"

Robert opened the other copy and flipped to the back. Grabbing his pen, he carefully thought out each individual word as he wrote them on the inside of the back cover.

'But he was wrong, for in six months he received a letter which, in part, read as follows:

Do not think me indifferent or ungrateful. I have watched from a distance while you made your wonderful fight for your old standards. You have won, and I am glad and I congratulate you. But Myra will not let me rest. She asks for you continually and cries at times. I can bear it no longer. Will you not come and see Myra?

And the man went to see Myra.'

"So much better," Morgan said after reading the handwritten words out loud. A profound sense of satisfaction showed on his face. "At last, this book feels finished after 14 years." He carefully took the pen from Robert and tapped it against the book. "So tell me, is there a new title you have in mind, a name that will sear this tragedy deep enough into public consciousness?"

Robert couldn't help but smile, a genuine, hopeful expression spreading across his face. Morgan wouldn't refuse the recommendation; this was a shared burden, a shared calling. Robert opened his mouth, then paused. The soft wind seemed to hush, just for a breath.

As soon as he answered, the words hung in the air, a

testament to both their shared past and their intertwined future, a promise that the truth, no matter how inconvenient, would eventually surface. It was no longer a warning unheard but a truth reclaimed. From *Futility*, they shaped a future.

"Yes," he said quietly. "I've been thinking of a phrase you used in the book when the *Titan's* loss made the papers. But instead of *Futility*, what do you think of calling it…" He looked directly into Morgan's eyes.

"… *The Wreck of the Titan*?"

11

AFTERMATH: ECHOES IN INK

Monday, April 14th, 1913

In the rhythmic clatter of steel wheels beneath the Pullman car, Robert found, not only physical comfort, but an odd sense of peace. A year ago, he had stepped off one small vessel and onto a much larger, very different one. Full of questions and vastly different expectations. Now, with copper-stained mountains sliding past, and sunlight filtering through the sooty train window. Glass and memory alike. He reopened his worn leather journal; the same one he had carried aboard the world's most well-known ship.

He stared at the half-filled page and wrote slowly, deliberately: '*We yearn for simple answers to difficult questions. We want clarity. We desire to cut through the entanglements to the heart of the matter.*

But there is a profound difference between a simple answer and a simplistic one. The simple answer is hard-won. It accounts for all the evidence and endures rigorous questioning. It survives.

The simplistic answer, though tempting, is a counterfeit. It may offer temporary relief, but it quickly dissolves under scrutiny. It does not satisfy in the long haul.'

He paused. The wet ink shimmered slightly in the slanting light as it began to harden.

He had spent the last twelve months haunted, not only by the memory of that night, but also by the many well-meaning people who tried to wrap it in tidy phrases like "God's will," "a lesson for progress," and "a test of faith."

All simplistic answers. Each one avoided the weight of truth. The truth was that the *Titanic* had not just gone down, it had taken with it a generation of hopes, and it had nearly taken Robert's own soul with the lives of over 1,500 people.

He glanced out the window as the train rounded a bend. In the distance, nestled among the hills and draped in the early hue of dusk, lay the small merchant town of Trinidad, Colorado. Robert reached into his pocket and pulled out a folded note. It was walking directions and an address where he would soon be speaking to a group of people who wanted to meet him. It was almost time.

The train gave a long, tired exhale as it pulled into the station, as if it, too, had made a difficult journey.

Robert stepped down onto the platform alone. No one had come to meet him and that was intentional. Robert had asked for directions from the train station so he could have quiet time to reflect. He hadn't even known about this place until a few weeks ago, but it felt right. The air was thinner here, cleaner, carrying the crisp scent of pine and damp earth. The sky hung lower over the Sangre de Cristo range, a vast, pale canvas stretching above. Even in the fading light, it seemed to press down with silent intention, a vast, watchful presence. The quiet hum of the small town settled around him. It was so different from the big city's ceaseless clamor.

Robert slung his small bag over his shoulder. Just enough for a few nights. The journal was tucked safely inside with a few other books. Two of them were old, and two were new ones. Relics, maybe. Or evidence.

He turned onto Main Street and walked slowly, his shoes crunching softly against gravel and brick. He passed shuttered storefronts, quiet homes, and the occasional dog barking behind a fence. Familiar, but changed. Or maybe he was the one who had changed. Each step toward his destination was not only a physical ascension but another type as well. Recalling Psalm 130 that Leo had recounted in English on the *Titanic*, Robert focused on part of those ancient words. "Out of the depths, I cried out..."

It didn't take long to see the soft brick façade rising up ahead. The unique-looking building was only 23 years old, yet it seemed dignified, eternal in a way Robert no longer trusted anything to be. Its windows caught the last glint of daylight, glowing gold for a brief moment as they faded into evening shadow.

Robert stopped across the street and stood still for a moment to take it in, his heart a steady drum against his ribs. A year ago, he had been fighting for his life in freezing water. Now, he was here, about to speak in a house of worship very different, yet in some ways much like so many others. A place Leo would have cherished. "Leo would have loved this place," Robert said quietly to himself, feeling a pang of familiar grief quickly followed by a quiet sense of purpose.

Before his treatments with Dr. Freud, Robert didn't want to live anymore. One night on the *Mauretania* or the *Titanic*, Robert wasn't exactly sure, maybe both, he had thought about jumping off the back of the ship and into the propellers, the churning blades offering a perverse, final escape. Convinced that no one would have cared or even known. But life got better. Leo had taught him to choose life, to cherish each precious breath. Now he could commemorate the lives that were gone, not just for himself, but for a world that needed to remember. Before it forgot.

Tonight, he walked toward a place built on memory, faith, and the fragile persistence of hope.

Before dusk settled over the small mountain-surrounded town, Robert checked the address he had carefully written down in his journal days earlier: '*407 South Maple Street.*' Facing the front of the unique building, Robert noticed on the right side a golden Star of David and the name of the place above the year it was founded: 1883. He had found the place.

Looking past the synagogue, Robert noted the most prominent mountain nearby rising high above. Fishers Peak. A flat-topped mesa.

Since his first encounters with Leo, Robert had wanted to learn more about Jewish people. So when he got an invite from a synagogue not far north of where he lived to come speak to them about what had happened, he couldn't pass up the opportunity. The invitation, as well as transportation and housing, had been arranged by one of the synagogue's founders who had heard of his story. Robert would stay for a few days before returning home.

As he ascended the fine stone steps that led to the main doors behind the rock columns holding up the facade, someone stepped out to greet him.

"Welcome to Temple Aaron, Mr. Morganson! We thank you for coming. Please, come in. I'd be honored to show you around and answer any questions you have."

The soft glow from the upstairs sanctuary's stained-glass windows illuminated the red brick walls and the iconic onion-shaped dome outside. "I'm very sorry to hear of your friend who died when that great ship went down last year," the man said as he led Robert up one of the side stairways and opened the solid wooden doors to the sanctuary, which filled most of the top half of the structure. Robert couldn't believe it had already been a year.

As the guide opened a few of the stained-glass windows to allow fresh air to flow, Robert was captivated by the furnishings. Many were familiar from the church he'd grown up in, but clear differences stood out as well.

"Over here, this lamp you see hanging in front of those thick curtains is what we call the *Ner Tamid*, which means 'Perpetual Light' in English," the man explained, gesturing toward the softly burning lamp above the ark. "It reminds us of God's constant presence. It's the only light we keep on at all times.

This raised platform we're standing in front of is called the *bema*. On each side, you can see modern replicas of the golden lamp-stand, *menorah* in Hebrew, that stood in the original temple built by King Solomon. And over here... follow me, please; this is the Holy Ark. Inside rest the Torah scrolls, carried with us through generations. Each one is hand-copied by skilled scribes in the same language as the first Torah written by Moses. All are identical inside. They contain the five books of Genesis, Exodus, Leviticus, Numbers, and Deuteronomy. If there is a single error anywhere in a scroll, it cannot be used in religious services, and it is repaired as quickly as possible. This is the same text that Jesus of Nazareth would have read from in his synagogue and taught in his public sermons."

He paused, then added, "We also have printed copies of these scrolls in book form, along with the rest of our Holy Scriptures. We call it the *Tanakh*, but you may know it as the Old Testament."

He completely opened the sliding doors of the Ark and parted the thick velvet curtain, revealing the large scrolls. Robert could smell the tanned leather and the scent of polished wood. It reminded him of being on the *Titanic*.

One of the scrolls was taken out, laid carefully on the pulpit, uncovered, and gently unrolled. Robert was astounded to see only consonants. Unlike the *Union Prayer Book*, there were no vowels or punctuation marks. The tour guide explained that the Hebrew Scriptures were originally composed without written vowels or punctuation, and for that reason, Torah scrolls are not permitted to include them.

"This scroll is currently rolled to the portion covering Leviticus Chapters 14 and 15. Chapter and verse numbers were added many generations after the text was written. We follow a much older system of divided portions that predates the wonderful referencing system developed by Christians. While we have it out," the guide continued with a warm smile, "I'd appreciate it if you would help me roll it to the next reading, please."

Robert felt an immense sense of reverence as he carefully helped the man roll the sacred text, his fingertips brushing against the ancient, cured leather, feeling the slight resistance of the parchment. It was a tangible connection to centuries of faith, a living link to the words Leo himself had surely revered. He thought of Leo's quiet dignity, his unwavering faith, and the simple kindness he'd offered a cynical stranger.

The idea of acquiring a Hebrew Bible for his own home, even if he never planned to learn the language, felt like a silent promise to carry a piece of Leo's world with him. When they finished, he also assisted in recovering the scroll and returning it to the Ark with the others. Before placing it back into the Ark, Robert held the scroll in his arms for a moment… not wanting to let it go, feeling a profound sense of peace settle over him, as if he were hugging a fragment of Leo's soul. An image of the iron gate on the *Titanic* flashed for a moment in his head. The sound of water flowing through the corridors and rising up the steps.

Afterward, Robert was shown the library and other historical parts of the synagogue. He listened in quiet respect as the man described more of the sacred space. The *bema*, the readings, the structure of prayers, it all stirred memories of his own church growing up.

Robert couldn't stop thinking of Leo Zimmermann. Robert had always been open to other faiths, and several of the synagogue's founding members planned to meet him afterward.

As time passed, people began entering the building to ascend both of the stairways in preparation for the memorial service. Robert found a seat near the back in a corner, not wanting to draw too much attention to himself.

As the service began, Rabbi Alfred Freudenthal addressed the congregation: "Welcome, everyone. Welcome. Thank you to all for coming tonight. This evening, we gather to remember those who perished one year ago tonight. It was, by all accounts, the worst maritime disaster in history. We gather this evening not only to memorialize those who have passed, but also to offer thanks for those who were spared when the great ship *Titanic* met its tragic end. Nearly fifteen hundred souls were lost. Only 706 people survived. We have among us now someone who experienced those events firsthand: a survivor. He has journeyed a considerable distance to be with us so that he might share some of his experiences. Mr. Robert Morganson, would you now please come forward and join me on the *bema* to tell us what transpired?"

With a heavy heart and his satchel in hand, Robert stepped forward, the weight of the moment pressing down on him. He placed *Futility*, his journal, and Leo's *Union Prayer Book* on the pulpit for everyone to see, tangible evidence of his journey and the lives intertwined with it. Rabbi Freudenthal sat in one of the decorative chairs behind Robert, a silent pillar of support.

"Shalom, everyone. I believe that's the correct

pronunciation. Thank you for inviting me to come and visit your beautiful temple. I am not Jewish; I was raised in a Christian family. We are God-revering, just as all of you are also. Please be assured that I am not here to proselytize anyone," he began, his voice surprisingly steady despite the tremor in his hands, "but I have come to honor the memory of someone I met on that ship and who was lost just a few nights later. I wish to share these words so his memory will not fade." Robert grabbed his journal and held it up, a symbol of his transformation. "I wrote in this very journal before, during, and after my travels on the *Titanic*. I'm still writing in it." Opening his journal near the beginning, he found the entry he planned to read, the words a familiar echo of his past self. "While I was waiting to board the *Titanic* near Cherbourg, France, I wrote, '*we travel, not to escape life, but for life not to escape us.*'"

He paused, letting the simple truth hang in the air, a stark contrast to the complexity of the tragedy. Closing his journal, he placed it on the pulpit and then lifted the novel for everyone to see.

"I noted my observations while I also read parts of this short novel. It's originally called *Futility*. It tells the story of the world's largest steamship, called the *Titan*, which sank in the North Atlantic in the month of April after hitting, of all things, an iceberg. In this book, there was a great loss of life because there were not enough lifeboats for everyone on board. Sounds very familiar now, doesn't it? But this novel was published in 1898, 14 years before the *Titanic* was built.

While I was in New York, I met the author in Central Park. At first, I was convinced *Futility* foretold the *Titanic's* fate. But when I met Morgan, he explained how his years at sea and knowledge of shipping had shaped the story. What I mistook for prophecy was really his pattern recognition. Even the vessel's name had already existed. And that realization humbled me. A few weeks later, a new edition was released. It is now titled *The Wreck of the Titan.*

As I look around your gorgeous synagogue, I see copies of the *Union Prayer Book* in your sanctuary. I have this one that was given to me by a Jewish passenger who didn't survive that night. His name was Leo Zimmermann. He was just 29 years old. I only knew him a few days, but he left an indelible mark on my soul. And I miss him terribly! I once arrogantly asked him if his prayers for a safe journey were really necessary on a ship like the *Titanic*. He told me a well-known Yiddish proverb that you are possibly familiar with: '*Man plans and God laughs.*' Maybe God finds certain things hysterical.

When I was rescued by the *Carpathia*, I was consumed by such anger toward God that I nearly cast all of these books into the ocean! But I now understand that had I done so, I would not be standing here today, one year later, visiting your community and speaking with you."

Everyone was silent as they listened. After Robert spoke more of what happened, the rabbi led the congregation: "The Book of Ecclesiastes tells us in Chapter 3, 'To everything there is a season, and a time to every purpose under the heaven…'" The rest of that chapter was recited responsively by everyone in English.

After some traditional Jewish liturgy, the congregation joined in the six verses of *Psalm 23*: "*The Lord is my shepherd; I shall not lack… and I shall dwell in the house of the Lord to the utmost length of days.*"

When it came time for *Kaddish Yatom*, Robert was invited to step forward again. He placed on the pulpit a bound memorial book containing the name of every soul lost aboard the *Titanic*, Jew and Gentile alike, for the congregation to keep.

The rabbi rose from his seat and stood next to Robert. "Our friend, listen to me carefully. The Mourner's Kaddish we will soon recite together is not a prayer for the dead. Nor is it a prayer to the dead. In fact, it doesn't even mention death at all. It is one of our oldest prayers. Instead, it thanks God for the lives of those we knew. Robert, in Leo's copy of our *siddur*, you'll find an English translation next to the Aramaic text… Yes, sir. This is the page where it is found. We all now recite together. *Yisgadal v'yiskadash sh'may rabo…*"

Though the ancient Aramaic words were foreign to him, their meaning, the sanctification of life and the remembrance of the departed, resonated deeply. A woman sitting on one of the long wooden benches stood up, balancing herself on her cane.

"Excuse me, Mr. Morganson, would you please be so kind as to repeat that in English for everyone?"

When the final *Amen* echoed through the sanctuary, Robert took the deepest breath his lungs could hold and looked past the doors of the sanctuary. In that moment, he felt the presence of those lost in the icy Atlantic, carried not by the waves but by the spoken words of the living.

After the service had ended and the sanctuary emptied with reverent hushes, Robert found himself in the downstairs social hall, surrounded by low conversation and the scent of warm stew. A few members of the congregation had prepared a modest dinner of lentil soup, hand-braided loaves of fresh-baked bread basted in egg white, and simple roasted vegetables. They invited him to eat with them.

He sat at the back corner near a long wooden table. The wooden bench built into the walls, with the backs of each where the lower stained-glass windows were, made an ideal place to sit. He was next to a noticeably older couple who'd emigrated from Odesa in Russia. Now they lived in Odessa, TX, not far from Midland, directly south of Lubbock. They mentioned plans to build new synagogues in those two growing towns. One was recently founded in Amarillo.

"We remember what it meant to leave," the man said, his accent thick but his tone gentle. "We remember what it meant to survive. To carry names in our pockets."

Across from him sat a girl and her brother. Each no older than 8 or 9, sketching ships in crayon on some scrap paper. One of them looked up and asked, not innocently but curiously, "Did the people know it was sinking?"

Robert hesitated, then said, "Some did. Some just hoped it wouldn't." She nodded like that made sense. Both showed him their drawings. Each had an iceberg at the side.

As the meal concluded, Robert gathered his things. He walked to the base of the twin stairways and lingered near the main entrance to the street, facing eastward. Beyond the horizon, the *Titanic* now rested on the ocean floor. But here, in this temple, their memory would live on. For the first time in nearly a full year, Robert no longer felt so much rage and anguish. Instead, he found so much to be grateful for. The sun had already set, and the stars shone brightly like they did in the lifeboats a year ago. But for Robert, something long frozen had, at last, been thawed. He let the silence settle for a moment. Then he whispered, "Dear God… If you must laugh, then please laugh with me, not at me. But I have an idea…"

Thursday, April 15th, 1915
Robert's home in New Mexico

'Futility of futilities, all is futile, to paraphrase the character

known only as Kohelet. For almost a full year now much of the world has been at war. Some are saying that this will be the war to end all wars. I question that. Everyone is calling this the Great War. But what is so great about it? As the Ottoman Empire continues to collapse, the longstanding balance of power weakens for our allies across the ocean.

History doesn't just repeat. It gets published. I'm very concerned that Morgan's 'Futility' *was just the beginning. True, it was not a prophecy of a doomed ship, but simply patterned recognition that is repeating. News from Europe reaches us daily, carried by letters and the scattered headlines of newspapers. Each word feels heavier than the last, as though pulling me eastward once again. Am I really ready for this?*

However, reading about my fellow survivors beginning again, braving the unknown to rebuild their lives, I realize I've been given another chance as well. A chance to learn from the mistakes of others, to carry those voices of the past forward, and perhaps to finally let go of what I can't change. What will I make of this second chance?

For the past few years, many have spoken about what the iceberg did to the Titanic. *But my question at the moment is, what did the* Titanic *do to the iceberg?*

I know that we can't change the past, and rewriting it, however tempting, does nothing to soften its truths. But from deep within that cold, star-filled darkness, I've seen sparks of warmth, courage, sacrifice, and love. If there is hope for what lies ahead, it depends on our insistence to learn from what has been, to continue with all that is good, and to leave behind what is now broken beyond recovery. Perhaps then, from that wreckage, something much better can finally arise.'

The sounds of the ship breaking apart and the screams of so many in the water that night continued to echo in his mind. Robert wondered if they would ever stop. But at least they had faded slightly.

On the shelf above his desk was the first edition of

Futility, printed in 1898, that he read that fateful night in the library on the *Titanic*. It was placed next to a reprinted edition that Morgan Robertson marketed one month later after learning of the tragic sinking. Both editions were almost the exact same on the inside. Only the title was changed when the copyright was renewed, and a new, more hopeful ending that Robert had written was added.

It was a brick-red-covered book. On the spine it read *'Morgan Robertson, The Wreck of the Titan. Autographed Edition.'* This copy that had been given to Robert had a short note written on the inside cover; it contained the words: *'With thanks and acknowledgements, I am sincerely yours, Morgan Robertson.*

Turning to the back of the new edition, he saw another note written below the new ending. *'My friend, thank you for making the true ending possible. Nothing futile about it. Without you it would have never happened!'*

Where Morgan Robertson failed to succeed with his original novel, this new edition was selling so fast, the manufacturer still couldn't produce enough copies to meet the demand. The once failed "*Futility*" had become far more successful as "*The Wreck of the Titan.*"

Robert closed the book and placed it next to the original. On a small shelf in his desk, Robert's watch was propped up to display its face, still frozen since that night. It still read 2:15. Robert decided not to have it repaired. Instead, he bought another watch but left the other sitting there silent.

Robert thought often of his visit to Temple Aaron two years prior, but it had not even been a full month since Morgan died unexpectedly, and he was still grieving that loss. They had corresponded by mail numerous times. When Robert was able, he would send some funds to

Morgan to help him out. Then one day a letter was returned with his money.

Marked on the envelop was a simple notice. Resident deceased.

The void left by their brief but profound connection weighed heavily on him. Writing was his only temporary escape from the mental torment, a solitary act of defiance against despair. He now wrote in smaller script, trying to fit every last thought before the pages ran out, as if racing against time itself to preserve the flickering truths.

'Life is full of ifs. That's why the word "if" is in the very middle of the word "life." Always choose life. Judge not a book by its cover until you have read the pages it contains. Morgan Robertson believed he had written a work of fiction. But after meeting him and reflecting on this more, I'm no longer sure. If someone should ever read this, if these pages are found long after I am gone, then I ask only one thing: please listen. Not only to me, but to the echoes buried within these words. Because history never truly dies. What happened was real. It matters. And when the world forgets, and it will, a voice from the past always returns. Sometimes in ink. For me, it was a novel. For you, perhaps next time, it will be this very journal. The past always speaks. If only we're willing to listen.'

Looking over those words and contemplating the distant future, Robert shook his head.

Man plans, and God laughs, he thought to himself, recalling the old Yiddish proverb Leo had once shared aboard the *Titanic*. Remembering that he had shared it at Temple Aaron, he decided to write it in his journal.

Leo's *Union Prayer Book*, notably worn, now rested in a place of honor on a nearby shelf. On the inside of its front cover, Robert had carefully recorded his friend's birth and death: February 20th, 1883–April 15th, 1912. Beneath that, Robert also noted the names of any relatives he'd been able to locate.

To his left, next to the small prayer book, lay Robert's old family heritage Bible. It sat open on his desk, as he had recently been reading from the book of Genesis. An idea came to him. He flipped through Chapters 6 to 9, pausing briefly to reflect. Then he reached for his pen and wrote down another thought: *'But don't ever be afraid to try something new. Noah was a total amateur when he built the Ark. Yet it was the world's best professionals who constructed the mighty* Titanic. *Even the great titans have knees that can buckle beneath the weight of hubris. Greatness moves in silence right up to the moment it breaks.'*

Pausing, Robert suddenly realized he was almost completely out of room in his journal. He looked back at one of the first entries he had written aboard the *S.S. Nomadic* near Cherbourg, France dated Wednesday, April 10th, 1912: '*... a new Titan, in every sense of her great name.*'

Now, he finally knew how best to conclude this book: that history or perhaps fate had guided his hand to the very end. By estimating the size of his handwriting and how many letters each word would take, he managed to barely fit one final thought at the bottom line on the back of the final page.

He glanced up at the 1898 *Futility* and the 1912 *The Wreck of the Titan*, the exact same story in two editions. Both were signed by Morgan Robertson. So much had changed in just 17 years. While on board "the unsinkable ship," he had once thought, *What could possibly go wrong?*

He took a deep breath and wrote one last line before finally closing the filled journal and placing it on the shelf directly between *Futility* and *The Wreck of the Titan.*

The original title may have been *Futility*, but for Robert, the story, like life itself, had found new meaning. There would never be anything *futile* about it.

'Now a lost wreck, but she still remains a genuine Titan in every sense of her once great name.'

He ran his fingers along both covers, marveling that though only the title had changed the most, the world could now read it differently. The way it was always intended to.

As he looked toward the horizon, Robert felt the weight of history pressing forward, carrying lessons yet to be learned, challenges yet to be faced. The world was changing. Chaos erupting from distant lands, echoing the uncertainty of a time that would test courage and resolve.

He did not know what lay ahead, but he knew one thing: the past had prepared him, and he would meet the future as he had survived the *Titanic*. With vigilance, gratitude, and a mind still open to wonder.

For some reason, a specific thought refused to leave his mind. For the rest of Robert's life, it would remain. He wondered if, long after he was gone, someone else might one day read those very pages of *Futility: The Wreck of the Titan* or perhaps even parts of his own journal. The idea lingered like a whisper in the quiet room.

He spoke aloud, his voice barely more than a breath: "Let that past now speak. Not as a warning, but as a witness. The ending, perhaps, has not yet been written..."

Passage Ticket No. T.C. O 26830

NEW YORK TO Liverpool

in the British Steamship Lusitania *sailing from Piers 53, 54 and 56, N. R., foot of West 14th Street, on the* First Day of May 1915 *M., unless prevented by some unforeseen circumstances.*

ECHOS THAT REMAIN

Coincidence, if you believe in such things, had me standing in my synagogue, a sacred space filled with the murmurs of generations, more than a year before this book began to take shape, co-leading that week's evening service and delivering a sermon. But not on sacred texts, nor on anything overtly religious in the traditional sense.

Rather, it was on something that had long fascinated me, a subject that had captivated my imagination for numerous years: the sinking of the *R.M.S. Titanic* and a short, largely forgotten novel by Morgan Robertson, originally titled *Futility*.

Today, of course, it's more commonly known as *The Wreck of the Titan*, a title far more fitting for the chilling reality it described. Many people still mistakenly think it was written originally in response to the *Titanic*, a clever piece of post-disaster commentary. But the available evidence, meticulously researched and widely documented, proves that is emphatically not the case. The book predates the ship by 14 years.

I began my message that evening with a deliberate theatricality, a storyteller's hook. I read selected lines from the novel, paraphrasing the words slightly to focus on the most striking details: the description of an "unsinkable" vessel, the grandest ever built, speeding across the Atlantic, carrying the wealthy and the hopeful, ultimately meeting its doom by striking an iceberg in the North Atlantic with insufficient lifeboats for all on board.

After a moment, allowing the descriptions to settle and resonate, I asked my fellow members what ship that book was describing. The immediate, collective response was a resounding murmur, almost a single voice: "*Titanic*."

I then asked my fellow congregants what year it sank. Without hesitation, someone from the front row, his voice clear and confident, said, "1912!" The night I gave this sermon happened to be the 111th anniversary of the sinking, further deepening the uncanny parallel. The irony hung heavy in the air, a palpable tension.

Finally, I revealed the stunning truth: the words I had just read, the details they had so confidently attributed to the *Titanic*, were written 14 years prior to the great ship's launch.

None of them, seasoned readers and history buffs though many were, had ever heard of the book, *Futility*. Many assumed it was a hoax, a trick of words, until I held up a reprint edition, faithfully reproduced from the 1898 original. Then I told them the name of the ship in Robertson's novel: the *S.S. Titan*.

The entire sanctuary fell silent. A profound, almost reverent hush descended. Even the choir, usually so lively, remained stunned. They listened intently to everything I had to say, their disbelief slowly giving way to awe, then to a thoughtful, somber understanding. The initial shock transformed into an eagerness to comprehend.

Toward the end of that service, seeking to broaden the discussion and introduce another perspective, I invited one of the board members, a respected man in our community, to come forward and share his own thoughts and respond to what I had said.

He is also deeply interested in maritime history and ships, having spent much of his life around the sea. He had sailed on the original *R.M.S. Queen Mary* during the 1950s, a testament to an earlier era of ocean travel, and had recently completed a transatlantic crossing on the successor, *Queen Mary 2*, the largest and most technologically advanced ocean liner of our time. And sadly, possibly the last. He shared anecdotes of safety drills and the vast, unsettling scale of modern ships, hinting that perhaps, despite all our learning, some old vulnerabilities still persist.

One year later, the uncanny echoes continued. I was invited to speak again. But this time as a returning guest at a local Unitarian Universalist Church, a community known for its open-mindedness, commitment to social justice, and acceptance of not only many different religious texts but also an insistence on accepting secular sources. One of the lay service leaders, Joshua Salmans, who served as a test reader for my manuscript, has been a longtime friend of mine with a keen intellect and a shared passion for exploring life's deeper questions and had extended the invitation.

Near the end of their Sunday service, my friend asked me up to their pulpit, the wooden lectern worn smooth by countless hands. Like before, I read those same haunting lines, leaving out certain key words that gave away the answer. And just like before, the answer came without hesitation: "*Titanic*."

Once again, people were wrong. I asked this congregation to look up the date the *Titanic* sank. And yet, as I revealed, it was not. Well… not exactly. The *Titanic* had almost perfectly mirrored the *Titan*.

My congregation, and then the Unitarian Universalists (UU for short), were horrified, their faces etched with disbelief and a growing unease, to learn that there are once again ships, the largest in the world, veritable floating cities, sailing the same vast oceans without sufficient lifeboats for all people on board. The regulations, they discovered, often rely on the ship itself being a "lifeboat," a chilling echo of the "unsinkable" myth.

History, it became painfully clear, has a habit of repeating the lessons we fail to internalize, reminding us that arrogance, complacency, and a blind faith in technology, no matter how advanced it is, are perennial dangers. The room buzzed with concerned whispers, a collective realization that the past was not merely history but a living, breathing warning.

At the end of my message, we had a time set for me to listen to their responses. Their questions to me and their responses to what I had to say helped me see different viewpoints. The feedback from both congregations gave me the faintest idea of writing this book.

The Spark of a Story: Not long before my visit to the local UU, a quieter, more personal journey had led me to step into the historic sanctuary of Temple Aaron in Trinidad, Colorado.

I'd gone to visit for a Shabbat morning service, seeking a deeper understanding of the more Classical Reform Jewish traditions Leo Zimmermann may have held so dear, and to celebrate their momentous occasion of being designated a National Historic Landmark. It was a quiet pilgrimage of sorts, drawn by an almost spiritual curiosity.

The warmth of the community, the ancient prayers, and the sense of enduring heritage all resonated deeply within me. Had Leo and other Jewish passengers arrived safely, some of them very well could have worshiped at Temple Aaron.

I remember standing in their sanctuary after the service had concluded, the last worshippers having departed, sunlight spilling through the magnificent stained-glass windows, painting the polished wood and worn pews in kaleidoscope colors. I looked out the same grand doors that thousands had passed through since the late 1800s. Immigrants and pioneers, all seeking solace and community in this remote mountain town.

I stood there longer than I expected, allowing the silence and the history to wash over me. The very air felt thick with generations of prayers, of hopes, of resilience.

I didn't know it at the time, but something settled over me in that moment, a profound inspiration. Alone in the sanctuary, picking up a copy of their *Union Prayer Book* from a pew, a later edition than what Leo could have used, I prayed.

It wasn't a formal prayer, not a structured request. It was a conversation, intimate and informal, yet steeped in newfound reverence.

"Hey God, it's me again," I whispered, my voice echoing slightly in the quiet space. "Listen, I want to run something by you. I have a plan for something. I'm thinking of writing a book, a novel actually. I think this idea needs to be told…"

Something, or rather, someone, was forming in my mind, coalescing from the disparate threads of history, coincidence, and ideas. A name. A voice. A story. A novel. A direct sequel, in spirit, to Morgan Robertson's *Futility*, picking up in some ways right where his chilling foresight left off.

It felt like a whisper, not from the distant past, not from the echoes of 1912, but from somewhere directly ahead, a call to a future purpose. As if the building itself, with its sturdy walls and 134-year-old rafters, had caught a memory, a truth suspended in time, and handed it down to me, a sacred trust.

His name would be Robert Morganson. He is a fictional survivor, yes, born not out of pure fantasy but conceived inside a house of memory, of tradition, of loss and endurance.

A character crafted to carry voices not often heard. Those relegated to the lower decks, the forgotten, the unseen.

A character to pose questions not often enough asked, questions that cut through the simplistic narratives and demand deeper truths.

A person who, much like me, often struggles with faith and occasionally gets a bit too blunt with God.

Robert wasn't created to rewrite history, to twist facts for dramatic effect. He was meant to listen to it, to internalize its lessons. To grieve with us, to mourn the collective losses. To walk forward from it, transformed but not broken, carrying the weight of remembrance into a hopeful, more aware future.

This story rose out of those moments, out of the profound experience in that sacred space and others. Out of the lingering mystery that exists between stark fiction and undeniable fact. Out of the many questions we still ask more than a century later, questions that continue to reverberate through time.

Listening to History: How could something so close to the truth have been written so far in advance? Was it really a coincidence, a blind stroke of luck? Or something more, a deeper current of understanding that some individuals, like Morgan Robertson, are uniquely attuned to?

The very notion challenges our comfortable assumptions about linear time and predictable progress. It forces us to confront the possibility that history isn't just a sequence of events but a series of patterns and repeating warnings, if only we have the courage and clarity to see them.

I invite you, the reader, to think about it. I earnestly hope you'll share your thoughts, your own insights into this. The conversation is as important as the conclusions.

While writing this book, one question kept surfacing, gnawing at me, refusing to be dismissed. I chose to let Robert Morganson ask it first, giving voice to a thought that had begun to define my own understanding of the *Titanic*'s legacy.

Many have written about what the iceberg did to the *Titanic*, the devastating force of nature, the crushing impact that tore through the hull. But I've been wondering: What exactly did the *Titanic* do to that iceberg? It's a seemingly absurd question, yet it carries immense symbolic weight.

The *Titanic* didn't just meet a floating island of ice. It collided with human hubris. With the illusion of invincibility. It left a mark, not only on the ocean floor, but also on the human psyche. That iceberg, in a way, became a temporary monument to that illusion. Scarred by the encounter, a silent fellow victim of a lesson learned the hardest way.

Robert Morganson is fictional. You won't find him on any passenger lists of ocean liners in the early 1900s. I've already checked, meticulously pouring over the remaining records, confirming his place only within these pages.

But many of the journal entries he writes aboard the *Nomadic*, *Titanic*, and *Carpathia* are real. They are found in a journal I bought, lying here on my desk, filled with my own scribblings, my own observations, and my own attempts to inhabit that time and that experience. They have been slightly edited to conform to early 1910s English.

But Robert speaks with the real people who were there. They are not fiction. Only their possible reactions and conversations with him are from my own imagination, being as close to the known historical records as possible.

When Robert is not directly interacting with anyone, just observing, those are their own words recorded later.

The meticulous details of the ships, the sensations, the immediate aftermath, much of that is drawn from the authentic historical record, combined with my own imaginative empathy.

But the emotions Robert felt, the awe, the doubt, even the anger, and the aching, desperate need to make meaning from tragedy, to find purpose in immense loss, that is all very real. It lives in every survivor's testimony, in the quavering voices that spoke of unthinkable horrors. It resonates in every grainy photograph of the departed, their faces frozen in time. It echoes in every unanswered letter that never made it to shore, wishes and goodbyes swallowed by the deep.

It is palpable in every artifact recovered from the wreckage, each a silent witness to a moment of terror and sacrifice. Many of them I've seen for myself when they were on display at the National Harbor in Washington, D.C.

In writing this novel, I have not sought to rewrite history, nor to impose a new narrative. But to listen to it more closely. To hear the whispers between the lines and the stories unspoken. To give voice to those whose stories were lost in the cold, unyielding embrace of the Atlantic.

And to the quiet warnings we too often ignore, the subtle signs that, only in hindsight, seem so glaringly obvious.

This is not the end of Robert's journey. His story, like the flow of time, will continue. But for now, his first journal is full and closed, a testament to a pivotal time of transformation. He has already pulled a blank one from the shelf and begun writing in a new one, embarking on the next volume of his life, carrying the lessons forward.

And I, the author behind his voice, wish to thank you. For reading. For remembering. And perhaps for wondering too, for allowing these questions to linger within you.

Please feel invited to contact me and share your thoughts, your own reflections on these unending lessons. I'm looking forward to hearing from you.

And now that the end has come… did you find it? The hidden message I left?

Not in the margins, nor in footnotes. But perhaps at the beginnings. In the very first words you read. The truth often hides where we rarely think to look, in plain sight, disguised as something else. I said that the first clue was in the prelude, and your final clue is in this very epilogue!

You were told to notice what was different from the rest. Did you see it? If so… you've already begun listening. I would love to hear from you about what you discovered!

The Unending Lesson: I conclude here with the closing lines from my original sermon, which also served as the powerful conclusion to the guest message I delivered at the local UU community. These words, born of contemplation and a profound sense of responsibility, encapsulate the core message I hope to impart to anyone who will listen.

It has often been said, so often it risks becoming a cheap cliché, that those who don't learn from history are doomed to repeat it. But I would add a sharper, more urgent warning: Anyone who actively prevents history from being taught, from being examined, from being grappled with, be warned, for they fully intend to repeat that history once again.

Too many have largely forgotten, and too many were never even taught, the hard lessons our predecessors learned at immense cost. We must always be very careful not to put too much trust in our modern advancements, in our technological marvels, or in our perceived invincibility. For, just in case there is a great danger somewhere in front of us that we cannot see, a hidden threat that our own hubris prevents us from acknowledging.

Because the next time it happens, it could very well be hidden within the quiet darkness of a cold, moonless night in the very middle of April!

17-ton bronze propeller of RMS Lusitania (1909-1915). Salvaged from the wreck near Ireland in 1982. Dallas, TX.

SS TITAN & RMS TITANIC

Category	(Fiction)	(Historic)	Notes
Name and Type	**Steamship Titan**	**Royal Mail Steamship Titanic**	R.M.S. carried mail & cargo
Nationality	British Built and Owned	Irish Built - British Owned	Both British Registered
Length	800 feet	882.75 feet	1898 largest was *Cymric* at 585 feet
Tonnage	45,000 tons	46,328 tons	May 1912 edition: 70,000
Horse Power	40,000	46,000	May 1912 edition: 75,000
People on board	3,000	2,224	*Titanic* was capable of 3,000
Average Speed	25 knots	22.5 knots	Both near top speed
Engine Type	Three Triple Expansion Reciprocating	Two Triple Expansion Reciprocating	*Titanic* also had a central turbine
Propellers	3 screw type	3 screw type	Identical/Similiar
Funnels	3 as depicted on the cover	4 in total with 3 functional	First 4 funnel ship built 1897
Sections	19 Watertight Compartments	16 Watertight Compartments	Both had auto closing doors
Watertight Doors	92	62 in total	*Titanic* had 16 auto closing doors
Lifeboats	24 (half destroyed in collision)	16 with 4 collapsable = 20	Insufficient for all
Reputation	"Practically unsinkable"	Thought to be "Unsinkable"	Both made of riveted steel
Voyage	On Third Return Trip	Halfway Through Maiden Voyage	Both described as the largest
Cause of Loss	Struck iceberg nearly head on	Struck iceberg on right side	*Futility* only hinted right side
Sinking Time	Very Quickly	Almost 3 hours	Quite Different
Time of Incident	Midnight in April	11:40 PM April 14th 1912	Nearly identical
Weather	"...the salt air was chilly..."	Very cold night	Identical
Wreck Location	Between 450-500 miles from Canada	400 miles from Canada	May 1912 edition: 900 miles
Journey	New York to Southampton	Southampton to New York	Opposite Direction
Casualties	Only 13 survivors	About a third (706) survived	Similar outcome
Rescue	S.S. *Royal Age* arrived days later	R.M.S. *Carpathia* hours later	

SS signifies that the ship is powered by steam, a revolutionary innovation in the late 19th and early 20th centuries. During the transition from sail to steam power, the SS prefix helped distinguish steam-powered vessels from traditional sailing ships. While most large vessels today use diesel engines, the SS prefix can still be seen, though it is much less common than it once was.

RMS indicates that the ship had a contract with the British Crown to carry mail and cargo. Dating back to 1840 with Cunard's *RMS Britannia*, this designation was awarded to ships that provided reliable and timely mail delivery. It was a mark of prestige and trustworthiness, as Royal Mail contracts required adherence to strict schedules. The *Titanic*, perhaps the most famous ocean liner ever built, was originally designated **SS**, but also carried the **RMS** prefix due to its mail contract. If the contract was not renewed, *Titanic* would have reverted back to **SS**. Lifeboats on all **RMS** certified ocean liners carried the designation of **SS**.

With the rise of air travel, mail transport by sea has diminished, and the number of RMS vessels has decreased significantly. However, a few notable examples remain. The *Queen Mary 2*, the last true ocean liner still in active service, retains the RMS prefix ceremonially in recognition of its historical connection to earlier ships.

Other historically significant ocean liners include the original *RMS Queen Mary* (QM1), retired in 1969 is now a floating museum and hotel in Long Beach, California and the *RMS Queen Elizabeth 2* (QE2), retired in 2008 is permanently docked in Dubai and also operating as a hotel. Both vessels continue preserve the legacy of the RMS designation and the golden age of transatlantic travel.

Currently the *SS United States* is being prepared to become the world largest artificial reef off the coast of Florida.

SOURCES CONSULTED

Most of the following are public domain and freely accessible online or through affordable reprints. These works shaped both my research and Robert Morganson's journey. Most of these books were the same texts he could have read or even written in response to.

Futility (1898) by *Morgan Robertson* – Much better known as ***The Wreck of the Titan*** since May 1912. This short novel eerily mirrors the fate of *Titanic*. It served as the inspiration for this story *Futility Foretold.* A physical copy of the original is now kept in the Rare Book and Special Collection Reading Room of the Library of Congress in Washington D.C. A hardcover facsimile edition available through the SeaWolf Press.

The Loss of the S.S. Titanic (1912) by *Lawrence Beesley* – A Second-Class survivor's calm and detailed recollection of the disaster. Most Second Class passengers didn't survive.

Sinking of the Titanic & Great Sea Disasters (1912) by *Logan Marshall* – A compilation of early survivor testimonies with illustrations.

The Truth About the Titanic (1913) by *Colonel Archibald Gracie* – A gripping firsthand account from a First-Class passenger who barely survived.

Titanic & Other Ships (1919) by *Charles Lightoller* – Written by the highest-ranking surviving officer, offering a rare glimpse into command decisions.

A Night to Remember ©1955 by *Walter Lord* – Not in the public domain until January 1st 2051, this account is considered one of the most compelling. Over 60 survivors were interviewed for this book. After the *Titanic* was located in 1985, Lord published ***The Night Lives On*** ©1987 (Public Domain beginning January 1st 2081.) These books were very instrumental in shaping both the public memory and historical understanding of the *Titanic* story. The titles for chapters 9 and 10 of my book are a respectful nod to his important contributions.

Union Prayer Book: Part 1 (1895-1922) by *CCAR Press* – The first widely accepted prayer book for American Jews. It received far better acceptance than *Rabbi Issac M. Wise's Minhag Amerika.* While still in use by some, it was replaced by *Gates of Prayer* and *Gates of Repentance* in the early 1970s. Now most use *Mishkan T'filah* and *Mishkan HaNefesh.*

Rubáiyát of Omar Khayyám – Title that *Edward FitzGerald* gave his 1859 English translation from Persian of a series of quatrains (*rubāʿiyāt*) attributed to Omar *Khayyam* (1048–1131). There was a valuable jewel-encrusted copy on the *Titanic*. Crafted in 1911 by Sangorski and Sutcliffe in London, it was won at a Sotheby's auction in London on March 29th 1912 for £405 (slightly over $2,000 in 1912) to Gabriel Wells, who had it shipped to New York. That book remains lost at the bottom of the Atlantic to this day.

ACKNOWLEDGMENTS

In gratitude to **Morgan A. Robertson** (11/30/1861–3/24/1915) for writing *Futility* in 1898 and later republished it as *The Wreck of the Titan* in May 1912.

In appreciation to **Walter Lord** (10/8/1917–5/19/2002), who preserved voices of *Titanic's* living survivors in *A Night to Remember* ©1955 and again in *The Night Lives On* ©1987.

In memory of the nearly 1,500 souls lost in the North Atlantic on that cold, moonless night in April 1912.

Dedicated to the remembrance of the 706 who survived and to those who rescued them.

Thank you, Dr. Robert Ballard, for finding the *Titanic* on 9/1/1985 and restoring her back to the world.

Finally, this novel is my gift to the living descendants of those who were lost and those who survived. May their names and their memories be for an abiding blessing!

-.-. –.- -.. ... — ... -.-. –.- -..

CQD was the original distress call used before the more well known *SOS* was adopted. *Titanic's* wireless operators famously sent both that night.

BIBLIOGRAPHIC NOTE ON MORGAN ROBERTSON'S NOVELLA "FUTILITY"

Today more commonly called *The Wreck of the Titan*, it was originally produced in New York by Milburg Francisco Mansfield's publishing firm *M. F. Mansfield & Co.* Measuring 6.5 x 4.25 inches, hardcover, 145 pages. 20,614 words. Originally priced at $0.75.

First listed publicly on May 28th 1898 in "Books Received" columns of *Chicago Tribune* and *The Literary World*. Reviewed in *The Book Buyer* (June 1898), *The New York Times* Book Review (June 11th 1898, p. BR382), and *The Detroit Free Press* (June 13th 1898, p. 7).

Often mischaracterized as a short story, *Futility* was originally published as a standalone novella or "chapbook," a common practice of the period for speculative or adventure fiction. A facsimile of the May 1912 edition is available as hard-back, soft-back, and ebook through the SeaWolf Press.

One physical copy of the original is known to be kept in the Rare Book and Special Collection Reading Room of the Library of Congress in Washington D.C.

Christo Chaney is a writer, lay spiritual leader, and seeker of meaning who explores forgotten areas of history.

A childhood passion with ocean liners eventually led him to Morgan Robertson's novella before entering the 136-year-old original doors of a National Historic Landmark in Trinidad, CO. There, inspired by the *Titanic* story and a very old book, he planned his debut novel, an unofficial sequel to Robertson's *Futility: The Wreck of the Titan* that reawakens history.

Like his protagonist, Christo keeps a journal, modified entries from which echo throughout this book. He once lived on a cattle ranch in New Mexico not far from Carlsbad Caverns, where the stars shine sharp and the wind whispers to anyone listening.

ChristoAChaney@Gmail.com

goodreads.com/christo-chaney

www.ingramcontent.com/pod-product-compliance
Lightning Source LLC
La Vergne TN
LVHW090556110826
845146LV00001B/156

* 9 7 9 8 9 9 3 4 5 7 4 2 0 *